CAN'T LOOK BACK

BACK

BOOK ONE OF THE WAR FOR DOMINANCE

Chris Kennedy

Chris Kennedy Publishing
Virginia Beach, VA

Chris Kennedy/Chris Kennedy Publishing
2052 Bierce Dr.
Virginia Beach, VA 23454
http://chriskennedypublishing.com/

Publisher's Note: This is a work of fiction. Names, characters, places, and incidents are a product of the author's imagination. Locales and public names are sometimes used for atmospheric purposes. Any resemblance to actual people, living or dead, or to businesses, companies, events, institutions, or locales is completely coincidental.

Ordering Information:
Quantity sales. Special discounts are available on quantity purchases by corporations, associations, and others. For details, contact the "Special Sales Department" at the address above.

Can't Look Back/ Chris Kennedy. -- 2nd ed.
ISBN 978-0990333586

As always, this book is for my wife and children. I would like to thank Linda, Beth, Dan and Jimmy, who took the time to critically read the work and make it better. Any mistakes that remain are my own. I would like to thank my mother, without whose steadfast belief in me, I would not be where I am today. Thank you.

Chapter One

John Gatsby hurried into his hotel room and checked the hallway behind him. He wasn't being followed. Slamming the door, he looked back through the peephole, but still couldn't see anyone. He started breathing again.

John usually loved FanCon. "A convention dedicated to fantasy in all its forms," it was a chance to catch up with some of the friends he hadn't seen in a while, dress up as his favorite character and generally get to be someone that he wasn't for a weekend.

Not this time.

John sat down on the bed and took a few more breaths to calm himself. The day had started out so well. He didn't have any problems crossing the border into the United States or driving to his hotel in Buffalo. It wasn't until he reached the hotel that things got weird. When the lady at the desk handed John his room key, she said that he was in luck; the hotel had been able to give him the room he asked for. He took the key the lady offered, although he didn't remember asking for a specific room.

The room seemed normal enough when he walked into it, and he forgot all about the lady's comment. Happy and excited, he changed into his costume and went down to give his presentation. He was responsible for three panels during the weekend, but this was his favorite: "How to appear as someone or something you're not, using only the things in your closet." He loved being successful, charming and witty in his presentation...all of the things he normally wasn't.

On a normal day, he was short, thin and nerdy-looking, with stringy brown hair and glasses. He had aspirations to do more than deal cards at the Niagara Falls Casino; he just hadn't done them yet. Maybe he would next year.

He had given this presentation several times before, and it went flawlessly. Except for the weirdoes in the audience. It takes a lot to be labeled a weirdo at a fantasy convention, as everyone in attendance generally has at least a few idiosyncrasies. There were, however, three people in the audience that were obviously weird, and it wasn't because of their costumes. The first seemed relatively normal, although he was either a midget or really young and extremely short; John couldn't tell which it was. Regardless, the person was tiny, and his costume was nothing out of the ordinary. John routinely did better with the odds and ends in his closet.

The other two were incredible. The second person was dressed as some sort of orc or half-orc. Almost six and a half feet tall, she was pale green and had what looked like tusks sticking out from both the top and the bottom of her mouth. The makeup job was outstanding; John couldn't see a single spot she had missed. She was also covered in coarse body hair. He didn't know how she got it to stick straight out like it did, but it was better than anything John had ever been able to do.

The third person was dressed as a devil, and it was by far the best costume John had seen in several years of attending conventions. Not because it looked like what you'd expect, because it didn't; the colors were way too garish. Purple eyes and purple hair? Those weren't normal eye or hair colors; the person had to have picked them to stand out. Like the orc, the devil's makeup was perfect. He was a uniform brick-red all over, without a smear, smudge or missed spot, but what really made the costume were the accessories. The horns were awesome; John couldn't see the line where they joined his head, nor did they ever appear to wobble. Even better was his tail, which gave every indication of being prehensile. John had no idea how the guy (at least he thought it was a guy) controlled it. He didn't appear to have a transmitter in either hand; the tail just seemed to move on its own. Barrel-chested and heavily muscled, the devil easily out-massed the orc by 50 pounds, even though he was almost a foot shorter.

The three watched John the whole time he was giving his presentation, and the way they stared at him made him very uncomfortable. It was almost like they were dissecting him with their eyes; they only looked away from him to talk to the others, and then they immediately looked back at him again.

As bad as it was to have them staring at him during his presentation, it was worse having them following him around the rest of the day. All afternoon, no matter where he went, he could always find at least one of them in his general vicinity. Although they glanced away when he looked at them, he could feel their eyes on him as soon as he looked away.

He didn't think it could get any worse, but when he finally went back to his room at the end of the day, it did. Approaching the elevator, he looked back across the hotel's open atrium and saw all three of them following him. Although they didn't get into the elevator with him, he saw the one that looked like a devil staring up at him as he walked to the door of his room. John didn't know whether to go past his door to keep them from finding out which room was his or to hurry in and lock the door. Having nowhere else to go, he went into his room and locked the door, figuring that he could call the front desk if he needed help. Happily, it didn't look like they had followed him.

John checked his watch. He would have to hurry in the shower if he was going to make it to dinner with his friends. Unlike a number of the convention participants, he had a sense of cleanliness and didn't like to smell his own stink. Some of his friends liked to play games at the convention, and they would sit at the tables for days without leaving. They reeked.

He had just taken off his pants when a large crow landed on the white molded-plastic table on the balcony. It hopped around on the table flapping its wings, almost as if it wanted his attention. The crow looked into the room, and their eyes met. John could feel an intelligence in the crow unlike anything he had ever seen in a bird. The bird hopped to the side and lifted a towel off something on the table. John knew that he hadn't left anything on the table because he hadn't even been on the balcony.

What could it be?

He glanced quickly out the balcony door to make sure that no one was around to see him without his pants and then opened the door. With a loud '*caw!*' the bird took flight, leaving a collection of things on the table. With another furtive glance at the rooms around him, John stepped out onto the balcony, picked up the objects and brought them back into the room. Setting them on the bed, he inspected each of them.

The first object was a crown. It appeared real, but it couldn't be, or it would have been in a museum or a castle somewhere. It was incredible the way the jewels sparkled in the hotel room's lights. Although he didn't know much about jewelry, the gems appeared real to him, and his eyes widened in shock. If they *were* genuine, this crown was more valuable than...he couldn't decide what. Certainly it was more valuable than anything he or his mother owned.

How could someone lose something that was obviously so valuable?

He looked at the other two objects he had brought in, a mirror and a small bag with a drawstring on top. The bag looked like the bags that gamers used to carry around their dice. He picked it up and found it to be far heavier than if it held plastic dice. It also jingled with the sound of metal as he lifted it. Metal? Coins? If it was filled with coins, there would be a lot of them.

He dumped the bag onto the bed and was amazed to see that it *was* full of coins, although they were unlike any he had ever seen. They appeared to be gold, and there had to be at least 100 of them. If they were solid gold, they would be worth a fortune. Maybe even more than the crown. What the heck was going on?

Dropping the bag onto the pile, he picked up the last object, a mirror. Three feet square, it looked cheap compared with the other two objects. The frame was some kind of light metal that had pieces of colored plastic in the shape of small gems in it. He touched one of the plastic gems and it depressed. He didn't get it. Why would someone make a mirror that looked so cheap, but had working pushbuttons? How did the mirror fit with the other two items?

He shook his head, not understanding where the things had come from or how they fit together. Putting the coins back into the bag, he decided to take a shower and then ask at the hotel's information desk if someone had lost the things. He pulled one of the gold coins back out of the bag to show the hotel staff so that they'd believe him; he wasn't sure he believed it himself. He glanced at the coin as he was about to drop it into his pants' pocket, and then stopped himself. What the...? The words and numbers on the coin weren't in English! They weren't in French or Spanish, either. He had taken a couple of years of both in high school, not liking either one, and knew that both of those languages used the same letters and numbers as English. The coin had letters that were unlike anything he had ever seen. If there were numbers on it, they were as strange as the letters and equally indecipherable.

That's it, he decided. They must be in Arabic, or whatever the Middle East used as its language. He had seen it once, and it had only looked like squiggles to him. Even some of the numbers looked like squiggles. The coins must be from the Middle East, he decided; the crown made sense then, too. Some Saudi prince must have stayed in the room before him and accidentally left the stuff on the balcony. No, a prince would have had a bigger room. It must have been one of his servants that stayed in the room...one that was going to be in HUGE trouble when the prince found out that his crown and gold coins were missing. The cheap mirror would have belonged to the servant; the rest of the things to the prince.

Having solved the mystery, John hoped that the servant didn't get in too much trouble for leaving the prince's valuables on the balcony. After considering it for a couple of minutes, he also hoped that there would be a big reward for the items' return. Satisfied that it all made sense, he put the coin into the pocket of his jeans so that he wouldn't forget it when he went downstairs. Taking off his shirt, he walked toward the bathroom, dreaming about how he would spend his reward.

As he turned on the water, he heard a knock on the door. It was too early for his friends to be coming by; they had agreed to meet in an hour. He walked to the door and looked out the peephole. There stood the creepy-looking devil and the orc from his presentation earlier. He looked down. The midget that had been with them was also outside his door. He was definitely *not* letting that group into his room. He was all for fantasy or he wouldn't be attending the convention; however, some people didn't know when to stop. Those three looked like they took it *way* too seriously, especially the devil, which looked like something from a freak show. Although the horns looked real, John still didn't understand why he had purple hair. What devil has purple hair? The devil was just doing it to get attention, John decided, although he wished the devil would do it somewhere else.

"I'm busy," he called, walking back to the shower.

The knock came again, harder this time. It was loud enough that it had to be the devil knocking, although the girl was big and could probably knock pretty hard, too. Knock as hard as you want, John thought, I'm not letting you in.

"I'm busy," he called again, a little louder this time. He turned again for the bathroom, but was interrupted by a sustained pounding on the door.

Oh! John realized, the stuff on the balcony must be theirs. If it was his, he would want it back pretty badly, too. He would probably want it badly enough that he would follow someone around all day and then keep banging on his door until the person answered in order to get it back. He knew they wouldn't go away empty-handed. With a sigh he went back to the door and put the chain on it.

He opened the door a crack. "Hey, I'm taking a shower," he began, but was hurled backward as the devil slammed open the door. Although the devil wasn't that tall, he was built like a bull and enormously strong; the force he used to push the door open tore off the chain and threw John to the floor.

Before he could move, the orc said "*Vincula!*" and something fastened him to the floor. Unable to move, he looked at his wrist and saw some sort of glowing shackle. John had no idea what it was made of; he was able to see through it, but it held him in place like it was made of steel. What the hell?

The devil spoke to him, but it was in some foreign language he didn't understand.

"I don't speak Arabic," John replied. "If those are your things, go ahead and take them. They were on the balcony when I got here."

The orc and the devil spoke to each other in their foreign language, with the midget interjecting something. From his viewpoint on the floor, he decided the smaller one was a young-looking adult midget and not a child. The group appeared to come to an agreement, as all three looked back at him. The orc said, "*Convertite!*"

"We finally have you," the devil said in English. He pointed to the crown on the bed. "With the evidence, too."

John shivered involuntarily. It never crossed his mind they might think that he had stolen the crown. "That's not mine!" John replied. "I never saw it before."

"I know it's not yours," the devil said with a smile; "it belongs to the queen. You stole it from her. I expect that the escape mirror sitting next to it isn't yours, either."

"No, none of that is mine," John said, not understanding why they were blaming him. "Who are you people?"

"We're here to bring you to justice," said the orc. "I'm sure you'll try to tell us next that you're not the Spectre, right?"

John wondered how they knew that was his stage name, but then remembered they had been at his presentation where he had introduced himself as that. "Well yes, I go by the name 'Spectre,' but I didn't do anything wrong," John said. "I didn't steal that crown."

The devil smiled at him again. It was probably the scariest thing John had seen in his whole life. The devil looked like he would enjoy causing him pain. "Ghorza," he said, glancing at the orc, "would you please do the honors?"

"My pleasure," the orc replied. "*Furta!*" she commanded. The crown glowed brilliantly, along with the bag that was sitting on the bed. She turned it over and dumped out the gold coins. They were glowing as well.

"The crown and the gold were all stolen," the devil said, "and they were stolen by the Spectre."

"But I didn't do it," John whined. "I don't know how those things got here." They *had* to believe him; he had never stolen anything in his life!

"They never do," said the orc, shaking her head.

The devil took off one of his boots. "Oops," he said as he smashed the mirror on the bed with it. "Seven years of bad luck for me; a lifetime of bad luck for you." He put his boot back on.

The midget scooped the coins back into the bag. "I claim these as my reward," he said. "You can have the crown; these are mine."

The devil shrugged and looked at the orc. She shrugged back at him. "Fine," the devil said to the midget, "I'm happy to get the crown back and strand him here." He turned to the orc. "How long will the chains last?"

"About an hour," the orc replied. "Long enough for us to get back and break the mirror, trapping him here forever."

"Good," said the devil. "Let's go." He picked up the crown and turned to leave.

"I'm staying," the midget announced, bouncing the bag in his hand so that the coins jingled. "I have money, and I like this world. The women are tall and pretty, and I'm rich. There are magic rooms to ride up and down in. This will be so much fun!"

The other two looked at each other and shrugged again. "Works for me," said the devil. "I'm happy to strand *you* here, too." They left, leaving John with the midget.

"Naughty, naughty, naughty," the midget said as he sat down on the bed. He shook his head. "You have been a very bad boy."

"But I didn't *do* anything!" John wailed. "I really didn't!"

"You can stop the denials," the midget said with a laugh. "I know you didn't do it." He pulled a small mirror out of his bag and gazed into it, saying something that John strained to hear, but couldn't. The midget's face melted, and John recoiled in horror as the midget's flesh turned liquid and rearranged itself according to some predetermined pattern. The midget's face took on a very sinister look.

"But, but, but," John stuttered, close to tears, "if you knew I didn't do it, why didn't you tell them?"

"That wouldn't have been very smart," the midget replied, patting his face into place as it hardened, "since I was the one that really *did* take those things." He got up. "That reminds me."

The midget walked out onto the balcony and pulled a handful of shelled peanuts from a pocket. Placing them on the table, he waved over the railing. Within seconds, a flock of crows flew in and started feeding. "Thank you for bringing those things up for me," he said, stroking the one closest to him.

"So you are just using me to take the blame?" John asked as the midget returned to the room.

"Of course I am," the midget replied. "You are as stupid as those other two fools. They got so excited when they saw the crown that they will go home and destroy their only way of coming back here before they realize it's a fake. You're helping me start my new life."

"But, didn't they do something to see if the crown was stolen?"

"Indeed they did," replied the midget. "They checked it the same way they always do, which is why I had the forgery made out of gold and gems I had stolen previously. She looked to see if it was stolen by "the Spectre." The crown glowed like it was stolen by me because it *was* stolen by me...just not from the time and place, nor by the person that they thought it was." He pulled a crown from his bag. The gems in this one shone with an internal light and brilliance that the other crown didn't have. John was awed; he knew it was the most valuable thing he had ever seen.

The midget began a belly laugh that was both gleeful and maniacal at the same time, leading John to decide that the midget was not entirely balanced. A shiver went down his spine. If the midget was crazy, he might do *anything* to tie up loose ends, and John was definitely a loose end.

"Wha...what are you going to do with me?" he asked, dreading the answer.

"With *you?*" The midget laughed, walking over to gaze at his reflection in the mirror on the dresser. He pulled a chair over to the dresser and reached forward to adjust something on the mirror. "Nothing. You are trivial to my plans. No one in my world knows you exist, and no one in this world will believe you if you tell them about me."

John knew he was right. He could never tell anyone about this; they would lock him up and throw away the key. "But what about you?" he asked. "What are you going to do?"

The midget smiled as he stepped up onto the chair. "What am I going to do?" he asked. "Anything I want to." He stepped through the mirror and was gone.

John passed out.

Chapter Two

John woke up to a banging sound. As he came to, he realized that the banging noise was someone knocking on his door. He rolled over, stiff and cold from lying on the floor wearing nothing but his underwear. Suddenly, it all came back to him. His room had been invaded by the three people in costumes. The two scary ones had left by the door, but the third one...the midget...had left through the mirror? He must have imagined that after hitting his head on the floor. He must have imagined the whole thing. Maybe someone had put something in his drink the night before. Maybe...he didn't know what, but it couldn't have happened the way he remembered it.

The knocking on the door stopped as he stood up and stretched. The mirror on the dresser looked normal, and he chuckled. People don't travel through mirrors. That was just in books and movies. He laughed at himself. He must have a concussion or something. He froze as he saw the reflection in the mirror. It looked like there was something on the bed. He turned. The cheap mirror sat in a pile of broken glass where the devil smashed it. Had it happened then, after all?

Wait, he thought; I put a coin in the pocket of my pants. Dreading what he would find, he picked up his pants from where he had thrown them. His hand shaking, he reached into the right front pocket. Nothing. He breathed a sigh of relief. He smiled at his gullibility as he threw the pants back onto the floor. They clinked with a metallic sound when they hit. He had forgotten to look in the other pocket.

He stared for several seconds at the pants lying on the floor, not sure if he wanted to know. Finally he decided that he *had* to know, whether he wanted to or not. With shaking hands, he picked up the pants. The coins in the other front pocket jingled. He reached in and grabbed the coins in a fist and pulled his hand back out. He could tell there were at least three coins, but he couldn't tell if any were different. Finally deciding they all felt normal, he opened his hand. A quarter, a nickel...and an indecipherable gold coin.

He hadn't dreamed it.

So if it *had* really happened, what should he do about it? Report it to the police? Like the midget said, there's no way anyone would believe him. "Really, officer, I was attacked by an orc and a devil at a fantasy convention." If he was lucky, they would only think he was joking; if they thought he was serious, they'd take him away as crazy. That was out.

The safest thing he could do would be to forget about it. He had just turned 21; he could head out to some of the party suites, have a drink or three and forget the whole thing happened.

But then the midget would get away. The orc and the devil were obviously looking for a criminal; they would never know that their midget friend was the person they were looking for. He had to tell them.

But how? When the first two left, it sounded like they were going back to wherever they were from. He had no idea where that was, or how to find them. Before he passed out, he *thought* he saw the midget go through the mirror. That couldn't have happened...but then again, none of this made any sense.

Before the midget went through the mirror, he had looked to see if John was watching. When he saw that John wasn't, he had done something to it and then had gone through it. John hadn't been watching him directly; however, John *was* watching in the reflection of the picture on the opposite wall. He had seen everything that the midget had done. There were three buttons on the bottom of the mirror; he had pushed them from left to right.

John went to the mirror. Push three buttons and then go through the mirror? That couldn't be right, could it? Before he could change his mind, he pushed the buttons like the midget had done. He reached out toward the mirror with a finger and tentatively poked it. His finger bent backward from the hard surface.

He sat down on the bed and looked at the mirror. Something was wrong. Well, lots of things were wrong, if he were being honest with himself. He probably had a concussion and was delusional. That was the most likely excuse, with alcohol and/or drug poisoning running a close second. If the events had really happened, and he wasn't delusional, then the midget had gone through the mirror. He was sure about what he had seen; the midget had pushed the buttons in that order.

Something didn't make sense.

He pulled his t-shirt back on and lay down on the floor. Looking at the picture on the wall opposite the mirror, he played the events back in his head. The midget pushed the buttons in order, from left to right. From the left, the button closest to the light, over to the...wait a minute. He jumped up and looked at the mirror. He ran his hand over his face, shaking his head. The light was on the right side of the mirror. When he looked at the mirror in the picture, what he saw was reversed. The midget had actually pushed the buttons from right to left.

John walked back to the mirror with a new purpose and pressed the buttons from right to left, then jumped backwards as the mirror shimmered. The glass now looked...fluid, somehow. He reached out to touch it with the index finger on his right hand, noticing that his finger didn't shake this time. He touched the mirror and found that it was no longer solid. His finger went into it. He could feel a tug on his finger, pulling him in.

He tried to pull his finger back out, but couldn't. The tug became more insistent, pulling his hand up into his wrist. He braced himself on the dresser, bent over at the waist. The lower half of his body kept him from being pulled any further into the mirror, but the pull only got stronger. His arm felt like it was going to be pulled from the socket, and there was no sign that it was letting up. The pull became stronger still, and John cried out as the pain in his shoulder became overwhelming.

He didn't know where the mirror led. He didn't know what would happen to him there. All he knew was that the pain was blinding, and he was about to lose his arm. A tear rolled down his cheek. He pulled the desk chair over with his right foot and stood up on it. The pain lessened as his arm went further into the mirror. The pull was unrelenting, though, and it again began drawing him further into the mirror. With no other options, he put his left arm up to the mirror like he was diving into a pool. It was drawn into the mirror the same way that his right arm had been. He leaned forward and pushed off the chair.

The mirror consumed him. He was gone.

Chapter Three

Solim strode into the room, secure in the knowledge that his personal secretary would close the hidden door that gave access to his lair.

"Welcome back m'lord," said his assistant, who stood up to bow as Solim entered. If he minded bowing to someone half his size, he didn't give any indication. Solim was a halfling, a race that looked generally human, but rarely grew taller than three feet. Tall for a halfling, Solim was just under three and a half feet, with large ears and straight black hair.

"Thank you," replied Solim. "Any problems while I was gone?"

"None, m'lord," his secretary replied. "Everything is in order and the instructions you left have been followed to the letter in your absence." He said it as if he had last seen his boss only a few days prior, when in reality a whole year had gone by. The secretary had long ago become accustomed to Solim's extended absences, as well as to the excellent salary he was paid to successfully complete the tasks he was given. No matter what they were.

"And Cuddles?" Solim asked.

"He is doing well, m'lord, and has grown to be bigger than his mother," the secretary answered. "I haven't had any problems with him."

"Good," replied Solim. "Please see that I am not disturbed."

"Yes, m'lord," the secretary said with another bow.

Solim went into his office. Closing the door, he was greeted by Cuddles, who came running up to Solim and knocked him over in its excitement. Most people would have experienced worse damage, as Cuddles was a five-year-old grizzly bear. The bear was just over nine feet tall when it stood up on its hind legs, and it weighed over 1,400 pounds. Solim on the other hand didn't weigh more than 40 pounds, except after the most strenuous of holiday eating festivals.

The only thing that saved Solim was his ability to control the monster, turning its wild charge into just a happy rush. It sat down expectantly and stared at Solim. "No, I didn't forget about you," Solim said, pulling a bundle from out of his pack. He unwrapped the bundle and threw the salmon inside to the bear.

While the bear ate his treat, Solim pulled his prized possession from his other bag. The crown looked as spectacular in this world as it had in the last. He smiled as he set it on his shelf. He pulled the bag of gold coins out of a belt pouch and put it alongside the crown. He didn't need the coins, it was just an added insult to the two Magisterium brats. As he thought about how successfully he had shamed the Magisterium, he shivered in delight. Flawless.

Solim had been a criminal all his life, ever since he had come into his magic as a child. He had been watching a beastmaster coax a kitten from a tree one day and had heard him say the word "*Guberno.*" The word had resonated in his head all day; he couldn't stop thinking about it. Finally, he had said it out loud that night while holding a kitten. Instantly, he saw himself through the kitten's eyes.

He hadn't let anyone know at the time, for even as a child he was aware that beastmasters were the lowest class of magicians. They were looked down on even more than people with no magic. As a halfling, he was already looked down on enough; he didn't need to give the other kids any more reasons to taunt or despise him.

He had grown his magic secretly, following established beastmasters whenever he could find them. Most didn't mind him tagging along; routinely reviled, they usually appreciated having someone to talk to. He listened intently to everything they said, memorizing it for future consideration.

He started small, using mice and other small animals to recover coins that had been dropped into confined areas. Sometimes he helped put them there by 'accidentally' dropping his change from a merchant. When retrieving coins became too trivial, he had mastered the avian art and started flying birds through open windows to see what he could steal from peoples' homes and shops.

Being a beastmaster was an excellent cover for his activities because no one thought that beastmasters were smart enough to be criminals. They normally weren't. When he realized that people thought that way, he let people know that he was a beastmaster, to the disgust of his parents. After that, he made sure that he followed the beastmaster stereotype. He developed a public persona of someone that wasn't very bright and made sure that he smelled bad. Really bad. Hiding in plain sight kept him safe. People had such little respect for beastmasters that he was never considered by the police when they tried to solve his crimes.

Before long, there was a string of unsolved crimes for which he was responsible. So many, in fact, that the police made it a priority to catch the person responsible. The police kept getting closer and closer, and he finally decided that he had to do something about it.

He framed his village's mayor, giving the secret police information on things that he had hidden in the mayor's home. Since then, he had continued to ingratiate himself with the secret police hierarchy, moving up their ranks until he was recruited by the secret police as one of their operatives.

People above him in the organization tended to have "bad luck" or make "bad decisions" that cost them their jobs, and he had advanced quickly within the organization to his present position. It had taken some time for him to put all of the pieces in place, but events were moving now, and it was almost time for him to advance again. One more step was all it would take. "King of Tasidar" had a nice ring to it.

Chapter Four

John woke up, cold and stiff. His head hurt so much that he was sure he was going to die. He hoped it would happen soon.

It didn't.

Spared the mercy of a quick death, he opened up one eye. The only thing in view was a rough wooden floor that ended in a rough wooden wall. He figured at least one of the numerous pains he felt was a splinter; the wood was that rough. Who builds with wood like that?

He opened the other eye, which let him see a little further up the wall. He saw the mirror and everything came crashing back to him. It was an exact replica of the one in the hotel room (his mind shied away from the term 'mirror image'). He realized in a flash that he had been transported somewhere far from home. As he looked at the rough floor and wall, he also recognized that it was a place far less advanced.

John rolled onto his back. Some of the aches and pains eased; others intensified. His head cleared a little, to the point that he realized the buzzing noise in his head was someone snoring. He rolled a little further and saw that there was a man asleep on some sort of no-frills bed. It was nothing more than a thin pad on a wooden frame, and it looked less comfortable than anything John had ever slept on in his life. The only thing it had going for it was that it was better finished than everything else in view; at least the snoring man probably wouldn't wake up full of splinters.

John levered himself onto an elbow, nearly passing out with the increased pain. Slowly the blackness faded back to the edges of his vision, allowing him to see again. Moonlight shone through the window, glinting off the blade of a very large sword leaning up against the head of the bed. It looked ready to use at a moment's notice...like if the occupant of the bed woke up and found a stranger in his room.

He needed to leave, and he needed to do it now.

John gathered his aching muscles and stood up. Being barefoot helped him be quiet until he stepped on another splinter. "Mmmph!" He tried to keep anything from coming out, but a small grunt escaped his lips.

The man in the bed twitched in his sleep and rolled over. The snoring stopped. John froze, hoping that the snoring would start again. It didn't. As he stood waiting, John realized that he needed to go to the bathroom. Badly. The longer he stood there with nothing else to think about, the more urgent the need became. The snoring still did not restart.

The urge to go changed from a need to a full-fledged pain that soon exceeded the agony in his foot from the splinter. John realized he had two choices, try to escape or relieve himself on the floor. As the second option also had the potential to awaken the man, he decided it was time to try to sneak out.

He tentatively moved one foot, easing his weight down onto it. Success. He took another cautious step toward the door, but then was doubled over by the wave of pain his bladder sent to remind him that he needed to relieve himself *now!* As the pain receded, he took two more steps and reached the door.

The moon went behind a cloud before he could get a close look at the door's locking mechanism; all he had been able to tell was that it looked unlike any door handle he had ever seen before. He waited, wanting to jump up and down like a 3-year-old, but after 30 seconds, moonlight flooded back into the room. The handle didn't look difficult after all; there was a lever to push down and a key hole under it.

He wondered what the odds were that the man had left the door unlocked. He pushed down on the lever and found his suspicion confirmed; it was locked.

He looked around the room wildly; fear and pain making his head spin. The bed! The key was hanging from the bedpost on some sort of weird-looking string. He walked warily to the end of the bed, pausing every other step to make sure the man's breathing hadn't changed. Reaching the end of the bed, he saw the key was actually on some kind of leather thong. He lifted the thong off the bedpost, his heart jumping to his throat when the lanyard hit a snag that threatened to pull it from his grasp. The thong slid from his hand, but he caught it just before it bounced off the bed post.

He crept back to the door, his bladder screaming its need with every measured pace. He had to go so badly that he turned the key faster than he should have. With a '*snock*,' the bolt was withdrawn.

The noise was too loud and woke up the man. "Grekle shamret?!" the man yelled.

John slammed down the lever and pulled. The door opened, and he threw it wide as he ran. He turned left as he went out the door, only to run into the end of the hallway. Dead end. He turned to go the other way and heard the bed creaking as the man got up. John ran back down the hall, barely seeing the stairs in time. His bare feet hurried down the stairs with a slapping noise, pain shooting through his right foot every time it hit a stair and drove the splinter deeper.

The room at the bottom of the stairs glowed with the half-light of a fire that had been reduced to embers. He made it to the landing and accelerated to full speed toward the door on the other side of the room. He might have made it, too, if a large man hadn't come around the corner to his right at the same time. They collided.

John went one way, crashing to the floor; the man was driven back the other. Although the other man didn't fall, the staff he had been holding was knocked from his hand, and it rattled across the floor toward the fireplace on the right side of the room.

The man asked something in a strange language, and then he began advancing on John. Looking up, John could see the doorway on the other side of a large table. Much smaller than the man, John went under the table on his hands and knees. The man tried to follow, but hit his head on the table and fell backward with what was probably a curse.

That was all the head start John needed. "Sorry!" he called as he ran across the room, "I didn't mean to do anything wrong!" He could hear other doors opening and excited voices calling out to each other. He didn't stop to look or listen to any of it. The main door was unlocked; he ripped it open and ran out into the night.

Chapter Five

The rest of the night passed by with tortoise-like alacrity; John couldn't remember a longer one. He had a splinter in his foot that he couldn't get out, despite several attempts, and he was walking through the woods barefoot. His feet hurt with every step. John also didn't know where he was going. He had run into a wooded area when he left the inn, with several people following him. After a couple of minutes, he heard his pursuers give up and go back to the inn. John stumbled on for a few more minutes, just to make sure that he had lost them, and then he had turned around, too.

However, John found that he had lost his sense of direction in the dark, and he had no idea which way to go. He desperately wanted to stop and rest, but the night was too cool. The one time he stopped, he was shivering uncontrollably within a few minutes of sitting down. A t-shirt and a pair of underwear briefs were not what the weather called for; unfortunately, they were all he was wearing when he came through the mirror. The only thing he had going for him was that he was finally able to relieve himself on a large tree.

John had no idea about where he was supposed to go, or what he was supposed to do once he got there. Unlike the orc that had come into his hotel room, none of the people at the inn had given any indication they could speak his language...however the orc had done it. As crazy as it seemed, it looked like she had cast a spell, and then they had all understood each other. Crazy...but no crazier than a mirror that transports you to somewhere else. He wondered how many people here were able to do whatever it was that she had done. Hopefully, more than just the orc. He didn't know how big a land mass he was on, but finding her was probably going to be difficult. Very difficult.

After several hours of walking, he came upon a road. At first he was disappointed that the packed earth track wasn't even as good as the road through his neighborhood back in Canada, but then he laughed at himself. Of course it wasn't; if this was some sort of medieval world, they weren't going to have paved roads...or cars. He'd have to find a way to get the splinter out of his foot soon; he was probably going to have a lot of walking to do in the upcoming days.

There wasn't a soul to be seen in either direction; apparently no one traveled by night. He had no idea which way to go and no way to find out, so he began walking to the right. At least the ground was fairly smooth and the splinter didn't hurt as much.

He walked about a half an hour, and then the sky began to lighten, and the sun came up. Although this was a good thing in that it let him see well enough to finally remove the splinter, it also let him see how badly torn up the bottoms of his feet were. After several hours of walking through the woods at night, they were bleeding in several places. He would have to get them treated when he got to where he was going...wherever that was.

With the sun's appearance, people also appeared on the road, almost as if by magic. While John had been hoping for this, the people presented a problem of their own, as it soon became apparent that all of them thought he was crazy. John couldn't blame them; if he saw people walking around wearing only what he was wearing, he'd probably think they were crazy, too. Or French...he'd seen some of the bathing suits they wore.

He tried a variety of approaches to interact with the people he encountered, but was unsuccessful. If he approached people slowly, they ran away in the opposite direction. If he tried to approach people quickly, they ran away even faster. Trying to speak to them in a strange language only assured them of his lack of sanity, causing them to run faster still.

Balling his fists in frustration after unsuccessfully trying to approach a sixth group, he gave up. The loaded wagon that he had seen was heading toward the rising sun; he guessed that the closest town was in that direction. As he trudged into the sun, he realized that the day was warming up rapidly and was already starting to get hot. Great, he thought. In addition to his feet hurting and being hungry and tired, he was about to add thirsty and sunburned to his litany of woes. What a wonderful day.

What had possessed him to go through the mirror in the first place?

Chapter Six

"*Aqua!*' said Solim. Water poured into the cup, and he smiled as he chewed on his day bread. The night before, he had experienced some sort of transformation while he slept. He woke in the middle of the night to find his mind seemed somehow larger. He really didn't know how to describe it in any other way. His mind just seemed larger. It was the same sensation that he heard mages reference when they moved up in level. But he wasn't a mage, he was a beastmaster, and beastmasters didn't level up...did they?

Arriving at the office, he sent his assistant to find out the cantrip words for each of the different elements. The cantrips were the lowest level spells that mages learned first. He cast the earth cantrip first and was amazed to find that it worked. He had created a piece of the magical day bread that was the 'fruit of the earth.' Now the water cantrip worked, too? Incredible. If this meant what he thought it meant—

The innkeeper strode into Solim's office, pushing past the scribe outside. He slammed open the door, and his eyes swept the room. He sniffed at the poor quality bookshelves and obviously faux bearskin rug to his left, figuring that Solim only had them to lend a pretense of culture. He *was* a beastmaster, after all; how cultured could he actually be? His eyes lit on Solim sitting behind a desk to his right, and he stomped over. Human, the innkeeper was almost three

29

feet taller than Solim, and he thought that the height difference would intimidate Solim.

It didn't.

"I am here for my reward," he said without indulging in any of the normal niceties of conversation.

"You are?" asked Solim, raising an eyebrow. "And what reward would that be?"

"The reward that you promised two years ago for letting you know if someone appeared at the inn," replied the innkeeper. "You haven't forgotten it, have you?"

"No, I haven't forgotten. Where is this person now?"

"How should I know?" asked the innkeeper. "He scared one of my guests and then ran off into the woods. I think he was crazy. He was running around half-dressed, and, as he went out the door he yelled something in a weird language I've never heard before. I've been an innkeeper for over 20 years now, and I've heard every language on the continent of Tasidar; this wasn't like any of them."

"I told you that you would get the reward if you found out where he went before you came here," said Solim. "You failed me. Can you at least tell me what he looked like?"

The tone of Solim's voice was beginning to scare the innkeeper, who was having second thoughts about coming to see the halfling by himself. Based on some of his past dealings, the innkeeper knew that Solim made a large amount of money in the black market...probably enough to afford a swordsman or two. He must have at least one of them somewhere out of sight, the innkeeper decided, which would explain why he wasn't able to intimidate the beastmaster. He decided that a little more discretion was probably in order if he wanted to leave with his reward...and possibly his life. "He was short and thin," said the innkeeper, in a more helpful tone of voice. "He was on the scrawny side; he didn't look like he had ever done any hard work or manual labor in his life. He might have been some sort of scribe. Certainly, he didn't get outdoors much; his skin was very pale."

"Is that all you remember about him?" asked Solim, his voice taking on a more distracted tone.

"One last thing," said the innkeeper, thinking back to when the young man had run into him. "He had some sort of things that sat on his nose. They made his eyes look big." He shrugged, not caring. He realized that Solim was distracted and decided on a bolder path. "I've told you all I know," he added. "Now, are you going to give me my reward, or am I going to have to take it from you?"

"Oh, you're going to get your reward," agreed Solim.

As the innkeeper watched, Solim's eyes went blank. Annoyed at the delay in getting paid, he didn't hear the bear rise from where it had been lying behind him. Despite its bulk, it made very little noise as it crossed the room.

"When am I going to get it?" asked the innkeeper.

"Right now," said the bear. The innkeeper turned around just in time to see the bear's paw that slapped him to the ground.

Later, when the bear had finished feeding and had gone back to lie down again, Solim's eyes refocused. He looked down at what was left. "They're called glasses," he said.

Chapter Seven

"I'm unarmed!" John cried. "I surrender!" John had hoped his troubles would be over when he reached a town, but he was coming to realize just how badly he had misjudged his situation. Some of the people he scared on the road had obviously run ahead to the small town he was approaching; he was met by five men with spears as he reached the town's outskirts. The men appeared to be dressed in some sort of uniform, as all were wearing leather armor colored in red and yellow. As the men surrounded him, John saw that their spear points were sharp and glistened in the mid-morning sun. He could tell their spears were weapons of war.

"Umtp glumgeth!" shouted a new voice.

John turned, carefully avoiding the spear points, hoping the new voice represented an island of sanity in his ocean of woe. Once again, he was mistaken.

The new voice belonged to the leader of the men, who lounged in the shade of a large tree while the troops guarded the road. Although the leader wore the same color scheme as the soldiers, he had a coat of mail that covered his upper half. As he approached, John could see that the leader didn't have a spear like his troops; he had a sword that was long, sharp and very, very pointy. John had a good view of the sword's point as the leader waved it in his face.

"I haven't done anything wrong," pleaded John. "I came here to help solve a crime."

John couldn't tell if they understood him, but his speech appeared to confirm something for the soldiers. They nodded their heads at each other, talking among themselves in their language. The ring of spear points drew closer to his waist.

The leader said something to John in what sounded like the same language, ending with a "Tongart grestch!" When John didn't move, other than to shrug his shoulders, the leader pointed to the ground at John's feet and said again, "Tongart grestch!"

Realizing that the leader wanted him to get on the ground, John started to kneel, but didn't do it fast enough for the soldiers. One of the troops behind him planted the butt of his spear in John's back and thrust forward, knocking John face-first to the ground. The soldier moved to stand next to him, the butt of the spear between John's shoulder blades, pinning him to the ground like an insect on a mounting board.

"Hey," John said in protest, spitting out a mouthful of dust. He noticed that several of his front teeth were loose now, too.

If the soldiers heard him, they gave no notice as they tied his hands behind his back with the professionalism born of many years of practice. John couldn't move his hands. Trying to do so only caused the rope to chafe his wrists. His shoulders felt like they were on fire and would both pop out of their joints at any moment.

The leader gave a command, and two sets of strong hands grabbed him and stood him upright. The tears of pain running from John's eyes made muddy tracks down his face. With another command, the soldiers pushed him forward. When he didn't keep walking, one of them shoved him with the butt of his spear, causing him to stumble forward. All of the soldiers laughed.

This is so unfair, thought John. All I wanted to do was help.

Chapter Eight

The soldiers marched John down the road and into the small town, going most of the way through it. His arms and hands went numb after a couple of minutes although John couldn't decide if that was a good thing or bad. While they no longer hurt as much, he figured the blood loss to his hands and arms was probably doing irreparable damage to them.

Hot, tired, hungry and near exhaustion, he didn't remember much of the walk. Most of the inhabitants seemed to be human in appearance, although some may have been too tall or short, or maybe even the wrong color. John couldn't tell; it was all a haze. It seemed like those that had small children tried to keep them from seeing him.

Eventually, the soldiers marched him into a building. It might have been 15 minutes later; it seemed like forever. The room they walked into had a desk and a table, with a number of doors ringing three of its walls. A tall man dressed in the same color scheme as the soldiers opened a thick wooden door on one of the walls. John was unceremoniously pushed into a small room on the other side of the door.

He stumbled, but before he could fall, strong hands grabbed him. The soldiers cut loose his hands and then shoved him forward again. His vision went red in agony as blood returned to his damaged arms and hands. He didn't see the low pallet in front of him which caught him in the shins. His arms were numb and useless, unable to break his fall, and his face hit the wall as he fell forward, splitting his cheek and cutting his temple. Unconscious, he fell forward onto the cot...

...only to be awakened some time later as a bucket of water was thrown on him. Cold water. John spluttered awake. With consciousness came pain, hunger and confusion. While the pain and hunger continued unabated, the confusion cleared as he remembered where he was, and how he arrived there. He looked up in time to see a man with a bucket leaving through the door, slamming it behind him.

Someone coughed politely from the end of his cot. Sitting up, John found a man waiting patiently for his attention. Like the majority of the locals he had seen on the way to town, the man wore a tunic that ended between his hips and his knees, held together at the waist by a plain leather belt. The parts that John could see seemed to be made of brown wool, as did the outer layer he wore over it. The outer garment was the only piece of clothing John had recognized since he came through the mirror. An oval poncho with a hole in the center, it appeared to fall almost to the stranger's knees in both the front and back. It looked like the same thing a priest wore over his clothes back home. On the front of the garment was the picture of a cloud with a hole. Several rays of sunshine shone down from the center of the hole, in shades of red and yellow that matched the soldiers' uniforms perfectly. A similar metallic emblem hung from a chain around his neck.

The stranger bowed slightly and said something. As toneless as the stranger's voice was, John had no idea whether what he said was a welcome, a benediction or his last rites. John carefully got up off the cot, his arms still feeling the pins and needles of circulation returning. His first attempt to get up was unsuccessful as his right foot wouldn't take his weight. In addition to the splinter, he must have picked up a thorn or nail or something; it *hurt* to put any weight on it. Hopping a little, he gained his feet on his second try, putting most of his weight on his left foot. He turned toward the stranger and bowed to him saying, "I have no idea what you just said, but I hope it was good." Realizing the stranger probably wouldn't understand him, he focused on projecting warmth and humility into his words. John tried to smile, but had to grimace again as his right foot spasmed in pain.

The stranger frowned at John and motioned him to sit down. John gratefully fell back down onto the cot. He misjudged its construction and almost overturned it, but caught his balance and set it right. The stranger came over and gently lifted John's right foot. The frown deepened when he saw the damage John had done to it in a night and day of walking on it unprotected. The stranger set John's right foot down carefully and picked up his left, shaking his head when he saw it. He carefully set that foot down, as well, before standing up.

The stranger smiled at John, before saying something brief to him. Looking up, he spread his arms and called out something in his language, before holding out his hands in the direction of John's abused feet.

John felt his feet grow warm for a second and then cool. As the warmth left them, he realized the pain left with it. He looked down to see a glow fading from both his feet. The skin on the bottoms of them was new and unblemished, colored the same as a newborn baby's. Overwhelmed with an absence of pain, John jumped up and hugged the stranger. "Thank you very much!"

The stranger calmly but firmly extricated himself from the nearly naked man's grasp, holding John at an arm's length. He pointed at John and then the ground, indicating that John should remain where he was. Walking to the door, the stranger called out something in a loud voice. The door opened, and a hand reached in holding a bundle of clothing. The stranger took it and returned to John. Handing the bundle to him, the stranger turned to look away.

John opened the bundle to find serviceable sandals made of leather, a tunic and a belt. The tunic was woolen and scratchy, but he pulled it over his head and belted it on. It came down past his knees, making walking difficult. At least he had his own clothes (or what he had of his own clothes) on underneath it which made the scratchiness more tolerable. He sat down on the cot and strapped on the leather shoes, happy to not be barefoot any longer.

"I'm dressed," John said, standing back up.

The stranger turned around and surveyed John from head to toe. He frowned at the length of the tunic but then shrugged and gave John a 'come along' motion with one of his hands. Turning, the stranger walked to the door of the cell and pushed it open. He walked out, John following closely behind his new benefactor.

Chapter Nine

Solim watched as the inn burned brightly, lighting up the clear night sky for miles. He gazed, unseen, as the area's farmers tried to put out the blaze. They would not be able to do much about it, as the inn had been completely engulfed in flames when they arrived. Some of them might have wondered how the flames could have spread from one end of the inn to the other so quickly, but he figured that most would just shrug their shoulders. They were in the middle of the dry season; sometimes, fires went rapidly out of control.

The flames must have spread very quickly; it didn't appear that anyone had made it out of the burning building. He smiled. Perhaps it wasn't the speed of the flames. Maybe it was the fact that the inhabitants were already dead before the fire started. It was a shame he'd had to leave all of their valuables behind, but it was necessary to maintain the illusion that the fire had been an accident.

He shrugged as he turned back toward the forest. He'd have more than enough treasure soon. Inspecting his companion, he saw that the package was riding nicely on the bear's back. Although the bear didn't like the smell of smoke, it was far calmer than one of its untamed brethren would have been. They walked deeper into the forest, leaving the shouting and the smell of smoke behind.

Chapter Ten

After two days of walking, John and his keeper arrived at a big city. John hadn't learned much in that time except for the other man's name, and the fact that he appeared to be a priest of some kind. The man's name was Theodicus. A man of few words, he gave every indication of being forced to carry out an unpleasant task that kept him from his normal duties. Theodicus kept up a brisk pace, rarely stopping, and didn't waste time in unnecessary speech.

Although Theodicus kept them going longer than John would have thought possible, only stopping for the night once full darkness fell, John had not tired during the journey. When John started to lag the first day, the priest had cast some sort of spell that refreshed him, leaving him able to continue walking. There was no denying it; the man was using magic. First he had healed John's feet, and then he had cast some sort of spell that had restored his energy. Wherever or whenever he was, magic was alive here.

His feet had been up to walking both days without stopping; whatever spell Theodicus had cast on them the first day healed them completely. John wished that he could take the magic home with him; he'd make a fortune when he got back. If he got back.

They didn't have any problems entering the city. Theodicus produced a piece of paper that he showed to the guards at the gate, who waved them through. People that didn't have a pass were not so lucky; several teams of horses were waiting at the gate as their drivers unloaded everything from the attached wagons for inspection. John didn't know what the soldiers were looking for, but the inspection appeared to be quite thorough. Even worse than U.S. Customs on a bad day going to Buffalo.

The city was immense; its suburbs alone dwarfed the town in which John was captured. They walked past shops and houses for 20 minutes before coming to a second wall, which fenced off the city proper. The trip through the city's outskirts was an interesting passage, and one that was completely outside anything in John's experience. While some of the scents of fresh-baked bread and other pastries made John want to stop, other odors reminded him that he was in a world that lacked central plumbing. People rarely bathed, and horses left trail markers down the main road. The city appeared to be well run, as there were people that picked up the horse droppings periodically, but the smell of horse dung added to an already miasmic barrage of aromas that made him wish he could turn off his nose.

Things improved once they passed through the next gate; they left the majority of the odors behind. The main part of the city was well-maintained, and the buildings and shops were in good repair, although the pace of life seemed to be far more frenetic than John would have thought normal. The inhabitants were rushing about, barely noticing or acknowledging each other. In just a few minutes' time he saw a variety of humans and other races. While some appeared to have characteristics that he recognized, like the pointy ears of elves or the squat shapes of the two dwarves they passed, other creatures were completely unknown to him. Although he looked everywhere he could, he didn't see the distinctive shapes of the devil or half-orc. In fact, he didn't see anything that even vaguely resembled either of their forms, leading him to wonder if he was in the right place.

The city was built on a hill, with the wall encircling its base. As they started climbing the hill, John looked up and saw his first real castle, perched at the top. The castle was so large that it could be seen above the intervening buildings. Goose flesh covered his skin as he realized that Theodicus was leading him in that direction.

After another 20 minutes of walking, John saw that the castle was not their intended destination, as Theodicus stopped in front of another large building. Almost as massive as the castle, the white stone building stood imposingly just down the hill from the keep's walls. Theodicus cocked his head as if considering something about it before continuing up the marble steps. As he had for the two previous days, John followed him up toward the entrance. While he hoped that a resolution to his problems waited inside the building's official-looking walls, a sense of nervousness came over him about what that resolution might be. He looked around quickly, wondering if anyone would try to stop him if he ran. Before he could make up his mind to flee, two young people about his age hurried out of the building. John could hear them laughing with each other, and his fears diminished slightly; at least it didn't appear he was going into a prison.

Theodicus led him inside the cool dimness of the building and into a small anteroom. The room only had one other door out of it, which was behind the room's only furniture, a high desk with a small man sitting behind it. The two travelers approached the desk, and Theodicus began a conversation with the man sitting there that went on for several minutes. Theodicus appeared to be relating John's story, as he kept looking over and pointing at John periodically.

When he finished, the man at the desk answered briefly, pointing at the door through which they had entered the building.

Rather than argue with the man at his obvious dismissal, Theodicus turned instead to John and indicated he should stay where he was. Before the man behind the desk could say anything, Theodicus turned and took several brisk steps toward the exit, opened the door and left. The door closed firmly behind him.

The man behind the desk yelled something at the door and then got up from behind the desk and ran across the room. As John got a full view of him, he saw that the man was only about half the size of a normal human, and he looked very much like the thief John had come to help apprehend. John decided he was on the right track but then had a bad thought. What if this was the home of the half-sized people, and the thief was about to come out and kill him?

The half-sized man opened the door and looked out, but Theodicus was gone. Turning back to John, he frowned, contemplating the problem that had been left with him. He shook his head a couple of times and then trudged across the room to the door behind the desk. Opening the door, the small man turned around to look back at John. He sighed and then waved for him to follow. John crossed the room to where the man waited and followed him as he turned to walk down the narrow stone passageway behind it.

The man led John down a flight of stairs and then along another passageway, stopping outside a door that looked the same as the rest of the doors they passed. He knocked, and a female voice answered from inside the room. The man opened the door and led John into a medium-sized office that had two women inside it. The first woman had the pointy ears of an elf but was a *lot* taller than what he thought elves were supposed to be. She stood at least three inches over six feet, with light brown skin, long white hair, and silver eyes. Not only did the elf have a regal look, she also exuded authority, giving every indication of someone well used to power. She was a woman to be obeyed.

He knew the second person, because he still had the unpleasant memories of meeting her a few days prior. She had pale green skin and tusked teeth, and was covered from head to toe in coarse tufts of body hair. At six and a half feet tall, that was a lot of hair. Her name was...Ghorza, John remembered. At least, that was what the devil had called her in his hotel room. Whether that was a name, a position or a reference to her race, though, John had no idea.

Their guide said something to them as he entered the room, and both of them turned toward John. When they saw him, both of them stopped talking. At first, recognition filled the half-orc's eyes. Recognition...and surprise. And then anger took over. She looked mad. Really mad. He was suddenly very frightened as more than six feet of angry orc stomped over to stand in front of him and glared down at him. "Gghghur sjsj pstttr!" she demanded in a foreign language.

"I'm sorry," replied John, "but I can't speak your language."

"*Convertite*," said Ghorza, casting a Translate spell. She then grabbed John by his tunic's lapel and slammed him into the wall, lifting him from his feet. "You've got a lot of nerve coming back here and showing yourself like this!" she exclaimed. "If you thought you could just come here and taunt us, and then get away without a serious beating, you are sadly mistaken."

"No, you don't understand—" John said.

"I understand you made a fool of me and got me suspended from my job!" exclaimed Ghorza.

"No, I didn't—" John said.

"Yes, you did," Ghorza replied, interrupting him again. "Where is the crown?"

"I don't have it," John said. "I tried to tell—"

"You sold it?" asked Ghorza, interrupting again. "Together or in pieces?"

"I didn't sell—" John said.

"Then where is it?" interrupted Ghorza for a fourth time.

"You know, Ghorza," said the elf, speaking for the first time, "he might actually tell us something if you let him complete a sentence or two." Her voice was intelligent and reasoned; it cooled Ghorza's anger as effectively as if the elf had thrown a bucket of cold water on her.

Ghorza released John's tunic, and he slid down the wall to stand on his own feet again. The elf came to stand in front of him. She looked down at him as if she were analyzing a lesser form of life; her eyes bored into him as if she could see into his soul. He knew that if he tried to lie to her, she would know it instantly.

She nodded her head once as if she were finished taking his measure. "Who are you?" she asked.

"Uh...my name is John, John Gatsby," he replied. "I didn't do it. Whatever she thinks I did, I didn't do it. I swear it! Please don't let her beat me!"

If his appeal had any effect on her, it didn't show. "Where are you from...John Gratsby?"

"Um, it's Gatsby, ma'am, not Gratsby," John said, earning a look of disapproval from the elf. "I'm not from around here," he added.

"That much is obvious," noted the elf. "Where *are* you from?"

"I'm not from this time, or planet, or something," replied John. "I'm not from anywhere around here. I came through a mirror. I followed the midget that Ghorza, is that her name? The midget that she and the devil brought into my hotel room. He has whatever crown it was that she was looking for. He showed it to me while I was lying chained to the floor where *she* left me."

The elf turned to the orc. "This, then, would be the Spectre that you caught when you went through the mirror?"

"Yes," replied Ghorza, "this is that Spectre. He even admitted to being the Spectre. He must have known we were coming for him because he had all of the things on hand needed to trick us. I don't know how he got the crown to glow like it was stolen, but we caught him red-handed with it, along with an escape mirror and a bag of gold coins."

"I can tell you why the crown glowed," replied John. "The midget explained it to me."

"Who or what is this midget that you keep speaking of?" asked the elf.

"He was a person about this tall," said John, holding his hand about three feet above the ground, "and he was with Ghorza and the devil when they came into my room." He paused and then added, "He looked like the man that led me into this room." He looked around, but the man had left while Ghorza interrogated him.

"He's talking about the halfling, Milos," explained Ghorza. "He was with us when we caught the Spectre."

"*He's the thief!*" exclaimed John. "After you left, he told me that he had a fake crown made with gems and gold he had stolen previously. That's why it glowed like it was stolen; everything on it *was* stolen. He's the real Spectre. I just used that name for the convention. He told me that he was using me, just like he used the two of you to start a new life."

"Ah...that is the missing piece," said the elf, nodding her head thoughtfully. "It all makes sense now. Milos was the Spectre all along. The only thing I don't understand is how you were able to come here if they broke the mirror he was using to come back."

"That's easy," replied John. "Just like the crown they brought back, the mirror they broke was a fake, too. The real mirror was on the table in the room. Once Ghorza and her friend left, Milos went through the mirror. I saw what he did to activate it, so I followed him through it once the chains went away."

"You followed him *as soon as* the chains disappeared?" asked the elf.

John nodded his head. "Yes, it was about 30 minutes to an hour later. Why?"

"That crime happened three years ago," Ghorza interrupted. "There's no way that you followed right after him." She turned to the elf. "See?" she asked. "He's a liar. He's probably lying about the crown, too."

"No," replied the elf, "he isn't lying...at least, not intentionally. He believes what he is telling us. Wherever it was that you and Dantes went, either time runs differently there or Milos set the mirror to return at a different time. He probably came back later because he knew that we wouldn't still be looking for him. No one would be looking for him. As long as he didn't come around you or Dantes, no one would even recognize him."

"No," John said. "No one will recognize him now, not even the two of them. Before he left, he did something, and his face shifted.

He looked completely different when he left my room than he did when he came into it. No one from here would recognize him; the only person that would know him is me."

"Is that so?" asked the elf.

"Yes," said John, "although the height stayed the same, even his mother wouldn't recognize him now."

"Please wait here," instructed the elf, before withdrawing to the other side of the room with Ghorza.

"This bodes ill," she said to Ghorza. "If he has come back here, it must be part of a bigger plan. The fact that he came back at this time cannot be an accident. The amount of planning and preparation that went into stealing the queen's crown was years in the making. He's here now for a reason. I don't know what could be more important than stealing the queen's crown, but I *don't want him to have it.*"

"Who are you going to assign to this case?" Ghorza asked.

"I'm going to assign you," the elf replied. "I think that you and Dantes have served your probation time and need to be reinstated. There was obviously much more to the Spectre than we knew at the time. You simply weren't ready to be matched up against him."

"What will the Council say?" asked Ghorza. "We've been on probation for almost three years. Our skills haven't improved much since we last went after him; how are we going to have any more success this time?"

"Leave the Council to me; I will handle them," replied the elf. "You focus on Dantes...bringing him back may not be easy."

"May not be easy?" asked Ghorza. "Magistra, that may be the biggest understatement I have ever heard. I will try, but I don't know whether I will be able to get him to come back."

"Think of it as an audition for your return," replied the elf. "If you can get him to come back, you are obviously ready to be reinstated."

"I will do what I can," Ghorza said with a sigh. She didn't radiate confidence. Head down, she turned and walked to the door.

"Just a second," said the elf. "Don't you want to take your new partner?"

"New partner?" asked Ghorza looking up hopefully. "Are you going to send someone senior to train us?"

"Unfortunately, there is no one else available," the elf replied. "The tension with Carpos continues to build. All of our best operatives are involved with that. There is no one else to send." She crossed the room to where John stood waiting.

"I'm sorry that I was not more forthcoming when we spoke earlier," she said. "You may call me Magistra. I am in charge of Norlon's Academy of Magic, the school in which you are currently standing. I am also in charge of the Magisterium, which is the home for the Kingdom of Norlon's special police. My operatives are responsible for solving the crimes local constables or city watches cannot, usually because they involve magic. You have already met two of my operatives, Ghorza," she nodded to the orc, "and her former partner, Dantes. He is the one that looked like a devil."

"My operatives are supposed to solve things quietly," the Magistra continued, "and they almost never fail." She shook her head. "Both of those things didn't happen in your case, of course. Unfortunately, I underestimated their quarry greatly, or I would have sent operatives that were more experienced. This was their first big case...and they weren't ready for Milos. Even more unfortunately, I don't have anyone else to put on this case now that he has returned.

While I normally do not involve civilians in our cases, I am going to have to ask for your help. It is the only way they will have a chance."

"*My* help?" asked John. "You mean like to help them catch him? I'd love to make sure that he gets caught, but I don't know anything about magic. How would I be able to help with that?"

"You are the only person that knows what he looks like now," answered the Magistra. "Assuming that they can keep you alive long enough, you're the only person that can identify him."

John gulped. "Umm...keep me alive? Is Milos dangerous? He didn't hurt me when I saw him the first time; why would he hurt me now?"

"He didn't hurt you then," the Magistra replied, "because he wasn't worried about you coming here. He obviously thought that you wouldn't be able to follow him. I don't know how you did it, but you are here now...and you are the only one that knows what he looks like. You are the only one who can identify him. If he has some nefarious plan, he might very well want to eliminate the possibility that he can be identified...and that would mean eliminating *you*."

The threat in the elf's words brought goose bumps to his skin. "I'm not sure that I want to do that," John replied. "Maybe I could draw his picture for you instead? I'm a pretty good artist..."

"No, it would be better if they had your active support, I think," said the Magistra. She frowned at him, causing John to feel unworthy. "If you don't help us, what are you going to do here? Where will you go?"

John was at a loss. "I don't know where to go," he said. "I guess I'd go back to my world."

"And how will you get there?" the Magistra pressed. "Through another mirror?"

"I guess I will go back to the inn where I arrived," John answered. "However, I don't know where that is. Or how to operate the mirror there, either."

"I will make you a deal," said the Magistra. "If you help Dantes and Ghorza find and apprehend Milos, I give you my solemn word that I will use the considerable resources of the Magisterium to return you to your world. If you do not assist us, I will not stand in your way, but neither will I do anything to aid you. I simply do not have the resources to waste on someone that refused to assist us in our time of need."

"When you put it that way," replied John, "I don't have any choice but to help you find Milos. There is no way that I can find my way back to the inn, or my world, on my own."

"Thank you very much," said the Magistra, gracious in victory. "I greatly appreciate your assistance. For my part, I have something that will assist you in your quest."

The Magistra turned to Ghorza. "Take him to Vishdink," she said, "and tell him to give John Gratsby the Necklace of Tongues."

"Yes, Magistra," Ghorza replied. She turned to leave.

"Thank you again for your assistance," the Magistra repeated to John. "Please know that once Milos has been caught, we will do everything possible to help you."

"Thanks," said John. "I'll look forward to it." He turned to follow Ghorza out the door. "Assuming I'm still alive," he muttered under his breath.

Chapter Eleven

John followed Ghorza another two levels down below the surface of whatever planet he was on, still worrying about everything the Magistra had said. In addition to the death threat, one other thing stood out. "I'm not sure I want to wear a necklace made of tongues," he said finally.

"Gruempt dakto?" asked Ghorza. She sighed. "*Convertite!*" said Ghorza, casting another Translate spell to replace the one that wore off. "What did you say?"

"I said, I'm not sure I want to wear a necklace made of tongues," John repeated. "You have to admit, that's pretty gross." Realizing that he knew nothing about Ghorza, he added, "Well, I don't know if it is for you, but it's pretty gross to me."

"Wearing a necklace of war trophies isn't gross in orc society," said Ghorza, confirming her orc heritage; "however, that certainly isn't something that would be worn in polite human company. In this case, though, I don't think that you have to worry about it." She stopped in front of an unmarked door and opened it before John could ask a follow-up question.

They entered a large room that was a little wider than it was deep, and was unlike anything John had ever seen. It looked like a cross between Frankenstein's lab and a corner convenience store. There were all sorts of racks and storage devices on the walls, but while the room might have been neat and orderly at some point, that point was long past. Metal rods were piled with large sticks, other piles might have been spell components...or yesterday's lunch, John wasn't sure. Several small tables were completely covered with piles of drawings, most of which had enough cross-outs and erasures as to be nearly unreadable. A bellows stood on the hearth next to a roaring fire, along with a wide variety of metal-working implements. Woodworking tools waited in one of the corners. The temperature in the room was well over 100 degrees, and enough things clicked, chirped and otherwise made noises that the room was a general cacophony.

In the center of the chaos was a large table in the middle of the room. Although there were several chairs around the table (and two more lying on their sides next to it), some type of small creature sat on top of it, oblivious to everything going on around it. The creature didn't acknowledge their presence; instead, it continued to draw on the blueprint it was sitting on. The creature had obviously been drawing for some time; it had blue all over its pants, most of its shirt, and the majority of the exposed skin that John could see. The skin that hadn't been colored blue appeared to originally be charcoal gray with splotches of dark red. The creature's skin color complemented its hair, which flowed down below its shoulders in waves of red.

"What *is* that?" whispered John.

"Vishdink is a fire gnome," replied Ghorza. "They like to tinker with things, especially new things. I'd say that they like to build things, but it isn't the completed product that interests them, as much as it is the process of figuring out how something works. Unless someone forces them to, it is rare for any of them to actually complete anything; they just keep improving whatever they're working on and never reach a final end product."

The gnome was erasing something on the blueprint, but stopped and turned to look at them when it heard their voices. It slid over to the edge of the table and dropped to the ground, and then it rushed over to stand in front of John. Although John was short by human standards, he towered above the gnome, which couldn't have even been three feet tall.

"What have you brought, Ghorza?" it asked. "It looks like a human, but it is shorter than it should be, and it smells different."

"You know I'm standing right in front of you and can hear you, right?" John asked.

"Oooh, and it is *so* sassy, too," said the gnome. "Vishdink thinks that Vishdink may like it." It peered up, squinting its eyes. "What are those things on its face? Vishdink see?"

"Yes, you can see them," answered John, taking off his glasses and handing them to the gnome, "but you need to be careful with them. They're called glasses. They help me see."

The gnome studied the glasses. "Help you see, do they? Are they magic?" Vishdink asked. It put the glasses up to its mouth and looked like it was going to take a bite out of one of the earpieces.

John didn't know if the creature could bite through the metal, but didn't want to chance it. The teeth that he could see were red and pointy and looked like they were meant to chop things up. "Hey!" he yelled. "No biting! I said you could see them, not eat them. Keep them out of your mouth."

"How is Vishdink supposed to tell what glasses are made of if you don't let Vishdink taste them?" grumbled the gnome. "Never mind, Vishdink can tell by the smell." It handed them back to John. "How do they work?"

"I don't know," replied John. "The shape of the glass bends the light waves so that they focus properly on the back of my eye. The shape is important; you have to have the right shape for the shape of your eye. Everyone's eyes are different, and even one person's two eyes may be different. My eyes have different prescriptions."

"Hmm...interesting," said the gnome, a faraway look coming to its eyes as it contemplated John's answers. "Vishdink doesn't know what a prescription is, but Vishdink guesses that means the shape of the glass within the metal frame. Is Vishdink right?"

"Close enough," said John.

The gnome muttered, "Hmm..." again and turned to walk off. Ghorza coughed. "Before you go build a pair of your own," she said, "we need some help."

"Yes, yes, of course you need help. Why else would you come to see Vishdink?" it asked. "You never come by to say 'hi;' you only come when you need something." It stopped at one of the smaller side tables and started writing on a scrap of parchment there. "One second."

"Ok," it said a few seconds later, "what is it you need?"

"The Magistra said to come and ask you for the Necklace of Tongues," Ghorza replied. "We are going on a quest to find a thief, and John does not speak any of our languages."

"It doesn't speak our languages?" asked Vishdink. "Where is it from? One of the moons in the night sky?"

"No," answered Ghorza, "he is from another world. We don't know where. Without the necklace, gherfu ksfrug prutlug mfrkond." The two of them continued speaking, but Ghorza's translation spell had worn off, and John was no longer able to understand them.

Lost to the conversation, John walked over to the smaller table where the gnome had stopped. There was a perfect drawing of his glasses on the scrap of parchment, as well as a representation of light being refracted through them to a single point. John was impressed.

He looked up as a loud crash reverberated through the room. Vishdink was standing in the remains of one of the sets of shelves, rooting through a basket that appeared to have been toward the top of it. He pulled something out and brought it over to John. While he had been impressed with the gnome's drawing skills, he was less than impressed with the gnome's necklace. It looked like something that a five-year-old might have worn. It wasn't gold but some brownish metal, and it was exceedingly tarnished. The necklace had little charms with crude sketches of various creatures on them. Overall, it didn't look like a magical device or anything that would be very helpful to him.

"What am I supposed to do with it?" he asked the gnome.

The gnome looked puzzled and turned to say something to Ghorza. She replied, and the gnome turned back to John. It motioned for John to put on the necklace.

John put the necklace on. "Now what?" he asked.

"Now what?" repeated the gnome. "Now you take the powerful artifact that will translate people's talkings, and you leave Vishdink in peace so that Vishdink can figure out this thing called 'glasses.' Bye bye." Vishdink took the parchment off the table and went back to the large table. The gnome brushed off the blueprint that it had been working on, and the blueprint fell onto several others that were already piled up next to the table. Vishdink picked up a blank blueprint and spread it out on the table, prior to climbing up and sitting down in the middle of it. The gnome started drawing, humming happily to itself.

"We might as well leave," said Ghorza. "Now that he has a new project, we won't be able to interrupt his thoughts again for some time."

Chapter Twelve

He would never live down the Spectre case, Dantes realized, throwing a rock into the lava pool far below him. He found he did his best thinking while sitting on the edge of the volcano's crater. Something about having his legs dangling over the edge was liberating. Maybe he would just slide in…one day…ending his need to think for all time. His father might have survived a fall into the molten lava, but he didn't think he would.

He had come to the conclusion a long time ago that it was his fault the case would never be solved. Dantes was the one that had broken the mirror, trapping the Spectre in a far off land…with the queen's crown still in his possession. Too young to have been trusted with such enormous responsibility, he had recovered a fake crown. Although Dantes had traveled the length and breadth of Tasidar, he had been unable to locate the land where they trapped the thief. That place was either across the ocean or on an alternate plane. The only thing he knew was that it wasn't on Tasidar. If it was, he'd have found it.

Being a member of the Magisterium had been the high point of his life. It was the only place that he had ever belonged, even a little. Although most of the humans had never trusted him, a few had, as had many of the demi-humans and other races. His partnership with Ghorza had been the pinnacle of his career. Even though she was a little flighty, they worked well as a team; each drew from the other's strengths.

That time was over, though, and he doubted that he would ever be trusted with that level of responsibility again. None of the good races would ever trust him; most of them believed that he had intentionally helped the Spectre escape. After three years, it didn't appear they had any intention of ending his probation, or they would have done so by now.

Perhaps it was for the best. The devil side of his personality had been calling him for the last year. Forsake the gods of good and come over to the evil side, it said. He could do what he wanted. He could kill whoever he wanted, and he could torture people at will. There was a considerable appeal to that...his powers would rise unchecked, and he could be the devil his father had wanted him to be. Maybe someday he would even take his place in the triumvirate of devils that ruled the second level of hell.

But that was not what he had promised his mother, and his word had to be good for something. It was the only link he still had to her. His father had destroyed everything else, not wanting Dantes to be 'soft.' He had even killed Dantes' mother. Dantes walked in as it was happening and had stopped his father the only way he could. He had killed his father, driving one of his horns through his father's heart. He was too late, though; his mother was only human and too far gone to be saved. Before she died, she made him swear to stay with the gods of good, and he had given his word to do so. The longer he sat looking down at the bubbling lava, the harder he found it was to remember her face...or his promise to her.

Chapter Thirteen

Although they started out early the next morning, John and Ghorza were delayed leaving the city. They made it as far as the gate, but were stopped there as company after company of troops was directed through ahead of them. In every military parade John had seen growing up, the crowd cheered the soldiers on. Not only were the people *not* cheering the soldiers marching by, they gave every appearance of actively disliking them. He saw several of the passers-by spit in the direction of the troops.

"What's going on?" asked John. "Where are the troops going? Why aren't the people cheering for them?"

"You've come here at a bad time," replied Ghorza. "Our country is at war. The armies of Salidar have come."

"From your tone, I'm guessing they didn't come bearing gifts," said John, "but I don't know anything about it. Is Salidar your enemy?"

"Don't you know *anything* about this land?" asked Ghorza, frustration heavy in her voice. John shook his head, so she continued. "Our world has two continents. You are currently on the continent of Tasidar, which lies to the north; to the south of us lies Salidar, separated by an ocean. It is a land of evil. Trolls, ogres and orcs all roam freely there, which until recently was the best thing that could be said about it. All of those races roamed freely. They fought and they died in their petty territorial squabbles, *and they stayed there.*

There was never a force to unify them, so they were never a threat to Tasidar. Every once in a while raiders would hit some of our southern towns and villages, but the raiders were always disorganized and easily driven off."

"Until recently?"

"Yes," Ghorza said, nodding her head. "Until recently. Something unified them. Now when the raiders hit our villages, they don't leave anything behind except the dead bodies of the village men. The women and children they carry off, along with anything else that has value to them. They burn the rest. They are so well organized now that they disappear before help can arrive. They've even hit some of the larger towns." She shook her head. "It's bad."

"So they're sending the troops out to defend the villages along the coast?"

"No," replied Ghorza. "That's not the worst of it. After months of increasing instability, a few weeks ago there was a coup in Carpos, the kingdom to the east of here. The new government welcomed in a contingent from Salidar, and within days there were ogres manning the castle walls during the day and hill giants at night. Our ambassador and all of her staff were killed, as were all of the people from our nation inside Carpos' borders. The fall of Carpos caught everyone here by surprise. Although we have a standing army, it was never intended to fight a land war against armies of ogres and giants. The navy was supposed to keep most of them from seeing our shores, and we counted on the armies of Carpos and the other countries to assist in fighting any of the Salidarians that made it to our shores. Not having Carpos' support completely undermines our war plans; having Carpos actively bringing in more and more of our enemies makes a war unwinnable."

"So, who are these soldiers?" asked John, looking at the mounted cavalry that was now passing by.

"These are mercenary troops," replied Ghorza. "I think this contingent was raised and paid for by the merchants' guild, under the direction of Solim Asmar. You met his younger brother Rubic at the Magisterium; he was the halfling that brought you down to where the Magistra and I were talking. Solim organized the guild and paid for these troops. They are barbarians from the Central Desert and are little more than savages. If their captains didn't watch them, they would probably loot the cities they were supposed to defend. That is why no one likes them; they can't be trusted."

"If these are mercenaries," John asked, "where are your real armies?"

"They are out on the front lines," replied Ghorza. "All of them. Every soldier and combat mage that we have is on the border with Carpos. There's no one guarding the southern villages except the local militias. These mercenary troops *were* going to assist with the raiders, but they just got called to the front lines, as well. A group of trolls were spotted in Carpos; it is hoped that the mercenaries on horseback can stop them, should they cross the border."

"Can they?"

"I don't know," Ghorza said with a shrug. "*All* of the skilled mages, even the ones that haven't been trained for combat, are on standby to assist the army with the defense of the capital. That is why it is up to Dantes and me to track down Milos; all of the senior operatives are with the army. There's no one else to send. If Dantes and I hadn't been on probation, we would have been there, too. His fire magic would be very welcome against the trolls."

"Can't you do fire magic?"

"Of course not," replied Ghorza. "You've seen me cast translation spells. My specialty is air."

"What do you mean?" asked John, confused. "You can't cast fire spells? Why not? Wouldn't that be a lot more useful in combat?"

"No, I can't cast fire spells," replied Ghorza, picking the easiest of the questions to answer first. "Let me guess, you don't know how magic works, either?"

"No, I don't," said John. "We don't have magic where I'm from, so I don't know anything about it. I mean, there are lots of games that pretend to use it, and tons of stories exist about it, but we don't have any *real* magic in my world. How do you start? Can anyone do it? If so, can you teach me to cast a spell?"

"Hmmm..." Ghorza thought a moment. She'd never been asked those questions before, nor had she ever had to explain magic; everyone grew up with it, and they knew everything they were supposed to know. "Well, first of all, not everyone can cast spells; only about 10% of the people are born with the ability to cast minor spells, which we call cantrips. If you aren't born with that ability, you will never get it."

"Most of the people that can cast cantrips never go any further than that," Ghorza continued. "No one knows why, just like no one knows why only certain people can cast spells at all. Only about 10% of the people who have the ability to cast cantrips also have the ability to progress and get better at it."

"I take it you are one of those people," asked John, "since some of the things I've seen you do have to be higher-level stuff."

"Yes, I am," said Ghorza, "I am a mage, which is what we call the people that are able to advance their skills in magic. I was rapidly advancing as a mage until the Spectre Episode, as it is called here. Things have slowed since."

"Why is that?" asked John.

"Simple," Ghorza replied. "If you use your talents in the service of your god, you advance your skills faster than any other way. After we made the mistake with you, we were removed from active questing for the last three years. Dantes and I were just reinstated yesterday. I wasn't sure we would *ever* be reinstated."

"Three years?" John asked. "You said that before, but it's only been a few days since I saw you."

"Only a few days may have passed where you live," replied Ghorza, "but here in Tasidar, three years have passed, and they have been long ones."

The last of the mercenaries passed through the gate. The soldiers that were manning the gate waved at them to hurry through, as if they were the ones that had been blocking traffic through the gate for the last 15 minutes. As they walked through the gate and into the city slums outside, John had a thought. "Why weren't you reinstated before now?"

"What do you see when you look at me?" asked Ghorza, happy to be on the other side of the questioning for once.

"I don't know if everything in my world is the same as it is here," replied John, "but if so, I'd have to guess that you are a half-orc."

"I am indeed a half-orc," said Ghorza. "The question remains, though. What do you *see?*"

John looked at Ghorza, trying to determine what it was that she wanted him to see. The green skin? The small pig tusks? The fact that she had more hair than any other girl John had ever seen? "I don't get it," he finally said. "What is it that you want me to see?"

"How about this, then. Do you remember Dantes? What did he look like?"

"Um, no disrespect meant to your friend," replied John carefully, hearing an edge to Ghorza's tone, "but he either looked like a devil or had the best devil costume I've ever seen."

"Exactly," Ghorza said. "Dantes is a teufling; half man and half devil. One of his parents was a full-blooded devil, but he's never said which one. In fact, he never talks about his family." She stopped walking and turned to face John. She was big enough to stop the traffic behind them momentarily, but then it flowed around them like a rock in a stream. Fists clenched in anger, Ghorza seemed oblivious to it. "Do you know *why* he never talks about them? Because people already don't trust us since one of our parents came from an evil race. *That* is why we haven't been reinstated. Most of the *humans* around here don't trust us and don't want to give us a second chance. They think we're responsible for stealing the queen's crown."

"Well, it doesn't bother me," said John, and he began walking again to break the mood. He hoped it would give her an outlet for her anger, but his plan backfired; Ghorza began walking, and her angry strides were much longer than John's. He almost had to jog to keep up with her. "What would have happened if he hadn't been reinstated?" he puffed. "What would he have done?"

"I don't know," Ghorza answered, "but I imagine his patience is running out. At some point, he'll probably give up on the Academy and will be lost to us."

"Why would he be lost? What does that mean?"

Ghorza sighed. "As I already said, you increase your magical abilities by using them in the service of your god. When Dantes came to the Academy, he swore to serve Incendius, who is one of the five gods of good. At some point, he will probably break his vow and choose to serve the evil god of fire. I hope he doesn't because I would hate to have to cross spells with him. He is almost like a brother to me." Ghorza shuddered unintentionally.

"Do you serve the same god?"

"No," Ghorza said, "each of the gods has an elemental sphere. There are good and evil gods of the four elements: earth, fire, water and air. My talents are in the realm of air; I serve Coelius, the good god of air."

"You said there were five gods of good," noted John. "What is the fifth god's sphere?"

"No one knows," replied Ghorza. "The fifth god of good disappeared sometime in the past, and the knowledge of the god's elemental sphere has been lost. Not only did the fifth god of good disappear, but the fifth god of evil, as well."

"I'm curious," John said. "I played a lot of magic games growing up. You talked about good and evil; is there a difference between law and chaos?"

"I thought you said that you didn't have magic where you came from," said Ghorza.

"We don't have real magic like you do," replied John, "with spells you can cast that actually do things. All of our magic was just pretend."

"Well, it is quite real here," Ghorza stated. "The first time you are the recipient of a flame strike, you will realize just how *very* real it is." She paused and then added, "As to your other question, if you believe in law, you are good. Those that are chaotic in nature worship the gods of evil. There is no distinction."

"Well that's at least easy to understand," John said. "So, how do I find out if I am a mage?"

Chapter Fourteen

"I see," replied Solim, pursing his lips, "the Magistra sent them to bring back the devil. I'm glad you came to tell me; the person I asked to watch the outlander failed me, and I didn't know where he had gone." He paused, stroking his goatee. He had grown it to further disguise his face but found that stroking it helped him think. "It is unfortunate that those two are to be paired up again, but it is too late for them to do the Magisterium any good. By the time they get back, it will all be over."

"If you say so, my brother," replied Rubic, who wasn't briefed on any of the overarching plans. He looked around Solim's hidden office to mask his annoyance. Although he didn't mind spying for his half-brother, he wished that Solim would trust him more. The room hadn't changed much since his last visit, although Cuddles had grown at least a foot.

"Did you learn anything else?" Solim asked.

"The mouse I was using to spy on them was on the other side of the room," Rubic replied, "so I couldn't hear everything. The Magistra sent them to get something, and then they were to go bring back the devil."

Solim stroked his beard a few more times and then nodded his head, coming to a conclusion. "I don't want them back. Follow them and find out what their plans are. If you get the opportunity, kill them."

Chapter Fifteen

Ghorza and John made camp as darkness fell. John looked up at the Mountain of Flames rising far above them. The lava inside the volcano's cone gave the mountain top a soft glow. "Is it safe to camp here?" he asked. "What if the volcano erupts?"

"It hasn't erupted in recent memory," answered Ghorza. "Some say that the gods of fire keep the lava at the same level because they use it to bathe in."

"Is that true?"

Ghorza laughed. "Who is to know?" she said. "The next time I see one, I'll ask."

She started to make the campfire. "This would be easier if Dantes were here," she said, trying to coax a spark out of her piece of flint. "Even the fire cantrip would be helpful in getting this lit."

"Can I try?" asked John. "You told me you'd let me try magic once we made camp. Maybe I can do it."

Ghorza tossed the knife and flint onto her pack. "Sure," she agreed. "I've never been good at lighting a campfire. That was always Dantes' job. I was the cook." She looked up the mountain where Dantes had been camping but couldn't see any signs of habitation. "If we find him, don't let him cook unless you like eating the soles of your sandals. He burns everything."

She waved him over to the shallow fire pit she had dug. John walked over and looked down, and he could see a little ball of tinder inside a tepee of kindling. "What do I need to do?" he asked.

She pointed to a little gap in the kindling that she had been trying to get a spark through to the tinder. "Put your finger right there and say, '*Scintilla!* That is the fire cantrip, which makes a spark."

"I thought you couldn't do fire magic," noted John.

"Just because I can't do it doesn't mean that I haven't heard Dantes say it a hundred times. Are you going to do it, or should I try some more with the flint?"

"Yes, I'm going to try," John said, looking at his hands. They were shaking. Badly. He didn't know which scared him more: finding out that he couldn't do magic...or finding out that he could. He blew out a large breath and knelt next to the fire pit. Holding out his finger like a wand, he cried, "*Skintilda!*" Nothing happened in the fire pit, and Ghorza began laughing.

"Skintilda!" she said, holding her stomach. "What's a skintilda? It sounds like some kind of rodent." She laughed some more, causing John's face to go red. "What I said was, '*Scintilla!*'" she added, once she had calmed herself.

"Ha, ha, ha," replied John in annoyance. "Why don't *you* do it if you're so perfect? Oh, yeah, I forgot. You can't."

"No, I can't," said Ghorza, sobering, "but I *can* do several other nasty things to you if you'd like."

"No," said John with a sigh. "Never mind; sorry. Just frustrated. My first chance to do *real* magic and I mess up the spell word." He rolled his shoulders several times, relaxing himself. Before Ghorza could comment, he pointed his finger and said, "*Scintilla!*" A spark leapt from his finger onto the tinder. It glowed for a moment and then went out. He felt somewhat...emptier in his mind.

He looked up to find Ghorza staring at him with an open mouth. "By the fifth god," she said. "You did it." She shook her head, clearing the disbelief from her face. "You need to blow on it gently once you get the spark on the tinder."

John wasn't listening, though; he was too busy jumping up and down. "I did it! I did it! I can do magic!" He ran over and started shaking Ghorza in his excitement. "You saw it! I can do magic! I'm a mage!"

The half-orc took hold of John's hands and worked her way out of his grasp. "Yes, you did magic," she said, "but it was only a cantrip. That doesn't mean you're a mage. The odds are still ten to one that you aren't." She tilted her head, peering down at him. "When you cast the spell, did you feel a little empty in your head afterward?"

"Yeah, I did. Is that good or bad?"

"It means that you have a mana store," Ghorza explained. "In nearly all cases, that means you probably *are* a mage. We won't know for sure for a while, though. You'll have to cast the cantrip many times before you're ready for a first level spell." She indicated the fire pit. "Cast it again, and this time blow gently on the tinder once you get a spark on it."

John focused on the tinder again. "*Scintilla!*" Once again, a spark leapt from his finger, landing on the tinder. He leaned forward and blew gently on it. The spark caught, and flames engulfed the ball of tinder. He continued to blow gently, and the flames grew, setting fire to the kindling with small crackling pops. He sat back, a satisfied smile on his face.

"Try casting it again," urged Ghorza. "Keep casting it until you can't do it anymore."

Leaning forward, John commanded, "*Scintilla!*" For a third time, a spark leapt from his finger. He thought he heard an intake of breath from Ghorza, standing behind him. "*Scintilla!*" he ordered for a fourth time. This time was different. Where he had noticed a feeling of...potential...when he had concentrated on the spell word the other times, this time he didn't feel anything. He just felt empty. "I didn't get anything that time," he said, stating the obvious.

"I saw," said Ghorza. "Still, most mages aren't able to cast the cantrip more than once their first time, and only a very few can do it three times. You have a larger mana pool than most mages."

"What is a mana pool?"

"That is the spell casting potential that a mage has, and every mage's pool is different. Yours is one of the biggest I've ever seen, although it is not unheard of for a new mage to cast three cantrips. That's how many I cast, by the way. As mages progress upward in level, their mana pools will grow, allowing them to cast more spells. Of course, as you move up, each new level of spell costs more mana to cast than the preceding level's spells did, so it is kind of a matter of diminishing returns."

"Can I try one of the other cantrips?" asked John.

"Not right now. Not only are you out of mana, which will replenish itself slowly over time, but it is also exceedingly unlikely that you will be able to cast any of the other cantrips. Only about one mage in ten thousand is able to cast a second element's spells, and no one can do three."

"Why not?"

"Just like the gods of good and evil are opposites, the elements have opposites, too. If you are a fire mage, you cannot cast water-based spells, and vice versa. Similarly, if you are an air mage, you cannot cast earth-based spells."

"Can I try one of those others in the morning?" John asked.

"You can," said Ghorza, "but you shouldn't hold your breath that it is going to work."

Chapter Sixteen

Dantes looked at the bubbling lava far below him and finally came to a decision. It was time to leave Norlon. He didn't know where he was going to go, but he had enjoyed traveling through Tasidar when he was looking for the land where the Spectre lived. He would journey to Harbortown and take the next ship to wherever it was headed, as long as it wasn't to Northshire. Although the halflings might like the weather there, it was too cold for his taste.

Maybe he would renew his search for the Spectre. Maybe he would just travel, looking for a place to fit in. If he was really lucky, he would find a small border war that needed his magical talents. That would probably be the most satisfying. If he couldn't find that, maybe he would look into freelance bounty hunting, as long as it was somewhere far away from Norlon. He laughed. Maybe he'd go to Salidar and start his own kingdom. There were always warlords starting new kingdoms there. Although physically smaller than most of the evil races that lived there, he knew he was much smarter than most of them, too, which would allow him to move up through the ranks quickly...as long as he stayed alive. His talents would be in demand wherever he went, especially his ability to work fire magic, and he was hard to kill. Going to Salidar might mean becoming evil...but thanks to his father, he knew he had it in him.

As he walked back to his tent, Dantes glanced down the mountain and saw a small flickering light at its base where someone was camping. He didn't feel like putting up with mountain climbers, so he decided to get up early and go down the other side of the mountain. Having spent three months by himself, he found that he was starting to enjoy his own company. Dantes went to bed early, but dreams of uncontrolled fires haunted his sleep.

Chapter Seventeen

"Ghorza, the sun is up."

The half-orc rolled away from John. She wasn't ready to get up yet, and the sun was *not* up. In fact, the sky was only just starting to gray. "I don't know why you're in such a hurry," she grumbled. "You do realize that Dantes will probably try to kill you when he sees you, right?"

"*What?* What do you mean?" John shrieked. "You never said anything about him trying to kill me!"

Ghorza's thick lips curled upward around her tusks in a grin. That will teach him to wake me up early, she thought. Realizing that was her mother's blood talking, she took pity on him. "Well, there's no doubt that he will be angry to see you, just like I was. That can't be helped. Until we explain everything to him, he's probably going to be pretty mad at you. After that, he'll just be angry in general, which won't be much better." She paused and then added, "Don't worry about it, though. I've been thinking about it, and I'll have a couple of spells ready that we can use to control him long enough to tell him what really happened."

"Umm, OK..." replied John, still sounding unsure. "Maybe it would be better if I just stayed down here, and you went up to tell him."

"Oh, don't be such a baby," said Ghorza. "It'll be fine." She stretched. "Well, I'm up now. Might as well get going. The Spectre isn't getting any closer." She started rolling her blankets.

"Before we go off to my doom," John said, "can I try one of the other cantrips? I'm dying to know if I can do it."

"That isn't the word I would have chosen to describe it," replied Ghorza. "People *have* died in the past trying to do too much magic too quickly. It doesn't happen often, but still..." Her voice trailed off.

That wasn't something that had ever been mentioned to John, but he was *really* curious to find out if he could do it. "I'd still like to try."

Ghorza shrugged. "It's your funeral," she said with a smile. John wasn't sure if she was just kidding with him or being serious, but he also wasn't sure he wanted to know.

The half-orc moved to stand next to John. "This is the air cantrip," she said. "It is a gust of wind."

"What does it do?" asked John.

"It is a gust strong enough to float on," Ghorza said. "It can be used to cushion a fall or keep you from breaking a dish if you drop one." She pointed her finger at him from about a foot away. "*Natate!*" she commanded. John could feel himself gently but firmly pushed away.

"That's cool!" he exclaimed.

"Well, it may not be a wall of flames, but it does have its uses."

John picked up his blanket and threw it up in the air. Just before it hit the ground, he pointed and said, "*Natate!*" The blanket came to rest about six inches above the ground, spreading out to lie flat on the cushion of air. "That. Is. Awesome!" he shouted.

Having fun, he cast the cantrip again and watched his blanket rise up into the air. He didn't see her jaw fall open in amazement. No one learned how to do two different types of spells that fast, she thought. No one. And no one was able to do it that well. The only spell that fizzled was the one he said wrong. It was impossible. It was...unnatural. It just didn't happen.

He cast the spell a third time and then turned around, grinning from ear to ear. "What's next, master?" he asked. "Can I try one of the other two?"

"Not now."

"Why not?"

"Well, you don't have any mana left, I'm sure," she said. "And besides, it's just not possible to do any of the other types. No matter which one you try, it is the opposite of one of the ones you already cast. You can't cast both fire and water spells. It can't be done."

"You sound like I just said that the sun would rise in the opposite direction," John said with a laugh. "Like I was going to break one of the laws of nature or something."

"If you knew *anything* about magic," said Ghorza, "which you obviously don't, you would know that casting one of the other spells *would* violate one of the laws of magic. Fire and water are in opposition, just like air and earth are. You can't do both. They are opposites. Being able to cast one of them means that you are physically unable to do the other. *You can't do both.*"

"Well it won't kill me to try, will it?"

"Maybe," replied Ghorza. "You are far too incautious. It *might* kill you. That is what I'm trying to tell you. They are opposites; maybe you will blow up if you do both. I don't know!"

"Opposites that blow up when put together?" asked John. "You mean like matter and antimatter?"

"I don't know what you just said," she replied. "The necklace only made a beeping noise for those two words. But if they are two things that blow up catastrophically when you put them next to each other, yes, just like that."

"Well, it can't be as bad as matter and antimatter," replied John. "Besides, they're just cantrips. How bad could it be?" He paused. "Tell you what, why don't I do the water spell. Maybe that will at least put out any fires that I start. It feels like I have enough mana for one more cantrip. I think."

"I will let you try it, outlander, but I am going to move a long way away. That way, if it goes wrong, you will only kill yourself."

"Fine," he agreed. "What's the word for the water cantrip?"

"*Aqua!*" Ghorza said.

"Really?" he asked. "That ought to be easy." He rubbed his hands together, and then he pointed at the embers of the campfire. "*Aqua!*" he ordered. A drizzle of water appeared where he pointed and fell into the fire, turning to steam. The hissing of the steam was drowned out by a loud crash from behind him. "*Now* I'm out of mana," John said, turning back around. Ghorza stood still, staring at the fire as if she had seen a ghost. All of her equipment lay at her feet where it had fallen. She shook her head, trying to clear it.

"I don't know what all of this means," she said, when she was able to speak again, "but I know we need to get back and talk to the Magistra. Let's get our stuff and get going."

She gathered her gear a second time and turned to look up the mountain. The peak was now in sunshine, although the mountaintop was too far to see clearly. "*Focus!*" she said, causing the light to bend and the distant peak to spring closer and into focus.

"Damn," she said. "We're too late."

"What do you mean?" asked John.

"He's gone."

Chapter Eighteen

The smoke rising from the city several miles away was coming from too many places and was far too thick to be cooking fires. The smoke didn't smell like cooking fires, either. The closer they got to the city, the more Ghorza found it impossible to deny. Parts of the city were burning. The attack they had been worrying about had taken place while they were gone.

"What's all that smoke?" asked John. "Is there some sort of festival today?"

"I'm afraid not," Ghorza said, whose half-orc nature gave her a better sense of smell. "The outskirts of the city are on fire. I think that the forces of Salidar have attacked Norlon."

"What are we going to do?" asked John. "Where are we going to go?"

Ghorza paused, estimating the fires. "I don't think they've made it up to the Magisterium yet," she said. "If we hurry, we can still make it there before they do."

"What?" asked John. "You want to go *into* the fighting? Are you crazy?"

"I am a trained member of the Magisterium, although a junior one," Ghorza answered. "That is where my place is. I need to go and see if I can help." She turned from the smoke to gaze down at John. "You don't have to go with me if you don't want to; however, if Norlon is no longer safe, it won't be long before all of Tasidar is under their boots."

"I'll go," replied John. "I don't know what help I'll be, but I'll go."

"Well, then, let's go with haste. I don't know how much longer we have."

Chapter Nineteen

Rubic found Solim at the command tent that had been erected just outside the walls of the suburbs. A squad of trolls was at the city wall, pulling it apart with their bare hands so that the command group could advance into the city. The trolls would jab their spade-like hands into the mortar of a joint, grab hold of a brick and rip it out. Periodically, sections of the wall would fall as they were undermined, and a squad of hill giants would move forward to pull the fallen sections out of the way.

The command tent was a bustle of activity, with messengers and leaders of all of the host's races coming and going. Finding a three-foot tall halfling among all of the giants, trolls and ogres might have been difficult at another time; today Rubic just followed a messenger to where things were the busiest, and there he found Solim.

Rubic could barely hear himself think among the ruckus; at least eight different languages were being spoken, and the hill giants were trying to out-shout the ogres. As bad as the noise level was, it didn't begin to compare to the smell in the tent. Rubic found himself barely able to breathe, and gagged when he tried to speak.

"You'll get used to it after a while," said Solim. "What news do you bring of the foreigner and his friends? Are they dead?"

"They did not come back together," Rubic said. "When the orc and the boy reached the mountain, the devil had already left. I didn't know if I should attack the two of them and risk alerting the demon that we were coming for him."

"Are you sure you didn't attack them because you were afraid of them?" asked Solim.

"No," replied Rubic. "I didn't have a chance to kill them all, so I came back to see what you wanted me to do. I trailed the orc and the boy back to the city; they're on their way to the Magisterium. You ought to be able to catch them there."

"I've already sent out several groups to find them and kill them if they could," Solim said, "but I think this may call for more drastic actions." He turned to the troll standing next to him. "Send a contingent to the Magisterium," he said, concentrating on focusing his words through the crown on his head. "Have them kill everyone they find there."

The troll's eyes glazed slightly as the magic worked through him. "Yes, master," he replied, looking at the halfling, who was less than half his size. "It shall be done as you order."

"As for you," Solim said, turning back to his brother, "I want you to go quickly to the Magisterium and see if you can find out what their plans are."

"Okay," Rubic said. He turned to go.

"One more thing," Solim said from behind him.

"Yes?" asked Rubic over his shoulder.

"You'd better hurry. I wouldn't want you to be there when the trolls get there."

Chapter Twenty

Ghorza opened the tunnel door a crack and looked around. A member of the Magisterium, she knew the locations of several tunnels that could be used to sneak in and out of the city. All were booby-trapped in case the enemy found them, but the one she led John through was still clear. So far.

Seeing no one around, she pushed up the trap door, which led into a small shed. Disguised by some of the best illusionists in Norlon, the shed appeared old, decrepit and unworthy of a second glance from the outside. The building was empty, although the smell of smoke was much stronger now that they were closer to the fighting. They could feel the pounding of siege machines trying to tear down the city's inner walls not far away. Ghorza didn't think that it would be long before the enemy forces were upon them, if they weren't here already.

She cracked open the door that led out of the shed and looked around to see what was outside. Satisfied no one was watching, she opened it the rest of the way and whispered, "Come on!" before running across a small lawn to a house. John followed close behind.

"Stay here," she ordered when they reached the cover of the building. "The owner of this house is a member of the Magisterium. I will see if he is home and can give us any information." John nodded, and she slipped through the back door of the house.

While he was waiting, John heard a commotion coming from in front of the house and went to look around the corner. The building next to the house was a small cafe. The restaurant was vacant, except for one table in front that was occupied. He was in luck! The devil they had been looking for was at the table, along with three of the largest creatures he had ever seen. John didn't know what they were, but they had to be at least nine feet tall, maybe taller, and weighed many hundreds of pounds. They almost looked comical, dressed in tattered furs and sitting on benches that were too small for them. All of them seemed oblivious to the events going on around them.

"Hey—" John started to call out, but a strong hand clamped over his mouth, lifting him from his feet and pulling him back around the corner of the building.

"Quiet!" whispered a gruff voice that smelled of sulfur. The voice pulled him back further and slammed him backward into the wall. His head snapped back against the building's bricks, causing him to see stars. As they cleared, he found himself looking into the face of the real teufling. John didn't have to be experienced with demonic facial expressions to tell the half-devil was angry. His tail flicked back and forth at the edge of John's vision; John knew it could strike him, and he would never see it coming.

"Come to gloat with the rest of your evil creatures now that you've taken the city?" the teufling asked. "If there's one thing in this life that I am sure of, it's that you won't last long enough to get that drink with your friends out there!"

"It's not like that at all!" John whispered back. "I'm here with Ghorza. We were looking for you. We went to find you at the mountain, but you were gone. We came back to the city, but it was already in flames."

"A likely story," Dantes said. "And you just happened to be going to meet that group out there?"

"I thought the teufling was you," said John. "I'm looking for you. I came here to tell you that you've all been tricked. The real Spectre is still on the loose!"

"The real Spectre?"

"Yes, the real Spectre. He used me to trick you. He got away and came back here...probably to take part in the destruction of this city."

"And I'm supposed to believe that?"

"It's true," said Ghorza's voice from behind him. "We've been looking for you, and if you would let him go, we can tell you all about it."

Her voice soothed his anger. Dantes let go of John and turned to find Ghorza looking down at him. Dantes gave an embarrassed smile. "It's good to see you," he said.

"It would be better if we weren't surrounded by the minions of hell," said Ghorza.

"Absolutely," said Dantes, who was more than passingly familiar with them. "I just got here, myself. I came through one of the tunnels hoping to reach the Magisterium, but before I could, I saw that group out there." He paused to glance around the corner. The sounds of fighting had moved on, and the group looked as if they had nothing better to do than stop and have refreshments. They had obviously been in the fighting earlier, as bits of gore were splattered all over them, and blood coated the clubs lying on the ground next to them. "I have to do something about the teufling. If I don't, he will bathe this town in blood, even more so than the other creatures."

"Wench!" they heard the devil call from around the corner, as if to prove his point. "We want food and wine! We hunger and thirst!"

His tone sounded full of promised pain to come. It made John want to go out and confront the teufling; at the same time, it also made him want to run away as fast as he could.

"Coming, gentlemen," replied a young barmaid in a tiny voice, hustling out with a tray of food and tankards of some sort of beverage. Her hands were shaking so badly that she almost dumped the whole tray onto one of the bigger creatures. Narrowly averting the disaster, she slid the food and drinks gracelessly onto the table in front of them.

"Don't make us wait again," cautioned the devil, evil in his voice, "or the next time we might have *you* for dinner instead."

Dantes turned to Ghorza. "He means to kill her. He's just playing with her until he's ready. Part of the fun for him is the fear he is causing her. He lives for that."

"How do you know?" asked John.

Dantes looked hard at John. "Trust me, *I know*," he said, his tone giving John goose bumps. Dantes turned back to Ghorza. "You can tell me how we got tricked by someone who is obviously brain dead later," he said, nodding at John; "for now, though, I have to do something about that teufling."

Ghorza snuck a glance around the corner. "You did see that there are three ogres sitting with him, right?"

"Yeah, that's the problem," agreed Dantes. "I can surprise the teufling and probably take one of the ogres, but the other two may tackle me and pin me down. I don't want to get trapped here any longer than I have to; it looks like all of Salidar is in Norlon today."

"I wasn't expecting combat today, but I do have a couple of chain spells and a haste that might help," said Ghorza.

"You're not ready for combat, but you have those available?"

"Well, I knew you might be less than happy to see the Spectre again," replied Ghorza. "I thought they might be needed to give me some time to reason with you."

Dantes snorted and a puff of smoke came out his nostrils. "*You* were going to use tact and reason with *me*? The world really has gone to hell today." He shook his head and looked around the corner. "Hit me with the Haste, and when I kill the teufling, Chain the ogre across from it to the table."

"What do you want me to do?" asked John.

"Stay out of the way," replied both Ghorza and Dantes, looking at him. Ghorza turned back to Dantes. "Ready when you are."

He nodded, and Ghorza commanded, "*Celeritas!*"

Dantes felt the world slow down around him as his movement sped up. He rounded the corner and walked toward the teufling. "Who's good for lunch here?" he asked by way of introduction.

The teufling and ogres turned to view the newcomer, and the teufling smiled in welcoming. Dantes felt himself ready to burst as he kept his movements as slow as possible. He knew from past experience that he would still seem a little faster than normal. "I've been looking for some fun all day," he said, hoping to cover the Haste; "it's great to finally find some!"

Dantes watched the teufling turn toward the interior of the cafe in slow motion. "Wench! Bring more wine and—*uh!*" it grunted as Dantes dropped down to all fours like a bull and sprang on him. Dantes cocked his head to the side, driving his right horn through the other teufling's heart. The only thing sharp enough to pierce a devil's heart was the horn of another devil, and he used his to great effect.

"What?" it gasped, as it fell to the floor. Dantes rode it down, twisting his head back and forth to ensure that he tore the teufling's heart apart.

The teuflings hit the ground, and Dantes jumped back up in time to see the ogre on the right upset his bench as it thrust itself to its feet. The better part of nine and a half feet tall, the ogre had light brown skin and a confused look on its face. Dantes didn't give it time to figure out what was happening. *"Globus Incendi!"* he commanded, sending a bead of fire into the creature's face. The fireball exploded on contact, cooking the ogre's face and bathing the entire group in its flames.

Counting on Ghorza to do her part, he spun toward the ogre on the left, jumping over the remains of the half-devil as he attacked. Hasted, Dantes looked like a blur as he dove at the monster. Already partially cooked, the ogre was just starting to get up from the bench when Dantes crashed into it headfirst, spearing it in the chest with his horns and driving it backward over the bench. Dantes' tail wrapped around one of the ogre's legs and pulled, helping to overbalance it. Holding onto the creature with both his hands and tail, Dantes rode it to the ground, twisting his horns to ensure he killed it. The ogre hit the wooden floor hard, and Dantes' horns drove all the way through it. Dantes felt the ogre relaxing in death, so he pulled out and spun toward the remaining ogre.

As he expected, Ghorza had done her part and Chained the ogre to the bench and chair, and it was awkwardly trying to lift itself up while still attached to both pieces of furniture. The animal skin on its back expanded as the creature took a giant breath, and Dantes knew that it was about to yell an alert. Drawing his knife as he charged, Dantes stabbed the ogre with all his might, driving the knife through the creature's back and into its heart. The only sound the ogre made was a gasp as it fell forward onto the table, which disintegrated with a wooden crash.

There was another crash, and Dantes spun with augmented speed to find the barmaid staring in horror, pointing at him. She had dropped her tray and was about to scream. Although Dantes was fast, he knew he couldn't close the distance to stop her in time; however, a small hand enveloped her mouth before she could scream.

"It's OK," said John, who had entered through the back of the cafe to try to keep her out of the fight. "It's all over now."

The waitress' eyes roamed the destruction of her cafe, taking in the devil and the orc standing over the remains of another devil and three ogres. One of the ogres was still rolling around, its face a mass of cooked flesh. She tried a second scream.

"That's not helping," John said through clenched teeth as she bit him. He turned her around so that she could see a fellow human. "It's OK," he said again. "We're the good guys."

Her eyes were wider than any John had ever seen before, and she was hyperventilating. He smiled at her in spite of his own terror. "Really," he said, nodding his head, "it's OK. I mean it."

She calmed a little, and he let go of her mouth. When she didn't immediately scream, he removed his hand and stepped back. "This is going to be a bad place to be, especially with the dead creatures here. You need to get away."

The girl nodded her head, still too scared to speak, her eyes flicking back and forth as if looking for a place to run. John told her how to use the secret tunnel system, and she turned and ran off into the restaurant. Turning back to the scene of the conflict, John found that Dantes had killed the last ogre, and both Ghorza and Dantes were going through the belongings of the creatures. As he walked over to see what they had found, a rank, unwashed odor caused him to gag as he got close.

"It's the ogres," explained Dantes. "They don't bathe much." He sniffed. "In fact, I'm surprised the teufling was with them. We usually have very sensitive noses, and it wouldn't have been pleasant to be in their company. Something must have been forcing them to operate together."

Dantes went back to searching the bodies, trying not to breathe around the ogres. It didn't take long to search them; there wasn't much to be found in their ratty and decaying furs. After a brief search of the teufling, though, Dantes held up a piece of parchment. "Success," he said.

Ghorza came over to look at the parchment. "I don't read Teufling," she said after taking a glance.

"They're orders for mopping up the city after it falls," he translated. "Damn. They're looking for us. How could they have known that we'd be together? Why would they care?"

"Are you sure it's us they're looking for?" asked Ghorza.

"Teufling, red with purple hair, medium-sized horns, found in the company of a female half-orc, greenish, six and a half feet tall, covered in clumps of hair. You tell me; it certainly sounds like us."

"That description could also fit almost any other teufling and half-orc," Ghorza argued.

Dantes raised an eyebrow. "Really? How many other teuflings have you seen in your life? Especially ones with purple hair?"

"Umm...With purple hair?" asked Ghorza. She sighed. "None; just you." Her brows knitted. "But why? Why would they be looking for us?"

Dantes turned to look pointedly at John. "I don't know why he's here, but I'd guess that he's the reason." He indicated the parchment. "This says that the two of us are wanted dead or alive. The human found accompanying us is to be killed immediately."

The color drained from John's face. "But, but..." he stammered.

"If you're not the Spectre, then I don't know who you are," Dantes said; "however, I see you make friends everywhere you go." He gazed at John with new respect. "I don't know what information you have, but obviously the enemy thinks it's worth killing you over. We need to get you to the Magisterium...assuming that it hasn't fallen yet."

"That's where we were heading," said Ghorza, "and his name is John."

"Good to meet you, John," said Dantes. "Let's get out of here before something else comes by and sees this mess. I don't want to have to explain it." He walked into the cafe. "There is a tunnel in the wine cellar; the barmaid's father is an acquaintance of mine." He led them down into the cellar. There was no sign of the girl; hopefully she had fled. She was better off on her own with nothing to her name than she was if another pack of ogres found her.

Dantes walked to the back of the cellar and reached under the cask furthest to the right. He pulled the lever underneath and was rewarded with a "click" as a hidden latch fell open. Taking hold of the cask, he rotated the entire rack forward and to the left. A secret passage yawned open behind it, dark and foreboding.

"You two go ahead," Dantes said, indicating they should precede him. "I'll close it behind us."

Ghorza looked at John. "You go first," she said. "There might be spiders."

"Really?" John asked, looking up at her. "*You're* afraid of spiders?"

"Not so much afraid as that I just don't like them," she replied. "I grew up near the desert, and we used to have some that were six feet tall."

Shaking his head, John walked into the tunnel. It was dark and damp. John knew it probably *was* full of spiders, especially now that Ghorza had put that thought into his head. He saw a torch located to the right as he entered the tunnel. "*Scintilla!*" he ordered, shooting a spark onto it. He blew gently and the flame caught. Sure enough, there was a big web about a foot further down the tunnel. John would have walked face-first into the hairy red spider sitting in its center. He touched the torch to the web, and it burned up, the spider falling to the floor. John started down the hall, wrinkling his nose at the musty odor.

Dantes put a hand on Ghorza's shoulder. Although she was taller, he was more massive, and he stopped her in place. She looked over her shoulder, and he gave her a quizzical look. "He's full of surprises," she noted in a whisper. "That's not all. He can do air and water magic, too." She turned back to follow John down the hall.

Overcoming his surprise, Dantes shut and latched the secret door and followed his two companions down the damp hallway. His eyes didn't need as much light as the others, and he was able to see quite well in the flickering torch light. He caught up with them in moments. "Let me lead," he said. "I know the way."

John and Ghorza moved to the side of the passage, and Dantes moved past them. Like most demons, he didn't have problems finding his way underground and was well-accustomed to subterranean passageways. He had also traveled through these particular tunnels before, and he went faster than John would have been able.

Several minutes passed, with the sounds of fighting getting louder and more violent. Judging by the feel of it, a catapult boulder landed nearby, and it shook dust down on them. Dantes could smell the fear coming from John. It smelled good. "Don't worry," he said. "The tunnels should hold together a bit longer." Another catapult stone hit close by and larger plumes of dust cascaded onto their heads. "Still, it might be best if we hurry," he added.

Dantes doubled his speed up the passageway. Ghorza's longer legs were up to the task, but John was forced into an awkward jog that hurt his shins. Within a couple of minutes, the sounds of clashing swords and screaming grew fainter, before nearly fading altogether. Dantes stopped suddenly. "We're here," he said. "Ghorza, if you could pull on that rope?" He pointed at the ceiling a few inches above her head.

Looking up, Ghorza saw the end of a small string hanging down about an inch. She would never have seen it on her own. Reaching up, she pulled down on the string. After six inches, she found that the string was tied to a rope. She pulled on the rope, and a ladder came smoothly down into the passageway on greased hinges. Dantes pulled down firmly on it, and a trap door about three feet wide opened in the ceiling. Dantes climbed up the ladder like he had done it many times before.

"Seems easy enough," Ghorza said. She took hold of the ladder and pulled herself up, leaving John in the tunnel by himself. He could see light in the room above, so he blew out the torch and set it down on the side of the passageway. Taking hold of the ladder, he climbed up into the center of a 30-foot square room.

As he looked around, he saw that he was once again in the center of a ring of spears, all of which seemed to be very sharp and pointed right at him. The men holding the spears looked both angry and afraid, a bad combination to see across the business ends of so many weapons.

Chapter Twenty-One

Solim surveyed the throne room. His troops had captured it in the assault, and he had decided to keep it as his command center. It was a place fit for...well, it was fit for a king, he thought, looking around at the opulence. Gorgeous tapestries hung on the walls for him to burn later, statues waited for him to pull out their gems and antique suits of armor were begging to be crushed into cookware. He couldn't wait.

The attack had been almost flawless. He had hoped to get the trolls a little closer before they were recognized, as it was never good for morale to have most of your front rank disintegrated before it reached the walls. It had almost caused his attack to fail, but he had been able to use the crown to drive the giants through the trolls, and everything had gone well after that...except for finding and killing the thrice-damned outlander and his companions.

"I want them found, and I want them found now!" Solim ordered, trying out the throne to see how it fit. He hadn't been told yet that he would be Norlon's new ruler, but he couldn't think of anyone that was a better fit for the position than he was. He was a far better choice than even that stupid anti-paladin who thought he was so high and mighty.

His eyes sought out the orc in charge of the beastiary and locked onto him. The orc's eyes glazed over at the contact. "Take your best trackers and *bring them to me!*"

Chapter Twenty-Two

"Uh, hi," said John, looking at all of the spears surrounding them. If anything, these spears looked even sharper than the ones that had been pointed in his face the last time.

"Are there any more of you down there?" asked the leader, who moved forward to hold the point of his sword on Dantes' chest.

"No, there are just the three of us," replied Dantes, reaching down to push the point of the sword away from his chest with a finger. "Despite our appearance, we are on your side, and you are holding us from our task."

The point of the sword returned to Dantes. "I'll be the one to say who goes where and when," said the man. "I don't know who you are, and there are all manner of foul creatures in the streets. If we hadn't come down here looking for an escape route for the Magistra, you might very well have slipped in unnoticed."

"I do not know who you are," said Dantes, his finger still touching the point of the sword, "but I am no enemy of yours, and our mission is vital. There are indeed fell creatures in the streets, which makes our errand even more urgent." He looked down and moved the point of the sword again with his finger. "Besides, if I wanted to take that sword from you, you would not be able to stop me. *Calefacite!*"

"There's no need to go name calling," the man said. "We just took over here, and it's our job to make sure that anyone coming in is supposed to be here, today more so than any other day. *Ouch!*" While he was speaking, the tip of his sword had changed color where Dantes' finger touched it, turning first red and then white as the sword heated. The temperature change traveled rapidly to the other end, and the soldier dropped the sword with a clang, to blow on his singed fingers.

"If you're done fooling around, we really are on an urgent errand," said Ghorza to Dantes, sounding annoyed. She turned to the soldier. "You may not have seen him around here recently, but some of your men have certainly seen me." Several heads nodded, and she looked back to the leader, who was still trying to cool his hand. "May we be on our way?"

"Yes, begone," replied the leader, and all of the soldiers withdrew their spears.

The three companions left the entry room. "Was that really necessary?" asked Ghorza.

"No," Dantes said with a smile, "it wasn't. Still, if he's going to guard the Magisterium, he needs to learn to respect magic."

The group went up several levels, the sounds of fighting growing more distinct with every passing floor. As they reached the third level, they heard a resounding crash echo down the corridor. "What was that?" asked John.

"I don't know," replied Dantes. "You two go find the Magistra; I'll check it out." He left at a run in the direction of the noise. Ghorza and John went up one more flight of stairs and then down a hall that went in the opposite direction from the way Dantes had gone. Halfway down the corridor they came to a door that was ajar. With a worried look, Ghorza pushed open the door the rest of the way. A young woman could be seen standing next to the Magistra, who lay in a bed along one of the walls of the chamber. The attendant looked up in surprise. Blood covered the bed, the floor, and most of the young woman.

"Help me!" she called. "The Magistra's dying!"

"Magistra!" exclaimed Ghorza, rushing to her side.

The woman moved to give her room, and Ghorza could see that she was one of the Magisterium's healers. Up close, the woman was much younger than she originally appeared. She didn't look like she was old enough to have completed the initial healer's training yet, much less be proficient enough to cure whatever had happened to the Magistra. "I can't save her!" the woman said, falling into hysterics. "You've got to *do* something!" She began sobbing.

"What happened?" asked Ghorza.

Hearing Ghorza's voice, the Magistra's eyes fluttered open. She reached out for Ghorza and pulled her close. "Don't have...much time," she gasped. "Did...find Dantes?"

"Yes," Ghorza replied. "I brought him back with me. We'll get you out of here and to a healer."

"Too late...for me," the Magistra said. "Must find...Milos. Crown...Most important."

"We will find him," Ghorza said. "Also, the human may be of more help than we thought. He is able to cast at least three types of spells."

The Magistra's eyes opened wider and her grip tightened on Ghorza's tunic. "Three? Forget Milos!" she forced out with a new determination. "Must take him...Mountain of Frost. More important. Prophecy..." Her grip faltered and she fell back to the bed.

Ghorza looked up to see Dantes run into the room. He had been fighting; steam was rising from his head and shoulders. "We've got to get her out of here," he said. "They're close. Too close."

"She can't be moved," Ghorza and the woman said together. "She won't survive it," added the healer.

"She won't survive what?" asked a high clear voice from the doorway. "There's not going to be any dying here today, at least not while I'm around."

John's head spun around to see the morning sun burst forth from the doorway. As the brilliant object entered the room, John saw that it was a woman...the most beautiful woman he had ever seen...dressed in plate mail that reflected every bit of light in the room with a crimson overtone. Her silver hair hung down below her metal collar, almost appearing to blow in some non-existent wind. The woman was a knight, and she was stunning. And she was good. She was very good.

"Damn," Dantes said, having to avert his eyes. The evil part that he kept locked up inside found it very hard to look at her.

John knew what Dantes meant. She radiated good, but not in the same way the teufling at the cafe had given off evil earlier. Where evil seemed to cling to the devil like black oil that had a hard time separating itself from him, good emanated from the knight like a sunburst, cleansing the air around her. Her faith was strong, and that belief radiated from her in every direction.

As she crossed the room, John could see that her initial appearance was only an illusion. She was a mess, and appeared to have been in some heavy fighting. The silver armor that reflected the light with a red hue was in fact covered in at least as much blood as coated the Magistra's bed. In the case of the paladin, though, none of it appeared to be hers. She was strong and confident as she strode across the room to where the Magistra lay.

It was only then that John noticed her companion, a man wearing a rough brown woolen robe, who trailed behind her like the morning followed the sun. His head bent, the priest followed the paladin to the bed and spread his hands out over the Magistra.

"She is in grave danger," said the robed man in a soft voice. The emptiness in his voice spoke volumes about what he had already experienced that day. "She will die without aid and comfort," he continued, "and alas, I have no more to give. I used all of the healing granted unto me out on the city's walls. If you have nothing left to give, then I am afraid she is doomed."

The young woman stifled a small sob. The cleric had been her last hope of saving the Magistra.

The paladin nodded in understanding, obviously familiar with what the man said. "Throughout the battle on the walls," she replied, "I knew that there was something that my god was calling me to do. Something that I needed to save myself for. It is obvious to me that this is the moment." Looking up to the heavens, she said simply, "In your name," and laid her hands on the Magistra. Healing emanated outward from her touch, and John could see ripped flesh knit itself together and the Magistra's breathing ease. "Thank you," the paladin added as the healing touch receded, leaving the Magistra in a much better condition.

"Well done," said the cleric; "you have saved her life." He turned to the rest of the people in the room. "Her condition is improved; however, she is by no means well. She will not be able to travel far or without aid until she has rested."

"We will need to fashion a litter," said Dantes, looking for poles.

"We can use the sheets from the bed if we have to," added the young woman.

"We just need some poles," said Ghorza.

"*Excuse me!*" interrupted a voice from the bed. Everyone turned to find the Magistra up on an elbow. "I am pretty sure I remember giving you an order, Ghorza. Why are you still here? Oh, I see you found Dantes. Good. Why are you still here too? I'm unconscious for a few minutes and everyone forgets what I told them to do?"

The cleric stepped in between the Magistra and her charges. "Lady Magistra, you need to lie down," he said.

If he hoped to calm her down, it didn't work. "Ah, Father Telenor, you are here, too," she said. "Is Lady Ellyn here also? Wonderful. You need to go with Dantes and Ghorza and...John Gratsby. Must...go...Prophecy..." she began weakening again at the same time as the squad of men from the basement burst into the room. They were followed closely by the halfling that John recognized as the one that had initially taken him to meet the Magistra.

"We must get the Magistra into the tunnels," said the leader of the soldiers as he came through the door. "The enemy will be here in seconds, not minutes."

"I will go...with them," the Magistra said. "But you must," she grabbed the paladin's arm and pulled her closer. "You *must* go to the Mountain of Frost. Prophecy...Fate of world..." She collapsed onto the bed again.

"We can't just leave her here," said Ghorza.

"We can and will," said the paladin. "I do not believe there can be any dispute over what the lady intended. We are to go to the Mountain of Frost, with all due haste. These other men will see to her needs. It is obviously urgent; we must accomplish the task she has given us."

"Follow me," said Dantes. "I know where the mountain is, as well as how to get out of the city. Getting there will not be any fun, but it appears that's where we are supposed to go, regardless."

"Wait..." said the Magistra as they turned to go. She was back on one elbow, her other hand pointing unsteadily at the wall. She waved her hand and a chest of drawers appeared where she had been pointing. "Take book...in dresser. John...must have it."

Ghorza opened the top drawer and removed a large hidebound book from it.

"What is it?" asked Dantes.

Ghorza looked up, shock evident on her face. "It's her spell book."

Chapter Twenty-Three

Dantes led the group through the tunnel. Compared with the din they experienced on their earlier trip, the relative silence seemed eerie. Only a random shriek every few minutes pierced the muffling nature of the tunnel complex. Lady Ellyn winced every time she heard one. Even in the minimal light, John could see that she wanted to be out among the civilians, saving as many as she could, for as long as she was able.

After a particularly long scream, Father Telenor put his hand on her arm, offering her the simple comfort of a human touch. It seemed to work...until the next scream.

After 10 minutes, they arrived at the changeover where they had to go above ground to get to the shed tunnel that would take them back under the wall and out of the city. Dantes led them up from the wine cellar and cracked open the door to leave the cafe. He closed it again quickly when he heard a voice close by. The man's voice was loud, though, and the group could hear him even with the door shut.

"All right, me laddies," it said, "who wants to step up and try out the new points o' my arrows? They're not fire, but I'm told that they'll light you up just as brightly."

A chorus of growls answered his questioning.

"Well now, laddies," the voice said, "I have to tell you that, while I can usually hold this bow a good long time, I'm a wee bit tired right now, what with all the fighting this morning, so I'm going to be asking you to decide who dies first a little more quickly than normal, if you'd be of such a mind."

Lady Ellyn pushed past Dantes toward the door. "I'm out of spells," Dantes said. "I won't be able to help much, and we don't know how many there are."

"I care not," replied Lady Ellyn. "I have listened to these beasts tear apart the people I've sworn to protect since the beginning of our journey. If I can help just one person on our way out of this godsforsaken city, I intend to."

"M'lady, you know that I am also out of spells, correct?" asked Father Telenor.

"I do," replied Lady Ellyn. "Can I still count on you to guard my off side?"

"Always, m'lady."

"Then let us go," she said. "For the gods of good!" She burst out of the door at a run, with Telenor close by her side. After a moment's hesitation, the rest of the group followed.

John trailed the warriors around the corner of the nearest house, and found himself much closer to three large evil-looking creatures than he *ever* wanted to be. Dark green in color, they each stood over nine feet tall and had some sort of rubbery, moss-covered skin. The fetid stench coming from them threatened to overwhelm him.

"Trolls," said Ghorza, coming to a halt. "I hate trolls."

"I hate them too," said Dantes. "Normally they're a lot of fun to burn. Unfortunately, we're going to have to do this the hard way, as I'm out of spells."

Lady Ellyn hadn't waited for the rest of the group, and as Ghorza and Dantes continued their advance, she charged up and sliced through the hamstrings of one of the trolls facing the other way. It crumpled, and she continued on to the next one.

The troll screamed in anger and frustration as it tried to get back up, but was unable. As John watched, the muscles that had been sliced off and left to dangle from the troll's legs began to heal.

"Quickly," said Dantes, "we have to kill it before it regenerates."

The scream of the first troll caused the other two trolls to turn and face the new threat. That was all that the person trapped in the corner needed, and he launched an arrow dripping a black liquid. It hit the troll closest to him in the chest, and the wound began hissing. The troll screamed even more loudly than the first one.

"Can you do something that doesn't make them scream so much?" asked Dantes as he and Ghorza threw oil onto the troll from bottles they pulled from their packs. "'Ware the arms!" he added to Ghorza. Nine feet tall, the troll had arms that were almost seven feet long, giving it a considerable reach as it continued to flip around.

Ghorza tried to light the oil, but one of the troll's arms flicked out and slapped her down, stunned. Seeing the easy prey, Dantes was immediately forgotten by the troll as it pulled itself around toward the semi-conscious half-orc. "*Scintilla!*" John commanded, sending a spark onto the troll. The oil caught fire, and the troll was covered in flames. It began rolling around, trying to put them out. Ghorza was forgotten as the troll burned to death.

The third troll was trading blows with Lady Ellyn and Father Telenor. Although the troll could reach much further with its club than the humans' weapons, it couldn't attack and defend at the same time. Lady Ellyn was protected from the troll's attacks by Father Telenor's shield, though, and she was able to make attacks of her own nearly unhampered. It didn't come without cost; the troll's attacks were far stronger than those of a human, and Telenor's shield was soon shattered. "Can't hold...much longer, m'lady," advised Father Telenor. "I'm down to almost splinters as it is."

With a massive swipe that the two humans barely ducked under, the troll caught the shield's iron edge on its club, and it flew out of Telenor's grasp. The troll roared in satisfaction as the shield went spiraling through the air.

As the troll celebrated, Lady Ellyn dove forward in a half-roll. She used the momentum of the dive to stand up underneath the troll, and she stabbed upward, transfixing the troll on her blade. The troll's roar turned into a scream of pain, which ended suddenly as an arrow flew up into its mouth, piercing its brain. The tip of the arrow burst forth from the top of its head and a loud hissing sound could be heard as the acid ate into its skull. The troll toppled to the ground, seemingly in slow motion.

All of the humanoids turned to the last troll, which had the arrow in its chest. It hadn't attacked further, as a large brown owl was harassing it, fluttering in and out of its reach. Any time the troll tried to attack the archer, the owl would swoop in and claw the troll's eyes, momentarily blinding it.

The archer whistled, and the owl flew up out of the way. The troll reached up to grab it, leaving itself undefended, and another arrow sprouted from its chest. This one found its heart, and the troll's attacks began to slow. With a groan, it swung one more time at the owl, and then it collapsed to the ground. The owl returned to alight on the archer's shoulder, nuzzling his cheek and then preening a wing.

"Many thanks, me lords and ladies," the archer said, flourishing his hat. John could see that the humanoid was even smaller than he first thought; without the large hat, the archer was barely three and a half feet tall. John thought that the creature looked similar to the fire gnome he had met earlier in the week, with pointed ears and angular facial features, but where Vishdink had been red and gray, the archer was light brown like the trunk of a tree. Complementing this color, the archer had tufts of forest green hair sticking out all over the top of his head, which he quickly covered back up with his hat. The eyes that faced the group were solid black.

"You're welcome," said Dantes, helping Ghorza to her feet. "However, those things were far too loud. We need to leave, *now*." He turned toward the shed.

"Wait!" said the archer. "Do you hear that?"

Dantes listened but didn't hear anything other than the sound of combat in the distance. "What do you mean?" he asked. "I don't hear anything."

"Aye, laddie, that's just what I was sayin'," replied the archer. "While we were tusslin' with the beasties, I heard the braying o' worgs." The tracking abilities of the oversized evil wolves were legendary.

"I don't hear them now," replied Dantes.

"Aye, and that's what's worrying me," agreed the archer. "If they've gone quiet, they've got the scent." He held up his head and sniffed the air. "They're here," he said. "*Run!*"

The sounds of running feet and the booming of drums calling the evil creatures to battle could be heard from the street in front of the cafe. The group ran toward the shed and went through the door.

As they started climbing down into the tunnel, a shout rang out from the yard. The door had been left open in their haste, and they had been spotted. "Climb faster," Dantes urged. "Go, go, go!"

Spurred on by the shout, the rest of the group hurried past him and down the ladder. The last member of the group went down the ladder as the first orc entered the shed. Seeing that everyone else was clear, Dantes dove into the ladder well and fell to the floor of the tunnel 10 feet below. Picking himself up, he ran forward and grabbed the end of a rope hanging 15 feet further into the tunnel. He pulled with all of his infernal might, and ripped out the key stones holding the tunnel's roof in place. The tunnel collapsed behind them, sealing off their enemies as the first orc started down the ladder.

Dantes turned around to find everyone staring at him. "Didn't that hurt?" asked John.

"Yes, quite a bit," Dantes replied as dust trickled down all around him. "But it will buy us a little bit of time. Come on; we need to hurry."

Chapter Twenty-Four

"They escaped into some tunnels and then destroyed the entrance," reported the troll scout in its deep voice. "We have troops opening it up, but it will be some time."

"They are beginning to get on my nerves," Solim said. He motioned for the troll to return to his duties and turned to his brother. "Did you learn anything from them before their escape?"

"Yes, Solim. Before she passed out, the Magistra sent them on some sort of quest. She was barely coherent, but she said that they needed to go to the Mountain of Frost for some sort of end-of-the-world prophecy."

"By the nameless *god*!" Solim swore.

"What is it?" asked Rubic. He had seen his brother get mad many times before, but couldn't remember ever hearing that level of vehemence.

"This is *exactly* the reason I have been trying to kill them," replied Solim.

He stomped over to a suit of armor and kicked it. It fell over with a tremendous crash that brought the rest of the room to silence. "No," he said in a quiet fury that Rubic had to strain to hear. "The Prophecy is *mine* to claim! I will *not* let them take it from me!" Solim kicked the suit's helmet, sending it flying through the air. It clattered to the floor on the other side of the room. A troll picked it up and looked at it curiously before smashing it flat. Solim glared at the leaders that had stopped what they were doing to watch. All of them found something better to do than meet his gaze.

Solim returned to the throne, now totally focused; his anger tempered into purpose. He glared at Rubic, who shrank from the malignance of his gaze. "It looks like you will get a second chance to kill them," he said. "They will be fleeing. Take a squad of orc trackers and go outside the city walls. Track them down and kill them. Bring me back their heads...or don't come back at all."

Chapter Twenty-Five

"I think we should probably stop and decide what we are going to do," said Lady Ellyn as the group came to a small clearing. They had been following the short archer through the woodlands for over an hour since escaping the city, as he seemed to know where he was going. Lady Ellyn nodded to the newest member of the group. "Why don't you start by telling us who you are, and how you came to be fighting the trolls."

"Aye, it's pleased I am that you came along when you did," replied the archer. "The name's Fitzber, Captain Fitzber if you must, o' the Earthen Gnome Rangers." He performed the flourish with his hat again. "I am at your service." He paused for a few moments. "Where to begin...where to begin...aye, at the beginning I s'pose. I was in charge o' a group of rangers that was sent to the frontier to watch the border with Carpos. We knew they were coming, but didn't know when or where. All o' a sudden, they were upon us. They used goblin sappers to tunnel under our lines. We were quickly overrun when they burst forth from the ground behind our defenses. I sent all o' my men to try and get the word back to Norlon, while I scouted behind their lines to find out what they were all about." He shook his head. "I wish I hadn't; the memories o' that time will be givin' me nightmares for the rest o' me life."

"Why is that?" asked Lady Ellyn.

"I saw their command element," replied Fitzber, "and I knew the lads back at Norlon would be in trouble. Their troops were led by some sort o' anti-paladin, astride a nightmare as dark as a witch's heart. Every time it snorted, smoke came from its nostrils. As dark as its steed was, the anti-paladin was even blacker. He seemed to absorb all o' the light around him, making it hard to see him in the darkness. He was hard to look at; he was evil personified." He shuddered at the recollection.

"What did he look like?" asked Lady Ellyn, her voice empty of emotion.

"He was a big human," replied Fitzber. "He had to be nearly seven feet tall, with armor black as the inside o' a cave in an eclipse. He was totally black; even his helmet was black...all except for his blood red hands. At first I thought it was the blood o' his foes still on him, but then I saw that his gauntlets had been painted red."

"He does that to terrorize his enemies," Lady Ellyn said. "When he pulls the hearts out of his enemies and holds them up, it makes them look bigger and him more ferocious by comparison."

"Oh, so you be knowin' that one, then?" asked the ranger.

"Aye, I do," replied Lady Ellyn. "It is worse than we thought. That man is the Dark Lord Kazan. No wonder he didn't show himself during the attack on Norlon; he would have wanted all of the paladins dead before he revealed himself, so that we couldn't try to guess what he would do."

"You said, 'worse than we thought,'" interrupted Dantes. "Why did you think it was bad to start with?"

"I was at the battle fought before the gates of Norlon," answered Lady Ellyn. "I saw the person I *thought* was leading their armies. There was a halfling riding on the shoulders of one of the leading giants...and he was wearing the queen's crown. That was bad enough."

"What is so special about the crown?" asked John. "I mean, I saw it, and it was pretty, but it's just a crown, right?"

"No," replied Lady Ellyn, "it's much more than a crown. It's a magical artifact. In fact, it's one of the three artifacts that will be brought together at the end of the world. It's all part of the Prophecy."

"The Prophecy?" asked Dantes. "The Magistra said something about a prophecy. What do you know about this prophecy?"

"I don't know a lot about it," she replied. "No one knows much about it for sure, as most of the details were lost after the Sundering. What knowledge remains didn't make much sense until recently. The one piece of information we have is a scrap of parchment that remains from before the Sundering. It says that at the end of times, a man will come from another world, he will gather the Three Items of Power and then...something will happen." She stopped.

"Something will happen?" asked Dantes. "Could you be any vaguer? What is supposed to happen? What kind of Prophecy is that?"

"No one knows," said Lady Ellyn with a shrug. "The parchment is torn at that point. It is hoped that this person will come and save the world from the darkness that is approaching. Half the people believe this. There are, however, cynics that perpetuate a rumor that the conclusion of the sentence is that the one that comes from another world will gather the items and thrust the world into a pit of darkness, from which it will never recover."

"What do you believe?" asked John. He tried to keep the quaver out of his voice, but wasn't entirely successful.

"Me?" asked Lady Ellyn. "I don't believe that either of these endings are what was originally intended, as the one true god would never preordain our lives for us. What would be the point if everything happened according to destiny and not free will? The point of living *is* the constant striving. Without free will, there is no good or evil. We can only achieve purity through struggle; it cannot be given." She looked intently at John. "You asked what I believe, and I will tell you. I believe that it is up to us. Whether this world rises or falls is dependent solely on our actions."

"Great," grumbled Father Telenor. "No pressure there."

Chapter Twenty-Six

"We are ready, brother of the overlord," grunted Khazatch, the orc platoon leader, in its language. Growing up on Salidar, Rubic had the misfortune of spending enough time with orcs that he spoke their language. While Rubic couldn't emulate all of the grunts that they made perfectly, he could understand their language without any problems.

"Lead on, then," replied Rubic, and the platoon leader barked out the command to advance. A giant of an orc, Khazatch was almost seven feet tall and 300 pounds, with a mix of features both ape-like and pig-like. Pig-like won out in the end, as tusks stuck out several inches from both his top and bottom jaws. His skin was a grayish green, indicating that he came from the southern part of Salidar. Immensely strong, he carried a double-headed great axe on his back and a whip at his side. Rubic also caught flashes of metal from all over his body as the giant orc turned and left at a jog, and he guessed the platoon leader had many hidden knives as well.

A squad of six large orcs followed Khazatch, each restraining a large worg. Although the orcs were six and a half feet tall and over 250 pounds, it took all of their strength to control the animals. Three feet high at the shoulder and weighing over 300 pounds, the worgs' eyes were right at Rubic's eye level. Rubic knew from experience not to look into the worgs' red eyes; the worgs were extremely intelligent and some of the most evil creatures he had ever met. Like the orcs holding them, they liked to kill for fun, often leaving their victims not-quite-dead for long periods of time, just so they could watch them suffer.

The six orcs of the second squad were normal-sized orcs, standing just over six feet tall, with the black hair, pointed ears and reddish eyes characteristic of their race. Like their leader, they were grayish green in color, and all wore mustard yellow pants and tunics that clashed garishly with their skin tone. Each of the normal orcs was just over 200 pounds and either carried an axe or a sword, as well as some sort of knife.

The last orc to jog past him was shorter and slighter than the rest of the orcs, and it was dressed in a variety of animal skins, bones and trophies. Armed with a staff and a bandolier of ceremonial knives across its chest, the orc shaman didn't look at Rubic as he ran by. He was focused on praying to his gods, which was quite all right with Rubic. He'd take all the help he could get.

Rubic chased after them, the orcs' jog translating into nearly a full run for the halfling's shorter legs. He was sure that they had enough combat power to kill the outlander's group; Rubic just hoped they would catch up with their quarry before his legs gave out.

Chapter Twenty-Seven

"What does the crown do?" asked Ghorza.

"It allows the wearer to control members of evil races," replied Lady Ellyn. "Whoever wears it can control orcs, hill giants, ogres, trolls, or any other evil humanoid that you can name."

"That's how they were able to unite all of the races of Salidar," said Dantes. He paused, deep in thought. "That also explains how they were able to make the teufling go with the ogres. It must have been under some kind of spell."

"I understand that the crown is magic," said the ranger, "but I canna' imagine that it would let the wearer control more than just a few o' the enemy at a time. How did it get them to storm the city? Commanding that big an army would not be easy."

"I was there at the gates of the city," replied Lady Ellyn. "The halfling did it by controlling a few of the leaders and making them do what he commanded." She paused, and then said, "Even so, it was a battle for the ages, full of fury and majesty. The enemy forces called forth a huge cloud bank, allowing their troll forces to move up unhindered. Our air mages worked to blow the clouds away, but the trolls charged before they could do so."

"I've been on the receiving end of a cavalry charge before, and it was horrific," she continued, her eyes distant as she relived the battle. "This was worse. Far worse. Although the average troll stands about nine feet high, they hunched forward as they charged across the field, looking much shorter than they actually were. We weren't even sure what they were until they were almost upon us. It was the king who first recognized them for the danger they were. The archers had been firing at them as they crossed the field, but as you saw earlier, trolls regenerate. Any that were hit simply pulled out the arrows or ballistae, and the wounds closed as they continued to run closer. Even the most grievous wounds had little effect on them."

"The ground shook with their approach, and lesser men and women on the wall began to quail. Then the king realized what they were, and cast a Smite spell on their leader. I have never before seen a paladin of his rank in combat; the way the king Smote his foe was awe-inspiring. Sent from the heavens, the power descended on the troll from above, shattering the cloud cover. The power of the one true god came down like a ray of sunshine, and he blasted the troll to dust. Following his lead, all of the paladins on the wall began Smiting the hells-brood charging at us, and we broke their charge. Once we realized they were trolls, the fire mages threw fireball after fireball into their ranks, and the screams they made as they burned up in front of us were horrible to hear. We finally killed the last enemy-controlled troll, and the rest of them stopped right in front of the wall."

"The trolls just stood there, almost within reach of us, but they were confused and without direction. With their leaders dead, they were not sure whether they were supposed to continue attacking or flee, and we threw everything fire-based we had at them. Fire arrows rained down by the hundreds, fireballs arced out and we dumped cauldron after cauldron of burning oil on them. It was a slaughter. We knew that if we could hold off the trolls, we could most likely fight off the giants we could see following them. The giants pushed forward, and the halfling riding the giant forced some of the trolls to continue the attack. The enemy began advancing again."

"We would still have carried the day," she said proudly, "were it not for the turncoats. The troops hired by the merchants' guild opened the side gate to the city while our attention was focused on repulsing the trolls. Our first indication that something was wrong was when the ogres hit us from behind. Their leader struck without notice, striking down the king. The ogres, ten feet tall and over 700 pounds, used their clubs to sweep the defenders from the castle wall. Those that fell were run down by the mercenary cavalry in the courtyard. The slaughter continued, but now it was our forces being slaughtered."

"Most of my squad of Silver Swords were killed defending the queen while the healers worked to save her life. When she heard that the Magistra had also been wounded, she sent Father Telenor to save her, with me to protect him. Unfortunately, we ran into several other pockets of fighting on the way to the Magisterium, and Father Telenor was forced to use the remainder of his healing spells on me as I fought through a band of hill giants. He had to use his last major cure spell on me when one of them broke my leg by throwing a donkey at me. Because of this, he arrived at the Magistra's bedside out of mana, even though he was tasked to save her. He had to use all of it to save me."

"To save both of us, if the truth be known," added Father Telenor. "Had the giants taken m'lady out of the fight, I wouldn't have lasted much longer, and certainly wouldn't have made it to the Magistra's bedside. Curing Lady Ellyn saved both of us, so that we could make it there, but it caused me to arrive without any healing spells. The rest of our story, you already know."

There was a momentary lull in the conversation, which was broken by John. "Hey," he said to Ghorza. "Can I see the book that the Magistra gave me?"

"Sure," she replied, handing him the large tome. Over five inches thick, John expected it to be heavy.

"That's weird," he said as Ghorza let go. "This book is really big, but it doesn't weigh a thing. Why is that?"

"Magic," said several voices around the group.

"What?" he asked, confused.

"The book is magic," explained Ghorza. "It is about magic, and it is full of magic; it's magic in every way. It's light because its last owner wanted it that way. It is also thick with hard covers for the same reason. If you wanted it to shrink or grow heavy, it would. The shrinking part might help, but I can't imagine why you'd want it to be heavy while you have to carry it around."

John concentrated on the book becoming smaller, and it shrank down to just about an inch thick, with thinner covers. Its weight never changed.

"Cool!" he said, opening it. As he looked at the first page, though, he felt something change.

"I think we need to have another talk about magic," John said to Ghorza.

"Why's that?" she asked. "You shouldn't be surprised that you can't read it. Until you become a first rank mage, you won't be able to read any of those spells. You can't read what you cannot use."

"Really?" John asked, flipping through the pages. "So I can use the Read Magic, Hold Portal and Invisibility spells? Cool!" He flipped to the red tab about a quarter of the way through it. "I can also use Flare, Burning Hands and Magic Missile? Oooh cool, Magic

Missile!" He flipped to the blue tab. "Ray of Frost, Shocking Grasp and Fog Cloud?" He turned to the brown tab. "Summon Monster I and Summon Monster II?" He looked up. "Awesome! What do I have to do to use them?"

The rest of the group stood frozen in place, staring at him like he had just grown two more heads or sprouted wings. "What?" he asked. No one said anything for several seconds.

"That cannot be," said Father Telenor finally, breaking the silence.

"What?" John asked again.

"Not only should you not be able to read them," said Ghorza, "some of those spells are second level spells. You'd have to be a third rank mage in order to be able to cast them."

"How is this possible?" asked Father Telenor.

"I didn't get a chance to tell you," said John, "but when I set the troll on fire, something happened. I don't know how or why, but my head all of a sudden felt emptier. Not like when I cast a cantrip, but a whole lot emptier. The only way I can describe the feeling is to say that it felt like part of my mind that was solid rock turned to water and that there is now a giant lake in my head. It feels like my perception of life has expanded to encompass this new reality." He shuddered. "I don't know. It's creepy."

"I wouldn't have believed it if I hadn't been there," Dantes said, "but you leveled up. That is exactly what it feels like when you level up. It feels like your mind expands; that is your mana pool growing."

"But that doesn't explain why he can cast second level spells," Lady Ellyn said. "How is that possible?"

"The thing that happened when I burned up the troll happened again when I opened the book and started looking at the pages," said

John. "What was it? Leveling up? Well, I think it actually happened a couple of times. It seemed like there was an expansion, and then there was another one that happened right after the first."

"It's the Spell Book of Aran-Than," said Ghorza, with awe in her voice. "It has to be. This book was thought to have been lost thousands of years ago. It's boosted you from first rank to third rank. While it is in your possession, you will function two levels higher than you actually are."

"The Spell Book of Aran-Than?" asked John. "If it's got a name, it's got to be something important, like some sort of artifact, right?"

"No," said Lady Ellyn, "it is much more important than that. It is the second Item of Power. We cannot allow the enemy to get its hands on it. Among other things, it turns single target spells into area of effect spells. Instead of allowing the enemy commander to command individual members of evil races, he would be able to control whole squads or companies of troops at once."

"The Spell Book also gives the holder access to every known spell," added Ghorza, "as well as an extra two levels of casting ability. The holder can cast spells as if he or she had that much more experience, and makes the spells that much more powerful, as well. Even without the other Items of Power, it is a very potent arcane item, and you are incredibly lucky to have it in your possession."

"Umm…maybe it would be better if one of you took it, then," said John. "You'd be able to put it to better use than I could."

"Perhaps…and perhaps not," replied Dantes. "I would only be able to use the fire-based spells and Ghorza would only be able to use the air-based spells. You seem to be able to use all four of the elements, even if you are not able to cast as high a level of spell as each of us." He thought for a moment and added, "Besides, the

Magistra gave it to you. She is far wiser and more acquainted with the Prophecy than all of us put together, I imagine. If there was a reason she thought you should have it, I for one am not going to go against her wishes."

"Nor am I," added Ghorza.

"I don't get it, though," said John. "How does it change my magical abilities?"

Ghorza slapped him on the forehead. "How can anyone be this dumb?" she asked Dantes. She turned back to John. "It's magic, of course. It does what it is supposed to do. Why? Who knows? Why do you have to ask so many questions?"

"Because maybe if I understood it better, I could use it better," John said, his fists clenched at his side.

Lady Ellyn cleared her throat, interrupting their discussion before it could get any more heated. "So in a brief span of time, the crown and the spell book have both made their appearances. The only thing missing is the Scepter of Decency. Does anyone doubt that our quest is to retrieve it?"

"The Scepter of Decency?" asked John. "What kind of name is that? It sounds like something that was made for a child."

"The Scepter gets its name from the fact that it has the power to command members of the good races," replied Lady Ellyn; "basically, people that are generally decent in nature."

"Even if we get these things," Father Telenor said, "what are we supposed to do with them? We can't just turn them over to someone so inexperienced, can we? He knows nothing about warfare or magic. We might as well go hand them over to the enemy ourselves."

"With our aid and assistance, I am sure that John will find a way," said Lady Ellyn. "This must be a trial that the one true god has put before us to test our resolve and our faith in her. Because John is unprepared to do it on his own, we have been called here because we all have a part to play." She stabbed her sword into the ground in front of John and knelt on one knee, her hands on top of her sword. Bowing, she said, "If you are to be our savior, I will assist you in whatever way I am able."

"So, he is to be our savior?" asked Father Telenor, sarcasm heavy in his voice. "I have to say I expected something... more."

"Who is to know the mind of the one god?" asked Lady Ellyn. "She sets things in motion for us, and she allows us to do our part in her service. You have to believe, Telenor. No one ever said serving her would be easy."

"No, that was never part of the agreement," replied Father Telenor with a sigh. "Still..." his voice trailed off.

"Still what?" asked John. "What was it you expected?"

"I always envisioned our savior would be someone full of religious fervor, for one thing," replied Father Telenor, "and would be someone with excellent leadership skills. I also thought our savior would have advanced magical skills, at least in the elemental, if not the clerical arts. Oh, and I would have expected you to be taller."

"Taller?" asked John.

"Yes, taller," agreed Father Telenor, who was less than six feet tall, but still much taller than John. "You know, someone I could really look up to."

"Are you done?" asked Dantes.

Father Telenor sighed again. "I think so, yes."

"Good," said Dantes, "then we can stop wasting our time. We have a long way to go."

"Why?" asked John. "Where is this Mountain of Frost?"

"The Mountain of Frost lies just off the coast of Salidar. We will have to start by going to Harbortown. While it's unlikely that we will find a ship there that will take us to Salidar, it will be almost impossible to find one anywhere else."

Chapter Twenty-Eight

"I don't know," said John. They had been walking for two hours, which had given him plenty of time to think. "Something just doesn't feel right about this."

"What do you mean?" asked Ghorza, who was walking alongside him on the forest path the ranger had found.

"I mean, the enemy's had three years since they stole the crown to work out their plans," he said. "They know what they're doing, and we're fumbling around trying to catch up, right?" John saw her nod in agreement, so he continued. "Don't you think they would have thought about this Prophecy and put something in place to keep it from happening? Maybe they know more about it or have a different interpretation of it. I mean, they *have* to know the crown is one of the three Items of Power, eh? That's got to be why they stole it, right? To use it to control the evil races and get them to do the thief's bidding."

Ghorza looked uncomfortable. "Well, maybe," she allowed. "But just because we know about it doesn't mean the enemy knows about it, too."

"Come on," said John. "That's what the good guys always do in the movies. They underestimate their opponents. We've got to be smarter than that."

"What is this thing you call 'movies?'" asked Ghorza.

"It's not important," said John. "What matters is that we can't underestimate them. If we know that they have one of the Items of

Power, they have to know it, too. They probably knew what it was when they stole it. *That's why they stole it.* They've been using it for crying out loud; they've *got* to know what it is. Not only that, they've had it for three years. I'll bet they've been looking for the other ones, too, including sending out spies to see if we've located any of the others."

"Nobody knows we have one of the others," said Dantes, from in front of Ghorza. "We just found out ourselves."

"See, that's what I don't get," said John. "If nobody knows anything about us or what we're doing, why have groups of the enemy been told to look for us? How does the enemy even know I'm here? The only people that know who I am are from the Magisterium, and there's only a very few of them. You must have a leak...a traitor...some turncoat that is giving information to the enemy."

"Impossible!" said Dantes. "There is no one in the Magisterium that hasn't been checked out. If there's a leak, it's not from within the Magisterium."

"No, it *has* to be from within the Magisterium," insisted John. "No one else knew who I was."

"It's not possible," said Ghorza. "There were only four people who knew who you were. The Magistra, Dantes, Vishdink and me. Dantes and I have been with you the whole time, and the enemy is hunting us. It's not one of us. It's not the Magistra; she had the spell book. If she was on the other side, she could have given it to them any time she wanted to. And it can't be Vishdink; he never leaves his lab. Like I said; it's not possible."

"It seems impossible, but it's not," said John. "It can't be. Someone else had to know." He took two more steps and then said,

"That's it! The halfling. He was there when I first came to the Magisterium. He brought me to the Magistra. He must have heard who I was. He's got to be the traitor."

"I don't see how," said Ghorza. "His family is relatively new to Norlon, but they are upstanding citizens. I mean, his brother is the head of the Merchants' Guild!"

"The head of the Merchants' Guild?" asked John. "Is that the same Merchants' Guild that hired the mercenary unit that turned on our forces at the crucial moment of battle? That one?"

"By the nameless god!" said Dantes. "He's right. Solim is the one that hired the unit that turned traitor."

"Solim?" asked John. "That seems familiar. Solim? Solim...Damn it, why didn't we see it? 'Solim' spelled backwards is 'Milos.' The head of the Merchants' Guild is the same person that stole the crown!"

"And he is also the same person that was leading the attack today," added Lady Ellyn. "He has been behind the enemy's plan the whole time."

"Oh, crap," said John, all of the color draining from his face.

"What is it?" asked Dantes. "You look like you've seen a ghost."

"We're in deep trouble. Milos' brother was there when the Magistra gave me the spell book and sent us on this quest. He heard everything...they know where we're going."

Before Dantes could reply, the ranger came jogging up to the group from wherever he had been scouting. "It's positive I am that we're being followed," said Fitzber.

"How do you know?" asked Lady Ellyn. "I haven't heard anything."

"Nor would ye, lassie," replied the ranger. "Even though your armor is oiled to perfection, it still makes a variety o' wee little noises that keep you from hearing as well as ye might. Twice during the last hour I heard dog or worg barks from behind us. There's something behind us that is following us. I'm going to drift back and take a look, if'n you don't mind. I'll be catching up with you by sunset."

"Don't get caught," warned Dantes.

"Don't trouble your wee red mind about it," said Fitzber. "I'm the epitome o' caution."

He mumbled a few words and then faded from sight as John watched, his colors blending in with the foliage. "Was that an invisibility spell?" John asked.

"No," said Ghorza. "Invisibility is an air-based spell. He just did some sort of ranger earth-based camouflage spell that allows him to blend in with the background. I hope he's of a high enough level to throw in some anti-odor protection, too."

"He did say that he thought there were dogs behind us, eh?" asked John.

"Yes he did," replied Ghorza.

"Then I hope so, too."

Chapter Twenty-Nine

"I smell rabbit," said Ghorza.

"Rabbit?" asked Dantes.

"Yes, rabbit," said Ghorza. "Someone up ahead of us is cooking rabbit." She paused. "It smells delicious, too."

"Should we continue on?" asked John. "If there's someone in front of us, shouldn't we try to go around them?"

"Well, they obviously aren't worried about being found," said Dantes. "It has to be someone that doesn't know there's a war on, so we should probably tell them. Still, we should be careful and watch out for the enemy."

Dantes slowed his pace. A short way ahead, he could see where the path through the forest opened up into what was probably a clearing or a glade. He approached the end of the forest cautiously, watching where he set his feet so that he didn't make any noise.

In the center of a large, 100 foot-wide clearing, he observed a small, nondescript figure sitting by a fire. "I was wondering if you'd make it here before nightfall," said Fitzber without looking up.

"You're lucky we didn't announce our presence with a fireball or three," said Dantes, walking into the clearing. From his new vantage point, he saw that Fitzber was rotating several large rabbits on a spit over a crackling fire. Ghorza was right; they did smell good. "You know you can smell those cooking a long way away, right?"

"Aye, indeed I do," replied Fitzber, with a smile. "You can't hide the smell o' a good hare cooking."

"So we are not being followed, after all?"

"Oh, indeed we are," replied Fitzber. "There are about 15 orcs trailing us, as well as 6 worgs and a halfling that appears to be in charge o' them." He looked at Lady Ellyn. "One o' the orcs is a shaman."

"*What!*" said Dantes. "There are orcs, *with a shaman*, trailing us *with worgs*, and you have a campfire going? They will home right in on us. They won't even need the worgs—the orcs will be able to find us with just their own noses."

"Oh, aye, indeed they will," replied Fitzber. "I expect that they'll be here in about two hours, which will give us time to eat and prepare for them."

"But there are 20 of them and only six of us," said John, "and I don't know how to fight. I don't even have a weapon!"

"That's true," said Lady Ellyn. "We will have to rectify that when we get to Harbortown. Without a weapon and some training, you will be a hindrance on the way to the Mountain of Frost."

"And with a weapon and some training," added Father Telenor, "you'll just be an annoyance."

"Let's focus on getting us *to* Harbortown first," said Dantes. He turned back to Fitzber. "I take it you have a plan?"

"Oh, aye," agreed Fitzber. "I wouldn't have hurried to get here if'n I didn't."

"Why didn't you rejoin us sooner?" asked Ghorza. "We could have gone further and faster if we'd known they were following us."

"Aye, but then you would have messed up your trail and tired yourselves out unnecessarily. As it is, you laid a nice trail, moving quickly but unhurriedly. Your trail makes it look like you don't know you're being followed. The campfire confirms it, and makes a nice beacon for the orcs to follow right to camp. Straight on, without worrying so much about looking to the sides. That's what I hope will happen anyway." Fitzber poked one of the rabbits with his knife. "They're done. Let's eat and talk about what we want to do," he said, pulling a rabbit off the spit. "I expect that they'll send the worgs in first..."

Chapter Thirty

"I'm not going to be very helpful with this," said John, indicating the dagger that Lady Ellyn had given him. "I don't know how to use it very well, and I don't think it will be much good against giant wolves or orcs with swords in any event."

"There's not much to using it," said Father Telenor. "Make sure you hold onto the round end and stick the pointy end into the orcs. Be careful; it is really sharp."

"Yeah, I think I got that part," said John. "What I really meant was that if you teach me how to cast spells, I might be more of a help than a hindrance."

"It takes years of preparation to be a good mage," said Dantes. "What you need to know cannot be crammed into one hour of instruction."

"Normally not," said Ghorza, from where she was preparing her spells and equipment. "Still, he has shown himself to have a natural affinity to magic that goes beyond anything I've ever seen." She walked over to where John was sitting at the edge of the clearing flipping through the Magistra's spell book. "In order to cast a spell, a mage has to prepare it first. The way you do that is to find a nice, quiet area to study, like you have already done. Then you choose the spell that you are going to cast, find it in your spell book and speak the spell up to the trigger phrase."

"Trigger phrase?" asked John. "What's that?"

"The trigger phrase is the last word or two of the spell. You will see it underlined in your book, but you will also know it as you get to it." She paused, thinking. "Casting a spell is like shooting a crossbow. You *do* know what a crossbow is, right?" John nodded. "Before you can shoot a crossbow, you have to arm it by pulling back the bowstring. That is the same as speaking the opening part of the spell. When the bowman gets the bowstring back far enough, there is a 'click' as the line snaps into place. A spell works the same way. When you get to the 'set' part, you will feel the spell settle in your mind. At this point, the spell is armed. You only need to memorize the trigger phrase and then speak it when you are ready to cast the spell."

"So I don't have to say the whole spell all at once in order to cast it?"

"That is correct. While you *do* have to say the whole spell, and say it correctly, you don't have to say the whole spell all at once. You speak the spell up to the trigger phrase and then stop. Then, when you are ready, you merely say the trigger phrase, and the spell casts."

"Cool," said John. "I wondered how anyone could cast some of these in combat, as most of them seem kind of long. My guess is that having someone trying to kill you while you are casting a spell would be very distracting."

"Having someone trying to kill you makes it extremely difficult to cast even the trigger phrase," said Dantes. "That is why it takes time to become a mage. Part of the training is to have people beat on you while you are trying to cast a spell. Devils prepare by having other devils stab them with white hot pokers if they take too long. Avoiding that kind of pain can be *very* focusing, to say the least."

"Okay, I get that," said John. "Having battled the trolls, I understand a little more about combat than when I first got here. All

I'm saying is that it's got to be helpful if you don't have to say the whole spell."

"There are also time and mana limitations to spell casting," added Ghorza. "Most spells will only stay ready for about eight hours. After that, they fade away and the first parts have to be re-spoken. You also can't memorize more spells than you have the mana to cast."

"Why not?" asked John.

"Because you can't," replied Ghorza. "It's just the way it works. You can only memorize the spells allotted to you by your level."

"How many can I memorize?"

"The number of spells per level is dependent on your rank," replied Ghorza. "A first rank mage is normally able to memorize two first level spells. I have no idea what you will be able to memorize."

"Why not?"

"Two reasons," answered Ghorza. "First, you have the Spell Book of Aran-Than. That *should* cause you to function as a third rank mage. If so, you would have three first level spells and a second level spell available. Second, I can't judge your ability because I don't know how it works when someone can cast more than one type of elemental spell. I don't know if that will give you extra spell capacity. It seems like it might, as you appeared to have more mana than you should have had for casting cantrips." She shrugged. "I think the only way we're going to find out how many spells you can memorize is to have you learn some."

"Ok!" said John. This was the moment he had been looking forward to ever since he found out that he could cast spells. He was going to learn to cast real spells and become a mage.

"I would start out with something easy to cast and control," said Dantes.

"Agreed," said Ghorza.

"How about 'Magic Missile?'" John said, pointing to the page. "That goes where it's aimed, right?"

"That's not an air-based spell," said Ghorza, "so I can't read what the book says; however, I believe that is true."

"Yes," confirmed Dantes, "Magic Missile goes where it is aimed. Unless a counter-spell blocks it, it will hit your target. It won't do much damage, but it doesn't miss. That is probably a good one to start with. I would also try the spray- and ray-based spells."

"Spray and ray?" asked John.

"There are first-level spray spells for most of the elements; I know for sure that there are ones for fire, acid and ice. They send out an elemental spray that damages any of your enemies that get caught in its cone. They don't do that much damage, but they're quick and easy, and they hit from a decent distance. There's also an electrical one, but I think you have to touch your enemy to use it, so that is probably not a good beginning combat spell. We want to keep the enemy away from you, as you can't cast spells very well with a sword stuck through your gut."

"Umm, no, that's the kind of the thing I'd like to avoid," said John.

"Good," said Dantes. "I don't know if Father Telenor has a raise dead spell or not, but I'd rather not have to find out. The ray spells work like the spray spells, but they are second level; they are more concentrated and cause more damage. I know there is a fire-based one called 'Scorching Ray;' you'd have to look up the other elemental ones because I don't have them in my spell book."

"Would it be better to just memorize several of the same one?" asked John. "If the fire-based spray spell works well, shouldn't I just memorize it as many times as I can?"

"It depends on the situation," said Dantes. "Sometimes, you will be going up against creatures that have a weakness to a certain element. In that case, it would probably be better to load up on a certain type of spell. If your opponent doesn't have a particular weakness that you know of, you might want to have a broad range of spells available. You might find that one works better than the others, which would be good information to have for your next fight against that type of creature. Also, getting hit by one element after another might cause additional system-shock damage."

"There are other considerations that go into the decision making, too," he added, "but much of that discussion revolves around various tenets of arcane philosophy that we don't have time for now. One quick example is my list of spells. As a devil-spawn, my spells with flame effects are more potent than if they were cast by you. Even against creatures that are resistant to fire, my spells are still sometimes effective due to their concentrated nature. Against creatures that are susceptible to fire?" He smiled, and John could see him reliving past battles. "They don't stand a chance."

"So I should try a little something from all of them?" asked John.

"Yes," said Ghorza. "I think Dantes' advice is good. Try the sprays and rays."

"Okay," John said. He went back to paging through the book, this time with a purpose and a happy smile on his face. He stopped on one labeled 'Spray of Flames.' In neat, crisp handwriting it read:

Spray of Flames

Evocation

Level: 1

Mana Cost: 1

Components: Verbal and Somatic

Range: Short/Cone AOE

Duration: Instantaneous

Description: Winter wolves threatening to put a chill on your day? Warm things up with a spray of flames.

A previous owner had also scribbled a note in the margin that read, 'Warning: do not cast this spell in front of the king's tapestries or anything else he finds valuable. He doesn't have a sense of humor regarding their accidental destruction.'

"This spell is fire-based," said John, looking up at Dantes. "Can you explain it to me so that I understand what I need to know about it?"

Dantes looked down at the book. "Yes, this is an excellent one to start with. In fact, it was one of the first ones I learned." He chuckled when he read the note. "It seems even the illustrious Aran-Than had accidents when he was first learning magic." He looked up. "This spell is quite simple. What do you not understand?"

"Take me through it, please. For example, what's an evocation?"

"An evocation spell taps into a source of power to create the desired effect. Basically, it creates something from nothing. In this case, it calls forth a spray of flames, without drawing that energy from your body. There is a wide variety of evocation spells, and many of them cause great amounts of damage."

"Got it," said John. "I guess that 'verbal' means that I have to say something, but what is a somatic component?"

"You're right; the verbal component means that there is a spoken incantation. Say someone casts a silence spell on you; if you can't say the trigger phrase, you can't cast the spell. The somatic portion means that there are also some very specific hand motions that have to be performed; you can see the drawings below the spell that indicate what you're supposed to do. If you don't do them correctly, such as if someone hits you or you are wearing armor, the spell can be ruined. If that happens, the spell might not cast, or it may cast incorrectly." John nodded, so he continued. "Some spells also have material or focus components. A material component is a physical substance or object that is destroyed by the casting process. If you don't have the required item in your inventory, you can't cast the spell. For example, I need a tiny ball of bat guano and a bit of sulfur to cast a fireball."

"Bat guano?" asked John. "That's gross. Do you have to collect it yourself?"

"Either that or pay someone to do it for you." He shrugged. "You get used to it. The last item is a focus item, which is a prop of some sort. Unlike a material component, the focus item isn't destroyed when the spell is cast, so it can be used again. One example is a cleric's symbol of faith, which is an item of divine focus. A priest needs his holy symbol to cast most of his spells."

"Okay," said John, "I think I understand. Can you help me with the fire-based ones, so that I understand how to say the words and do the gestures?"

"Yes I can," replied Dantes. "You are on your own for the ones that aren't fire-based. All I will see in your spell book is a smear of illegible writing and blurred pictures. If you can't cast the spell, you won't be able to tell what it says."

"It's time to get into position," Fitzber said a short time later as the sun touched the horizon. The group stood up and moved to their designated positions.

"You go to battle well-armed," said Lady Ellyn, looking at the scimitar hanging at Ghorza's side.

"I've found that it's better to go into combat well-armed rather than not," agreed Ghorza.

"More to the point," said Father Telenor, "I think Lady Ellyn is saying that we have never seen a mage carry a sword."

"I'm guessing you've never been to the orc lands either, eh?" asked Ghorza.

"No, I haven't," said Father Telenor.

"If you had, you would understand," replied Ghorza. "A sword keeps working when mana runs dry. It's kept me alive on many occasions when I would otherwise have been at my opponents' mercy."

Chapter Thirty-One

"Something is wrong," said Rubic, looking over the lip of the hill at the campsite below. "This soon after the battle, they wouldn't make camp and not post a guard, would they?"

"No, they would not," Khazatch replied. "Certainly, I would not, anyway." He looked again, using his ability to see into the infrared. Although more limited than many of the other races, the orcs had developed it when they lived underground, and many of them were still able to see the differences in heat. He scanned the camp again. "Wait. There *is* one guard, but he's hard to see because he's on the other side of the campfire." Khazatch slid a few feet to the left to get a better look that was less impeded by the fire. "How many were there supposed to be?"

"They left with five. They had the devil, the half-orc, the outlander, the paladin and the cleric."

"The one I can see is small, so it must be the outlander. Wait, they must have added someone else to their group, because I see five more heat sources in their bedrolls. There are six total."

"What do you recommend?" asked Rubic.

"Have the troops circle the camp, and then have the shaman cast a Hold Person spell on the guard. Send in the worgs, followed by the rest of the platoon."

"I agree," said Rubic. "Do it."

Khazatch gave the hand signals and the rest of his platoon deployed. When they were in place, he moved forward slowly with the shaman until they were in range of the guard. The shaman cast two spells, saying the words so quietly that Khazatch, who was standing next to him, could barely hear them. The first was cast on the patrol leader, helping him resist fire. When fighting a teufling, it was a wise precaution. The second was cast at the guard, after which the shaman nodded, indicating that the guard was held immobile. Khazatch gave the owl hoot to signal the attack.

The worgs raced into camp, followed by the orcs. As they entered the circle of light cast by the campfire, the orcs screamed their battle cry to help disorient their foes as they woke. The worgs gave a scream of their own, but theirs was one of pain as the ground grew spikes all around them. The orcs' screams of defiance turned to confusion as the undergrowth developed a mind of its own, and vines started wrapping themselves around the orcs' legs. The orcs were entangled, their motion slowed.

"They know we're coming!" yelled Khazatch, jumping back from several vines that reached out to grab him. "Rally to me!" He moved back outside the Entangle spell's area of effect; the rest of the patrol wasn't so lucky.

Chapter Thirty-Two

The mages watched as their enemies raced into the camp. "Now!" said Ghorza, who had the best night vision of the group.

"*Globus Incendi!*" commanded Dantes, and a bead of fire sprang from his pointer claw. The fireball traveled to the center of camp, growing slightly en route, before detonating with a low roar over the campfire. The worgs that had attacked the sleeping forms in their bed rolls were all roasted by the fireball. Most of the orcs were still outside the main blast area, though, and were only singed by the flames. The fireball also burned the covers off of the forms 'sleeping' by the fire...rocks, which had been heated by Dantes to give the illusion of body heat.

The sixth worg attacked Fitzber, who didn't move as the wolf raced toward him. As he had expected, he was held in place by the shaman's Hold Person spell.

Any time now, Telenor, he thought as he watched the worg lope toward him, saliva dripping from its fangs. Fitzber had plenty of experience hunting worgs on the frontier; he knew it wouldn't be distracted by his lack of movement. Although some bears wouldn't attack if you played dead, worgs would just chew on you until they got the reaction they were looking for.

"*Obstupefece!*" commanded Telenor, removing the paralysis.

Fitzber felt life come back to his limbs and shook out his arms. Although he hadn't been held long, he knew he needed to get the cast right the first time, or he would be dead, buried beneath a wolf that weighed three times as much as he did. *"Empathia Feri!"* he commanded, casting a Wild Empathy spell that befriended the charging worg. As the beast gathered itself to spring on him, Fitzber saw the worg's eyes glaze over, and the animal went into a head-first tumble as the expected pounce didn't happen. Fitzber stepped out of the way as it crashed past and then took a step over to it to scratch it behind its ear. "The green ones want to hurt us and our pack," Fitzber said. "Let's go kill them."

The worg bounced up from the ground and oriented on the closest orc. Nothing was allowed to hurt a member of its pack, and killing was not only something that the worg understood very well, but also something that it liked doing. A lot. It raced forward while Fitzber picked up his bow. The orc saw the worg racing toward it but didn't give it a second thought as it stumbled forward toward the patrol leader. He turned away from the worg, so he didn't see the giant wolf spring. It leapt onto his back, and the orc barely had time to feel the worg break his neck as it slammed him face first into the ground.

The rest of the companions dropped from the trees on the opposite side of the campfire from Fitzber and Telenor, and Lady Ellyn sprinted toward the patrol leader and the shaman, helped along by one of Ghorza's Haste spells. Telenor raced from the other side of the camp to join her.

Dantes' second fireball erupted in the closest concentration of orcs, killing several of them outright and burning two more that dove to the side. It also served to alert the orcs to the group's location. "Get them!" yelled Khazatch. "Kill the casters. I will take care of the paladin." The nine remaining orcs turned and charged the mages.

John had never been attacked by anything that intended to do him harm, much less things that were armed with swords and battle axes, and he felt his knees go weak. He couldn't think of any of the trigger phrases that he had labored to memorize just an hour earlier; all he could think about was running. John's eyes twitched to Dantes on his right. The teufling was gesturing in preparation for casting a spell. He looked to the left and saw that Ghorza was doing similarly.

"*Molaris!*" Dantes shouted, and two force missiles shot out from him. They started small, but then grew to almost a foot in diameter. The missiles hit the leading orc in the chest and face and exploded; what was left of the orc wasn't pretty. The dead orc fell backward, missing most of its head.

"*Segniter!*" Ghorza commanded. A crackling black ray shot out of her hand to strike two of the orcs behind the one that Dantes killed. As John watched, they seemed to shrivel and grow old as their life force was pulled from them. Their movements slowed, and they fell to their knees, gasping for breath.

"Don't just stand there, do something," grunted Dantes. "Cast Magic Missile, if you can't think of anything else."

John snapped out of his daze. He remembered the pictures in the spell book, how the movements went and... "*Missilis Magici!*" he commanded, and two missiles jumped from his finger at the next orc in line. Smaller than the ones that Dantes cast, the missiles sped unerringly to their target and hit the orc in the chest, knocking him backward. The orc wasn't dead, but he didn't appear to be an immediate threat any more.

"*Dormi!*" shouted Ghorza, casting a Sleep spell at one of the remaining orcs. Nothing happened; the orc kept coming. Ghorza drew her scimitar as the orcs were almost on them.

"Scorching Ray on three," said Dantes. "One...two...three!" As one, Dantes and John both commanded, *"Fluxum Ignis!"* and a stream of fire blasted forth from their outstretched fingers. The two cones of fire overlapped in a wave of blazing destruction that washed over the charging orcs. The orcs screamed, sounding like squealing pigs. Three of them didn't make a sound; they fell dead. The other two orcs pushed their dead bodies out of the way and leaped to attack the defenseless casters.

The first orc carried a battle axe, and it swung at Dantes and John. Both casters dove out of the way of the killing blow. John fell to the ground, and the orc took a step toward him, raising the battle axe over his head. Before he could chop down, he suddenly lurched, and the battle axe fell backward out of his hands to land on the ground behind him. His eyes rolled up into his head, and he fell forward onto John, an arrow sticking out of his back.

The second orc swung his sword at Ghorza, intending to take her head off. Having grown up with orcs, she recognized the attack and used her scimitar two-handed to block it, the two swords clanging together sharply. As the orc's sword rebounded, she let go of her sword with one hand, pointed at the orc and commanded, *"Dormi!"* The orc fell to the ground and lay still. After a moment, it started snoring.

Lady Ellyn approached the orc leader and his shaman with a speed born of Haste, while Father Telenor came as fast as he could to join her from the other direction. The shaman gestured behind the orc, and Khazatch momentarily glowed. Lady Ellyn had fought enough orcs to know that the platoon leader had just received a Protection from Good spell; he would now be harder to hit. She slowed, both to allow Father Telenor to catch up as well as to catch her breath. Running in armor was tiring, especially when Hasted.

The shaman gestured again with his staff, and Lady Ellyn was plunged into darkness. Stupid orcs, thought Lady Ellyn; they can never do anything honorably. She tried to back out of the darkness, but was unable; the shaman had cast it on her. She knew that while she was disabled, both of the orcs would attack Father Telenor, hoping to remove his support. *"Inveni Malum!"* she said, casting a Detect Evil. Sure enough, she could see two forms through the darkness, both circling her, one on either side. Based on where they had started, she was fairly certain the one on the right was the leader, so she backpedaled to the right to cut him off.

"Lux Diei!" said Father Telenor, casting a Daylight spell. Not only did it banish the darkness spell, but it turned night into day, taking away the orcs' better night vision. The orc leader *was* the one on the right. Lady Ellyn cut him off with a swing of her sword. Momentarily blinded, the orc blocked her swing with his battle axe. Unable to look directly into the spell, the orc drew a dagger and threw it at her, hoping to gain some time to let his eyes adjust.

Lady Ellyn advanced, not wanting to give up her advantage. She held up her left arm and the dagger bounced off the vambrace on her forearm. Pressing the attack, she used her Haste to swing several times at the orc. The patrol leader blocked her attacks with his axe as he continued to backpedal, reaching behind his back with his off hand.

Coming to Lady Ellyn's aid, Father Telenor saw the darkness envelope her and knew the orcs would come for him. He knew he wouldn't last long against the fighter, so he went around to the left of the darkness to intercept the shaman as he cast the Daylight spell.

Father Telenor saw the shaman gesture with his staff, and a thick mist surrounded the priest. Unable to see, Father Telenor held his mace in front of him as he tried to back away. He felt a presence to his left and heard the shaman say, *"Vulnera Mediocria,"* casting a Cause Wounds spell. He felt the shaman's touch, and a large cut opened up on his side. As he spasmed in pain, he swung his mace in that direction and was rewarded with a solid crunch as it hit the shaman.

Although Father Telenor gained a couple moments' reprieve, he knew the shaman would be back, and that he couldn't take many more wounds like the first one the shaman gave him. He could feel blood pouring down his leg and realized that he needed to even the odds. *"Flagra!"* he cast, calling down a flame strike. Although the mist caused him to almost completely miss the shaman, the divine flames were successful in burning away the mist that had been obscuring his vision. He caught the shaman circling around to his left, intent on hitting him from behind. The shaman's left arm was hanging limp; Father Telenor's mace had crushed his shoulder.

As Lady Ellyn pressed in on the leader, trying to beat down his guard with a series of strikes, the orc's left hand came out from behind his back holding a whip. He lashed out and wrapped it around one of Lady Ellyn's ankles; pulling with all his might, he threw her off balance, and she went down.

The orc took a step forward. Dropping the whip, he raised the massive battle axe with both hands. A giant of an orc, Lady Ellyn knew that if he hit her, the axe would split both armor and paladin, as well. *"Caede Malum!"* she said, casting her Smite Evil spell. A divine flame roared out of the heavens, hitting the orc on the head and blasting him with divine power. The orc was knocked backward, the axe falling from his suddenly numb hands.

Lady Ellyn used the respite to roll to her stomach and get back to her feet. She picked up her sword in time to meet the renewed assault by the orc but realized that her reflexes were back to normal; she was no longer Hasted. She saw that the orc's attacks were no longer as crisp; he'd been hurt by the Smite spell.

Father Telenor could feel his strength leaving him and saw that the shaman was beginning another spell. "*Consiste Hominem!*" he said, casting his last offensive spell. The Hold Person spell was effective, and the orc shaman was held in place, unmoving. Laying his hand on his side, he said "*Remedium Magnum,*" channeling positive energy into his injury with a cure spell. The wound closed, and he felt better even if he was still a little physically weak from the blood loss he had incurred. Before the Hold spell could wear off, he stepped forward and finished the shaman with a well-placed strike.

Lady Ellyn continued to trade blows with the orc leader. He had used a cleaving spell on her which had opened up a gaping wound; she had used her laying of hands ability to cure it and had continued on. The orc had been unable to recover completely from the Smite spell and was tiring fast. She began to beat his attacks back and came closer and closer to landing the blow that would finish him. She could see in the orc's eyes he knew it was coming, and Lady Ellyn knew she needed to end the fight before the orc did something desperate. In previous fights she had seen orcs that knew they were going to lose do a variety of daring things to kill their opponent, even though they knew it would open themselves up to be killed, as well. They were happy just knowing they were taking their opponents into the next world with them.

Lady Ellyn knew it wouldn't be long before this orc tried something similar. She needed to end the fight *now*.

On the orc's next strike, she blocked it less well than she could have, allowing the head of the axe to glance off her leg armor as she parried it down to the side. Stepping back, she stumbled, as if the axe had numbed her leg. She could see in the orc's eyes that he believed it. The orc followed her forward, putting all of its flagging energy into a swing that would decapitate her if it landed.

She was no longer there, though, having used her leg to push off and dive forward. As the orc leader overextended himself with the roundhouse swing, she came up on his side and drove her dagger into his kidney. As she stepped back away, she chopped down with her sword, severing his Achilles tendon. Lamed and mortally wounded, the orc attacked as well as he could, trying to kill her before he died. With two good legs, she was able to stay out of his reach until he wore down and fell to his knees. She stepped in and drove her sword through his heart, killing him. The companions had won.

Chapter Thirty-Three

"Sure'n I appreciated your assistance," Fitzber said, putting his arms around the worg's neck. The giant wolf was so big that the gnome's arms could barely reach around it. Lady Ellyn saw that he held a sheathed dagger in one of them. "Sorry I am to have to do this." As he drew the dagger, the worg's eyes changed. Although the intelligence remained, the feral ferocity disappeared. The worg bounded out of Fitzber's arms before he could slit its throat.

In a couple of bounds, the worg was up to full speed and on a direct course to where Dantes, Ghorza and John were dispatching the wounded orcs. The worg appeared to be headed toward John, who had his back to it.

"John, look out!" yelled Lady Ellyn as Fitzber picked up his bow and nocked an arrow. Knowing he would only get one shot, he focused as he drew the bow and fired. The arrow arced up and came back down to hit the worg as it leaped toward John, using an attack similar to the one it used to kill the orc. The arrow pierced the worg's heart, and the dead animal crashed into John. The two went down in a heap and lay unmoving on the ground.

"Nice shot," complimented Lady Ellyn. "The spell picked a bad time to wear off."

"The spell didn't wear off," replied Fitzber. "It had a little longer to run. That was something else." He looked angry and confused.

"What was it?" asked Lady Ellyn.

"The worg seemed like it was suddenly possessed," said Fitzber, "but that would mean... *beastmaster!*" He ran toward the woods. "Beware any animals you see," he called over his shoulder; "kill any that come close." He began fading before he entered the tree line; once he was past it, Lady Ellyn couldn't see him any longer.

Chapter Thirty-Four

Within ten minutes, Fitzber was back, prodding a halfling along in front of him with his dagger. "Look what I found hiding in the woods," he said. He brought the halfling to the fire and forced him to sit in front of it.

"Hello, Rubic," said Ghorza. "So it's true. You *were* helping the enemy all along."

"No, I wasn't helping the enemy," replied Rubic, "well, not at first, anyway. I started out helping my brother. It wasn't until much later that I found out he was working for the enemy. By then I knew too much. I could either continue what I was doing and lead a comfortable life, or tell everyone about my brother and lead a much shorter one. I chose the life of luxury."

"And how is that working out for you?" growled Dantes. He placed a clawed hand on Rubic's shoulder.

"It was going very well until the outlander showed up," he said. "It has not gone so well for me since."

"Why is he so important to you?" asked Lady Ellyn. "He can only cast low level mage spells and isn't much of a warrior." She looked at John and added, "No offense."

"That's fine," said John. "As that battle just showed, it's true; I'm not much of a warrior. Not yet, anyway."

"You don't know?" asked Rubic. "Well, I'm not going to tell; you'll have to find someone else."

"Is this related to the Prophecy?" Lady Ellyn asked.

161

Rubic's eyes glanced aside for the briefest of instants before coming back to Lady Ellyn. Rubic continued to remain silent, and Dantes squeezed a little harder. A red stain appeared on Rubic's shoulder, but he did not say anything else.

"Easy," said Lady Ellyn. "I have no intention of torturing the information out of him." Dantes looked annoyed, but he eased his grip. Rubic breathed a sigh of relief.

"Let's try something different," said Lady Ellyn. "How much does Solim know about our mission?"

Rubic began laughing. "How much does he know?" Rubic asked. "He knows *everything*. When I don't come back, he'll send out something bigger and stronger to kill you all. He knows where you're going, and he won't underestimate you again." He looked at John. "He will come for you, and he will take the spell book from you. Then he will have two of the Items of Power. With them, he'll go to the Mountain of Frost and get the Scepter. With all three of the Items, he will rule Tasidar, and then he will overthrow the Overlord and rule the world!"

"No delusions of grandeur there, are there?" Father Telenor asked Lady Ellyn.

"It's not a delusion," said Rubic. "My brother already controls the two most powerful nations on this continent. Who is going to stop him from ruling all of it? You? Ha!"

"There are plenty of free folk that will band together, once they see what he is up to," replied Ghorza. "There is no way he'll get away with this."

"Oh, but he will," said Rubic. "He will take the spell book, he will get the scepter and he will rule this world. It is preordained in the Prophecy. Say what you will and do what you want, it won't matter. Evil will win in the end."

"That's what my father always said when I was young," Dantes said. "He always said that an evil victory was inevitable."

"Did he give you a reason why?" asked Ghorza. In all her time with Dantes, this was the first time he had ever spoken about either of his parents.

"No, he didn't," replied Dantes. "He said that he wasn't allowed to talk about it...although if that was a rule and he obeyed it, it was the only one he ever followed in his life. He was a liar, and everything he did or said was always full of deceit. Most times, there wouldn't even be a reason for lying, other than the fact that he could."

"So you don't know why he thought that evil would be triumphant in the end?" asked John.

"No, I don't," answered Dantes, "although he always said that evil had the greatest number of forces, and the ones that were most committed to the fight. Look at the intelligent races on this planet, for example. There are no races that are inherently good. The closest to a 'good' race are the elves, but even the elves have their evil Dark Elf cousins."

"Humans, like most of the races, are mixed in their allegiance," Dantes continued. "Some are good, while others are bad. There are, however, entire races that are evil, like trolls, goblins and orcs, just to name a few. Some of the half-breeds, like Ghorza and me, are committed to stopping them, but we are vastly outnumbered by the purebloods."

"So, they will win because there are more of them?" asked Lady Ellyn. "Wars are not always won by the side with the greatest number of troops."

"That's what bothers me," replied Dantes. "He lied about everything; the fact that he always mentioned this reason leads me to believe that he was being deceptive about the *real* reason he thought that evil would win. One time when he was drunk, he mentioned some plan that the evil forces had. It was something he said had been decades in the making, with people and forces prepositioned where they would do the most harm when they were needed. He used to make up some of his biggest lies when he was drunk, and I thought this was just one of them. Now I'm afraid that there really is a master plan, and what we are seeing is the result of this plan."

"Now you finally see," said Rubic. "The Overlord has been planning this strategy for *centuries*. Nothing you can do will stop it. Join us, or flee to a far off land. Maybe you can live out your days there in peace before our horde gets there...but probably not."

"Okay, I think we've heard about enough of this," said Lady Ellyn. "This is getting us nowhere."

"Do you want me to kill him?" asked Dantes.

"No," said Lady Ellyn. "That would not be an honorable thing, even for him. You can't kill a prisoner. I said earlier that we won't torture him, and we will not. We don't need to anyway, as Father Telenor has a Truth spell. Once he casts it, Rubic will tell us anything we want to know."

"Truth spell?" asked Rubic.

"Oh, yes," replied Lady Ellyn. "With the force of a god behind it, the spell can't be tricked. You will tell us the truth about anything we want to know."

"Shall I cast it?" asked Father Telenor.

"No!" screamed Rubic. Turning around, he reached over the dagger and grabbed Fitzber's hands. Tilting the dagger up so that it rested on his chest, Rubic pulled with all of his might, driving it through his heart. "Won't tell..." he gasped, the light going out of his eyes.

"Bah," said Dantes. "Coward."

"Want me to raise him from the dead?" asked Father Telenor.

"No," said Lady Ellyn, "then we'd just have to drag him along with us until we got to a city and could jail him. During that time we'd have to watch out for every animal we saw. No, we will dispose of him with the rest of his allies. We'll travel faster without him."

"But what about the Prophecy?" asked Ghorza. "He may know something more than we do."

"I doubt it," replied Lady Ellyn. "He'll only know what his brother told him. Solim may have lied to him, too, in case he got caught. The only way we'll find out what Solim knows is to capture him. Besides, I know what the Prophecy says. Our order long ago saved the original lines of the Prophecy as were spoken by Aran-Than at the time of the Sundering."

"You do?" asked Dantes. "Why haven't you shared them before?"

"Because the words of the Prophecy are ambiguous. Throughout the ages, people have interpreted them to mean whatever advanced their cause the most. No one knows exactly what they meant." She paused. "And it was only recently that we recovered the information about what really happened at the Sundering. We're still trying to figure it out."

Lady Ellyn sighed and then continued. "I was sworn to secrecy, but if we make it to the Mountain of Frost, you're going to find out anyway. What most people no longer remember is that the last war started when the one true god was overthrown by the evil elemental gods. The elemental gods are children of the one true god, four that chose the way of the light, and four that chose the darkness. Having overthrown the one true god, the four dark elemental gods decided to do away with the good elemental gods, as well; however, the dark gods realized that the only way they could conquer them was through a battle of such magnitude that the entire universe would be unmade in its fighting. Seeing this, they challenged the good elemental gods to a war by proxy. The elemental gods would give gifts of their power to those who worshiped them, and whichever side won in the world would be the winner in the heavens. The evil elemental gods thought that they could easily win a battle of numbers; they had many more."

"But what about the one true god?" asked John. "What happened to her?"

"Somehow the four evil gods captured her," replied Lady Ellyn. "No one knows what became of her, and she hasn't been heard from since."

"How do you know she hasn't been destroyed," asked Dantes, "if no one has seen or heard from her since?"

"Every time I use a power or cast a spell, I know that she still exists," replied Lady Ellyn with a smile. "I wouldn't be able to do these things without her assistance." She held Dantes' gaze, and the smile faded. She sighed. "With that for perspective, we come to the end of the first War for Dominance."

"What is the War for Dominance?" asked Ghorza. "I've never heard of that."

"That name, like most of the knowledge from long ago, was lost in the Sundering," said Lady Ellyn. "After the elemental gods 'blest' us with their powers, the worldly forces began the War for Dominance. Back then, there was only one continent, not two, as Tasidar and Salidar were joined as one. The war raged back and forth across the continent, with one side holding the edge, only to lose it to the other. With so much death and destruction, advancement in the service of your god was rapid, and heroes of great power were made and unmade on both sides. After many years of constant warfare, the forces of evil achieved the upper hand. They captured nearly the entire continent, trapping the forces of good on a plateau in the center of the continent. The city was the City of Silver, the home to the Paladin Training Academy. Its walls were stout, and the legends said that the city could never be taken."

Father Telenor spoke for the first time. "The legends were wrong."

Chapter Thirty-Five

"Indeed," agreed Lady Ellyn. "They were wrong. The forces of evil were too strong. Their siege engines were more numerous than the stars in the night sky, and the plains surrounding the plateau were black with enemy forces. The war was sure to be lost. Most of the good forces gave up hope; they were so outnumbered they didn't see how salvation was possible."

"One man, however, didn't give up hope—the wizard Aran-Than. He alone reached the level required to cast a Wish. Through research, he knew that the Wish spell was not only the most powerful spell ever conceived, but also the most dangerous, as it was tricky and might not work out the way he intended. Even if Aran-Than got what he wanted, it might not be in the manner he originally desired. What Aran-Than was contemplating was especially dangerous. Because of the power necessary, he knew the spell would be incredibly difficult to control, and that there could be massive unintended consequences. He knew the danger, but as the forces of evil breached the walls of the City of Silver, he cast the Wish."

"Aran-Than knew that he was walking a thin line, as the War for Dominance was set in motion by the gods themselves. He suspected that wishing for victory wouldn't be allowed, as one side had to physically beat the other, and he doubted that the gods would see such a wish as 'fair.' He was also aware that when the war started, the forces of evil started out with a large advantage in the number of troops they had, and he thought that was where he had an opportunity. He Wished for the war to be restarted at the beginning, with both sides having equal forces *that were separated from each other.*"

"That Wish caused the Sundering. As he uttered it, an earthquake unlike anything ever imagined hit the world, and a rift cracked open the continent from east to west, breaking it in half. Where before there was just one land mass, Halidar, there were now two, Tasidar and Salidar, which were pushed away from each other in the devastation of the earthquake. The forces surrounding the plateau were destroyed, as were the majority of the forces in the City of Silver. The Sundering killed nearly all of the inhabitants of the planet; the only races that survived were some good ones living in the north of what is now Tasidar and some evil ones in the south of what is now Salidar. Some of the other races that lived at that time, like the cyclops and the unicorns, were lost for all time."

"When he saw the outcome of the Wish, Aran-Than knew that he had only postponed the inevitable. Although the forces were now numerically equal, all of the evil races bred faster than the good ones, and it wouldn't be long before the evil forces had a huge superiority in numbers again. With the two sides separated, the forces of good would be vastly outnumbered when the sides met once more. Good wouldn't have a chance...again. Faced with a no-win situation, he cast another Wish. No one had ever cast one Wish spell before, much less two, and the energy that he expended in it killed him. Legend has it that, in his frustration, the Wish he cast was 'I Wish I knew how to defeat the forces of evil the next time.' He was given the Prophecy as his answer, just before he died."

"Wait a minute," said Ghorza, "you are telling this story as if you were there. How do you know all of this?"

"Someone from the City of Silver recently contacted us," replied Lady Ellyn. "He gave us an ancient text with the knowledge we lost at the Sundering. We didn't know that the current fighting was anything more than just civilized forces fighting to keep the evil races from our towns. We didn't know that this is actually a war for control of the world and the heavens by proxy. After the Sundering, the good races forgot that this was the War for Dominance. The enemy, though, has never forgotten. They aren't just fighting for loot or a little more land; they are fighting for the dominance of their gods, and the only way they can do that is to completely wipe us out. They are in this war with one goal and one goal only—to win it for their gods. They will stop at nothing short of our complete annihilation."

Chapter Thirty-Six

There was a long pause as the companions digested the new information.

"I have a couple of questions," Dantes said. "You said you were contacted by survivors of the City of Silver." Lady Ellyn nodded. "Where have these survivors been for the past centuries? Why haven't they come forward before?"

"The answer to the second question is easy," said Lady Ellyn. "They have been on the Mountain of Frost."

"It can't be," said Dantes. "I have sailed past the Mountain of Frost, and there is nothing on it. The mountain top is covered with snow year-round."

"That is true," Lady Ellyn replied. "The peak is covered in snow, but what about lower down on the mountain?"

"I don't know," Dantes answered. "The lower half of the mountain is always shrouded in mist or smoke. No one knows which, because sailors won't go within several miles of it."

"Nor should they," Lady Ellyn agreed, "as that is the abode of Scylla, and Charybdis looms nearby, as well."

"Wait a minute," John interrupted, "I've heard of Scylla and Charybdis. That is a myth we have on the world where I am from. One of those is a sea monster, I think, and the other is a whirlpool or reef or something."

"Interesting," said Lady Ellyn. "That is also what Sir Luce, the knight that escaped the island, said. There is a whirlpool that completely encircles the island. In fact, that is what causes the mist that rings it, preventing anyone offshore from seeing that the island exists. There is, however, a finger of land that goes over one part of the whirlpool before going back into the sea. Underneath that is the lair of Scylla, the many-headed. It is a monster that eats anything that approaches the island. If you somehow escape it, the odds are that you will be swallowed up by the whirlpool, or Charybdis as the locals call it."

"How would I have known that?" asked John.

"No one knows where people that are sucked into the maelstrom end up," said Father Telenor; "perhaps there is a portal to your world."

"So you know about this island, too?" asked Dantes.

Father Telenor nodded. "I was there when we recovered Sir Luce," he said.

"Father Telenor is being modest," said Lady Ellyn, "as it was his healing spells that saved the knight, at least for a little. An elderly man, he passed away soon after, but not before he completed his mission."

"His mission?" asked John. "What was that?"

"He told us all of the things that I've already told you about the island and the war, and two things more," said Lady Ellyn. "First, he mentioned something about 'the Keeper,' a mystical being that lives high up on the mountain."

"The keeper of what?" asked Ghorza.

"No one knows," said Father Telenor, "although Sir Luce said that it was supposed to be something very powerful. Sir Luce also said that many people have tried to obtain it over the ages, but all have failed...failed and died. It is said that only the Chosen and the Unchosen, the champions of both sides, can pass his trials."

"That's comforting," said Dantes. "What is the other thing the knight told you?"

"After the Sundering, the people that survived thought that they alone had escaped the devastation. They could not leave the island, due to Scylla and Charybdis, but they could climb up the mountain and see that the continent of Halidar no longer existed. They thought that they alone had survived the cataclysm, so they had no reason to brave Scylla and Charybdis."

"And yet Sir Luce did," said Dantes. "What changed?"

"Over 200 knights set out from the island with Sir Luce, along with their retainers and support personnel; Sir Luce was the only one that survived long enough to make landfall in Tasidar. The island has no trees, so building a ship was challenging, and it didn't survive Scylla's attack. Sir Luce was the only person who lived long enough to gather enough pieces of the ship to form a raft and float it to our shores."

"That he lived that long is nothing short of incredible," added Father Telenor. "He should have perished long before reaching Tasidar. Only his incredible will kept him going, long past the point where anyone else would have given up and died."

"His will, and the blessing of the one true god," said Lady Ellyn. "Without her aid, he never would have made it to Norlon to give us warning."

"What warning?" asked Dantes, dreading the answer.

"A knight arrived on the island six months ago, riding a red dragon," said Lady Ellyn. "He captured and tortured some of the island's population. That knight was wearing black armor with red gauntlets."

"The Dark Lord Kazan," said Fitzber. "Aye? Wasn't that what you called him?"

"Yes," replied Lady Ellyn. "That sounds like the Dark Lord Kazan. If he tortured the civilians, he got the information from them. He knows the last Item of Power is on the island, and it is just a matter of time before the enemy tries to claim it."

"It's almost daylight," said Dantes, "and Harbortown is a long way away. If what you just told us is true, we need to get going. We don't have a moment to lose."

Chapter Thirty-Seven

"They're still closing on us," said Fitzber as he materialized next to Dantes.

"*By the gods!*" swore Dantes. It was the fourth time in three days of traveling that the gnome had done that to him. "Didn't I tell you not to do that?"

"You did, laddie?" asked Fitzber. "Sure'n I don't recall you *not* wanting a status report on the enemy forces. In fact, I thought that was what you said to do. 'Now Fitzber,' you said in that gruff devil voice o' yours, 'we want you to go find out where the enemy is, how far behind us they are,' and so on and so on. To me, that meant you *wanted* a status report. My apologies; my wee mind must have misinterpreted your meaning."

"That's not what I meant," said Dantes, steam starting to rise from him in several places.

"So the enemy is catching up?" asked Ghorza, stepping in between the two. "How far behind us are they?"

"Sure'n they're not more than four hours behind," said Fitzber. "Three and a half if they take to hurrying."

"How do they keep gaining on us?" asked John. He stifled a yawn. "We're barely getting any sleep, and we're going all day. How are they catching up to us?"

"It helps that most o' the beasties are twice as big as us," said Fitzber, "and more like three times bigger than you and me. They can take big steps and move a lot faster."

"They're most likely being magically aided, too," said Dantes, "and fear probably plays a part. You can get people to do a lot more than they ever thought possible with the correct application of a little fear."

"What do you recommend?" asked Lady Ellyn, who was used to working with rangers and knew their skills.

"Well, lassie, if we push hard the rest o' today and tomorrow, we can be there by midday. They'll be closer, but should still be two hours or so behind us. Is that enough to get us through town and onto a boat?"

"It should be, yes," said Lady Ellyn.

"Then you ought to get the devil to stop standing around. He needs to get going," said Fitzber, looking in Dantes' direction.

Dantes opened his mouth for a retort, but Fitzber faded into the forest and was gone.

Chapter Thirty-Eight

"I forget what we decided last time," said Fitzber, materializing next to Dantes. "Were you a-wanting a status report or no? Sure'n I remember having a wee bit o' discussion o'er the topic, but for the life o' me, I don't remember what was decided."

Dantes tried to grab the gnome, but only succeeded in grabbing a handful of air.

"Which way was the right of it?" asked Fitzber from the other side of Dantes.

Dantes stopped and growled, steam coming from his nostrils in two big clouds that smelled of sulfur.

Ghorza gave him a little push to get him moving again. "You know you only encourage him when you do that, right?"

"What's up, Fitzber?" asked John, who was coming to like Fitzber's pranks. Things had a way of going missing when he was around, and then turning up later in unexpected places. For example, Dantes' pack had been about 20 feet up in a tree when they woke up in the morning. Although Fitzber swore he didn't do it, John saw a glint in his eyes when he said it. He may not have done it himself, but he probably had a hand in it.

"Sure'n I don't know," replied Fitzber. "It's the darnedest thing I've ever seen. The forest ends about 15 minutes from here, and you wouldn't think that there was any sort of hostilities going on. Farmers are out in their fields, working at a normal pace, doing the things that they always do. Confused I am about how they don't know there is a giant army, no pun intended, just a couple o' hours from here. It's almost like they didn't know...or didn't care."

"It must be that the word has somehow failed to reach here," said Lady Ellyn. "It cannot be that they don't care. When the enemy arrives, they will all be killed. Of that, there can be no doubt."

The group continued on and found it to be as Fitzber had related. A farmer, along with his wife and son, were picking beans in the first field they came to, looking as if they didn't have a care in the world. The woman wore a white dress to reflect the sun as she worked, the man a brown tunic.

"Hello there, gentle sir," said Lady Ellyn in greeting. "Can I ask what you're doing out here?"

"Good day," said the man, wiping sweat from his brow as he looked up from a bean plant. "There's a water barrel over there if you need it."

"I'm sorry, I don't understand your meaning," said Lady Ellyn.

"Well, it's pretty obvious...to me, anyway...that I am a farmer out working in my field," he said, holding up a handful of beans. "If you can't see that, then I figured you were having some sort of heat stroke and needed water. I wanted to render what assistance I could."

"Are you not aware that there is an army no more than two hours from here?" asked Lady Ellyn in frustration. "Has no one given you the warning?"

"Of course we know there's an army coming," replied the man. Both he and his wife were wearing large straw hats; he removed his to fan himself with it. "We were told about that a couple of days ago. In fact, I was starting to get worried that it wasn't going to come.

You know, what with all the talk that the forces of Salidar are on the move, it certainly calms one's mind to know that there is a big army around to protect you...even if they do tend to eat up all of your crops and only pay you a pittance of what it's worth. Still, that's better than having trolls and such around, you know?"

"But sir, the enemy following us *is* the army of Salidar. No more than two hours behind us is a huge force of trolls, giants and ogres. You must flee now to Harbortown or you will be killed."

"I'm sorry, but you are mistaken," replied the man. "The mayor of Harbortown, himself, was out here in the fields just a few days ago to tell us that the Norlon army would be passing through here. He personally assured us that everything was okay, and that it would be even better once the army got here. Now, you're wasting my time, so if you could please move along, I have a lot of work to get done before the sun goes down."

The companions started down the road, all except for Father Telenor. "Can I ask your names for a prayer?" he inquired.

"Name's William James Rysanek, just like my dad and his two dads before him," said the man, "and this here's my wife Angie and my son Will."

"Thank you," said Father Telenor. He extended his hands in their direction, saying a prayer over them.

"Why did you ask their names?" asked John as Father Telenor rejoined the group. "Was that some kind of blessing?"

"No," Father Telenor replied, "it was their last rites. They're already dead; they just don't know it yet."

"This is craziness!" said Lady Ellyn as the group continued once more down the road. "They're expecting an army from Norlon? There no longer *is* an army of Norlon. There are probably soldiers on the run, maybe even a few scattered units that got out in one piece, but an army? I don't believe it. Where did they get that idea?"

"I don't know," said Fitzber. "He can believe what he wants to, but I've seen the army that's following us. It is not an army of Norlon. They have been tricked somehow. The army that trails us is the army of Salidar."

"We must hurry," said Dantes. "If this is the state of the outlying fields, I'm worried about whether the city is ready to receive an enemy army."

Chapter Thirty-Nine

It was as Dantes feared. As the group neared Harbortown, they could see the gates standing open. Four soldiers on guard duty lounged nearby, watching people pass back and forth through the gates. "I am going to do a little scouting," said Fitzber. "Something is very wrong here." He faded out.

The companions continued to the gate.

"What in the name of the one true god is going on here?" exploded Lady Ellyn when the soldiers waved her through, without even getting up to acknowledge her status. Although they looked a little chagrined at getting yelled at, they didn't appear to be terribly worried about any additional consequences of their actions.

"Uh, sorry ma'am, but what do you mean?" asked the soldier with the most stripes on his rank insignia.

"What do I mean?" asked Lady Ellyn. "I mean, there is an enemy army no more than two hours from here, and you are all sitting here like you have nothing better to do. You should be preparing for war!"

"Naw, you heard it all wrong," said the leader. "There is an army coming, but it's coming from Norlon. They threw back the forces of Salidar, and now the army is coming to help defend Harbortown."

Lady Ellyn drew her sword. "There is an army coming from Norlon, but it is a Salidarian army. Norlon was sacked four days ago. I know because I was there!"

"Naw, you couldn't have been there four days ago; it's a five- to six-day march to get here from there," said one of the men.

Lady Ellyn walked over to the leader of the men and put the point of her sword on his chest. All of a sudden, he didn't look bored anymore; now he looked scared. Lady Ellyn looked at the rest of the men. "Which one of you would like to spare this soldier's life by going to get the Sergeant of the Watch, *right now?*" she asked.

"Me!" said two of the men, not wanting to be in her presence anymore. They jumped up and ran inside the gate. Lady Ellyn removed the sword from the leader's chest, but kept it close by to let him know she was serious.

Within five minutes, the two men came back with the Sergeant of the Watch, who was armed only with a turkey leg. By the ruins of it on his face and hands, it was obvious that he had been interrupted at lunch. He had the foresight to bring along another six men in addition to the two that had gone to get him. All of the new men were armed with halberds, two-handed pole weapons that had an axe blade topped with a spike on one side and a hook on the other for grappling mounted warriors. The eight soldiers had on pieces of armor, but none had on a complete set. Even though their weapons were deadly, the men looked sloppy, just like their sergeant.

"Now, what's this all about?" asked the sergeant between bites. "These men 'ere said someone's been threatenin' the watch. We can't be havin' that in this town. We're an orderly sort, here."

"I was the one threatening him," said Lady Ellyn. "I wanted to know what kind of worthless piece of animal dung was running this watch. Now I know. For your information, oh piece of dung, there is a Salidarian army that is an hour and a half from here, and if you don't start organizing right *now*, you will all be dead within two hours."

"Hey now, for guests, you're not being very nice," said the Sergeant of the Watch. "Men, arrest the foreigners and take them down to the jail until they learn some manners."

The men with halberds lowered the points and advanced on the companions.

"By the seventh level of hell," spat Dantes. "This is not helpful. We should all be preparing for war, not fighting with each other."

"There is not going to be war," said the Sergeant of the Watch. "A knight arrived here a couple of days ago, and he let us know that not only were the Salidarian forces driven back, but the army of Norlon took so few casualties doing it that they were sending a contingent to help defend Harbortown, too. You are wrong, you have no manners, and you need to cool off. Men, take them to jail."

"Perhaps you'd like to re-think that last order?" asked Fitzber, materializing in front of the Sergeant of the Watch. His dagger was within a hair's breadth of the sergeant's crotch. "If you have any intentions of having children in the future, anyway, that is."

"All right, men, no sense getting hasty," said the Sergeant of the Watch. "Perhaps we might be better served by taking these people to the mayor's office and letting them hear it from him. Maybe then they will believe it."

"That would be fine," replied Lady Ellyn. "I would also like to meet this knight that came from Norlon."

"Shouldn't be a problem, ma'am," said the sergeant, sounding more comfortable now that the dagger had been removed from his privates. "The knight hasn't left the mayor's side since he arrived, I don't think."

The group headed through the gates and into the city. As they cleared the gates, Dantes felt a slight tug on his sleeve. "I will meet you on the other side of the merchant's quarter," said Fitzber. "At the base of the hill prior to the port complex."

"Aye," whispered Dantes, wondering where the gnome was off to. It was information they needed most, though, and the gnome was able to get it best on his own, so he let the ranger go.

The companions were led through the town to the new mayor's office. "Things have changed since the last time I was here," said Dantes, looking up at the official-looking building. The white structure was as big as the king's castle in Norlon.

The Sergeant of the Watch didn't answer. He had dropped his turkey leg on the way and spent most of the journey trying to wipe the grease off his hands and face, with limited success.

"No weapons inside the mayor's office," said one of the two sentries at the door going into the building. Unlike the city watch, these men's uniforms were crisp and their weapons spotless. "You can leave all of your weapons in here," he added, pointing to a table in a small anteroom.

"Do we trust them?" asked Ghorza.

Lady Ellyn walked over to the sentry that had spoken. Taking hold of the front of his uniform lapel, she pulled his face close to hers. "This sword was given to me by my father," she said in a voice laced with menace, "who got it from his father, who got it from his father. I will be back for it. If anything happens to it, I will kill you, then have Father Telenor raise you from the dead so that I can kill you again. Slowly. Am I clear on this?"

"Yes, m'lady," said the sentry. "I will guard it as if my life depended on it."

"See that you do," she said, "because it surely does." She glanced at Ghorza while still holding his uniform. "I think we can trust them," she said. The man nodded, and she let him go.

After the companions had stacked their weapons, they were led into a large open room. All of them drew a breath as they entered; the room was an exact replica of the throne room in Norlon, complete with a throne on which the mayor sat.

A majordomo stood at the door. He took their names and announced them, and then they were led forward to stand in front of the mayor. They got their second surprise in quick order as the mayor's advisors walked out to stand next to him. His chief advisor was a halfling, who stood to the right of the mayor's throne; to the left of the mayor stood a knight in dark armor. The man was easily six feet tall and looked incredibly strong. His dark hair, dark mustache and dark eyes complemented his dark aura. Lady Ellyn didn't need a Detect Evil spell to know the knight was evil; he radiated it from every pore of his being.

She also knew instantly that this wasn't going to end well. "We should leave now," she said under her breath.

"Kneel," said the majordomo.

"Why should we kneel?" asked Dantes. "He is the mayor, not royalty."

"In Harbortown, the mayor *is* royalty," replied the majordomo.

"We will not kneel to the mayor," said Lady Ellyn, eliciting a smile from the dark knight.

"If they will not kneel," said the mayor, "throw them out of town."

"We come with information that is vital you hear," said Father Telenor. "It would be best if you take a minute and listen."

The halfling leaned over to the mayor's ear and whispered something that the group couldn't hear.

"Take them outside of the gates," said the mayor. "If they won't go, kill them. If they try to come back in, kill them. If they try to talk to any of the city's inhabitants, kill them. They are known agitators that go around trying to incite riots. If they do anything out of line, *kill them!*" Before they could move, the companions were surrounded by ten men who had been standing guard in the room, each carrying a halberd. It was obvious that they weren't the first people to be expelled from the city; the men performed the drill better than anything else the companions had seen any of the city's soldiers do.

"Should we attack?" whispered Ghorza. "Even unarmed, we could still probably take these buffoons."

"No," said Lady Ellyn. "These men are basically good, they are just poorly led. I will not kill them. The city will need them soon."

"Soon?" asked Dantes. "They'll be dead inside of an hour."

"That is true," agreed Lady Ellyn, "but it won't be by my hand."

"How are we going to get to the port?" asked Ghorza.

"I don't know," said Dantes, "but we'll figure something out."

The soldiers escorted the companions out of the audience room. Although they were initially worried about getting their weapons back, the soldiers stopped and let them pick them up, perhaps to prevent problems with them in the small room.

The companions were then marched to the gate, very much aware of the passage of time.

"The mayor said that I wasn't allowed to talk to the citizens of the city, correct?" Dantes asked the Sergeant of the Watch, who had been put in charge of their expulsion. "He didn't say that I couldn't talk to you, right?"

"That's true enough," said the sergeant. "But if I were you, I'd be watchin' my tongue."

"Okay," said Dantes, "then I won't talk badly about the mayor, or the fact that his chief advisor looks to be the brother of the halfling that led the attack on Norlon. I won't even talk badly about the dark knight that is advising him."

"That's good," said the sergeant, "because if you do, me boys will have to stick you with their halberds."

"Okay," said Dantes. "Good to know. I won't mention that you are being led astray and are probably going to be dead inside of an hour."

"What? What's that all about?" asked the sergeant. "That almost sounds like you're doin' that instigatin' thing that the mayor warned me about."

"Nope, not me," replied Dantes. "I won't say a word about the fact that you're all being tricked. I also won't tell you that the city of Norlon is no more, nor that the army that is approaching is led by dark knights that are dressed just like the dark knight in the mayor's audience room. I'll just keep my lips shut about all of that." John could see that his words were having an effect on the men. The sergeant hadn't noticed, but some of them were starting to look *very* nervous.

The group reached the gate. In the distance a dust cloud loomed over the forest, the kind of cloud made by thousands of marching feet.

"I've got another question for you," said Dantes. "The mayor said to expel us, but he didn't say that you had to do it right away, did he? Maybe it would be better if you waited to see who was in the army drawing near. If it is an army from Norlon like he said, we'll leave, just as nice as can be. If, however, the army turns out to be one from Salidar, I'm sure you'd like to have our assistance in helping to turn it away."

"Gee, Sarge, a devil would be awfully handy to have in a fight," said one of the original soldiers. "I hear they're really hard to kill."

"That's true," said Dantes. "I am pretty handy in a fight."

"I don't know..." said the sergeant, not wanting to lose face in front of the men, but also not wanting to give up six experienced fighters. Wait. He counted again. "Where did the other one of you go?" he asked. "Where's the one that threatened me family life with his dagger?"

"To tell you the truth, I really don't know where he went," said Dantes. "He was going to try to find out what was going on in town. Does it matter? He wasn't with us in the audience room, so the mayor didn't really expel him now, did he?"

The sergeant looked confused. Although the mayor had expelled the group, the gnome hadn't been with them when the mayor had done so. Still, he was part of the group that had threatened the soldiers (and he had definitely threatened the sergeant), so he probably should be expelled, too. But how could he expel the gnome, if he wasn't around to kick out? In fact, he couldn't remember the last time he had seen the little troublemaker.

Dantes smiled to himself, he could almost see the wheels in the sergeant's head turning. Before he could pose his next question, the sentry on top of the wall called, "Sergeant, I've got movement in the distance."

"Well what is it?" asked the sergeant. "Tasidaran troops or Salidarian?"

The sentry peered harder into the distance. "Sergeant, I can't rightly tell. They don't even look like soldiers at all. If anything, it looks like a couple of farmers walking their dogs."

"Farmers walking their dogs?" asked one of the men. "At midday? That's odd. I grew up on a farm, and all farmers do is work the farm. They don't take afternoons off to walk their dogs."

"I've got a bad feeling," said Ghorza. "Sergeant, I have a spell that will help me see farther. May I go up on the wall to look?"

"Yes, but don't be thinkin' of doing anythin' tricky," said the sergeant. "If you do, your friends here will pay for it with their lives."

"I understand." Ghorza left for the stairs at a run.

The soldier met her at the top of the stairs and pointed to where he was looking. "See, they're farmers," he said. "Now that they're a little closer, I can tell for sure. They both have big straw hats on, like farmers wear. The woman is wearing a red dress and the man is wearing a brown tunic. They've each got two dogs that they've got on leashes. They must be coming into town for supplies or something."

Ghorza looked and saw that it was pretty much as the sentry described. Still, something was wrong. The soldier down below was right. Farmers didn't take afternoons off during the harvest. Ever. Especially with an army coming that was going to eat them out of house and home. If anything, they gathered their crops faster so that they could hide them away for their own use.

"*Focus!*" Ghorza cast the far-seeing spell, and the two farmers seemed to jump closer as the air magnified the light rays. The two people approaching the town were dressed very much like the two farmers that had been working in their bean field. She couldn't see their faces because of the big straw hats, so she couldn't tell for sure.

The only difference was that the woman had been wearing a white dress, not a red one. Looking closer, she could see that the dress had white spots on it; it wasn't uniformly red. Something seemed odd, but she couldn't place it.

The couple stopped and bent down to pet their dogs, and Ghorza's focus was drawn to the dogs, which seemed to be a little bigger than usual. Still, on the frontier, some people owned deer hounds or other big dogs for protection or to help them hunt. Deer hounds were big dogs, too, but these dogs were shaggier, almost wolf-like. And they had red eyes. And the farmers' hands that were holding the leashes, the only skin she could see, was green.

Realization hit her as the 'farmers' loosed their 'dogs' and began running after them toward the gate. "*Orcs and worgs!*" she cried. "Get inside and close the gates!"

"What's it going to be, sergeant," asked Dantes as the other members of his group started readying their weapons. "Want to let us in, or do you want to die out here?"

"Umm...umm...umm..." the sergeant stalled, unable to make up his mind.

"Sarge, I don't like this," said one of the soldiers. "I think they're right. We need to get inside." All 14 of the soldiers started edging toward the gates.

"*Globus Incendi!*" shouted Dantes, casting a fireball. The bead of flame streaked toward the four worgs and burst, enveloping all of them. Only two of the worgs emerged from the fireball, and both were injured.

"*Missilis Magici!*" John cast. Two missiles jumped from his finger and hit the worg in the lead, killing it. It rolled to a stop, and the last one vaulted over it.

"*Flagra!*" commanded Father Telenor, calling down a flame strike on the last worg. A vertical column of divine flames roared down from the heavens to strike the last worg. It was overkill for the already wounded worg, but served its purpose. When the flames cleared, there wasn't much left beyond the smell of burnt hair.

Suddenly outnumbered, the two orcs skidded to a stop. In their haste to charge the gate, their hats had come off, exposing them for what they were. They turned and began running back the way they had come. By now everyone could see that the dress was red with blood; it was the farmer's wife's dress.

"Umm...I think we should get inside and close the gates," said the sergeant, making up his mind. "Call out the alarm! Ring the bell! To arms! To arms!"

The companions rushed inside the gates and helped shut and bar them.

Ghorza, still on the wall, glanced up from watching the gates shut. She didn't need a spell to see the next creatures coming out of the woods. "Ready the fires!" she yelled. "*Trolls!*"

Chapter Forty

"Y ou there!" shouted Lady Ellyn. "Take that vat of acid to the wall." A natural leader, she easily slipped into the vacant leadership position and started organizing the defense. With mere minutes until the trolls arrived, she already knew there wouldn't be enough time. If the orcs and worgs had taken the guards unaware and been able to keep the gates open...she shuddered at the thought. Now at least they had a chance. She laughed. The only chance they had was to kill a few of the enemy before the walls fell and they were overrun. And they *were* going to be overrun, she knew. Of that, she had no doubt.

"You five with halberds, get to the left side of the gate," she yelled. She started to go redirect a load of crossbow bolts, but Dantes grabbed her.

"We've got to go!" he urged. "We've got to get to the port."

"Without me, they are going to lose the wall," Lady Ellyn replied.

"They're going to lose the wall even with you," said Dantes. "If there were 50 of you, even 100 of you, they'd still lose it. They're not ready, and *the wall is going to fall!*"

"He's right," said Father Telenor, "and you know it."

"I know...," said Lady Ellyn, "just as I know they're all going to die. Everyone here is going to die. I just want to give them a chance."

"All you're doing is ensuring that our quest will fail," said Dantes. "Even with your aid, the wall may hold for 10 minutes, but no more.

At that time, the enemy will be inside the city, and everyone is going to go to the port to try to flee. It will be a madhouse, and no one is going to make it out of here alive."

Lady Ellyn sighed again. "You're right," she said. "Let's go."

"You're not leaving, are you?" asked the Sergeant of the Watch. "We need you here!"

"We have to go meet the last member of our group," said Dantes. "Hold the walls until we get back. You can do this."

"I can?"

"Yes, you can," said Dantes. "There are a lot of people counting on you. Do your best."

As the companions jogged off, Dantes shook his head. It was obvious that the soldiers had never trained to defend the wall. They were running everywhere, and nothing was prepared. It was going to be a slaughter, whether they stayed or not. Everyone in the city was going to die.

"Who said to close the gates?" asked a loud voice.

The group turned to find that the dark knight had arrived. Without a word being spoken, all of them charged him. Seeing the group coming at him, the dark knight turned and ran off the other way. He reached the corner of a building and was quickly lost from sight. "Stop," said Dantes. "Let him go. There'll be another time to kill him. He's a distraction. Let's get to the port."

Lady Ellyn was the last to turn back to the port, watching where the knight had fled in the hopes that he would return. The knight was evil and needed to be dealt with. When he didn't return, she sighed once more and turned to follow her companions. She knew she would meet him again.

Chapter Forty-One

"I was wondering when you'd turn up," said Fitzber, materializing next to Dantes, causing him to jump. He looked like a turtle with a giant shield strapped to his back, and he had several large items in his arms.

"Even now you have to do that?" asked Dantes, resisting the urge to strike down the little gnome as his heart rate returned to normal. "Can't you ever stop?"

"Stop what?" asked Fitzber with a smile. "Showing up with presents?" He gave the load he was carrying to John. There was a wrapped package, as well as a short sword and a dagger. "I guess I could, but I thought it would be better if John were armed and armored, at least a little. And I also knew I owed the good Father a new shield for the one he lost coming to my defense, sure'n that's the truth." He climbed out of the shield and handed it to Father Telenor.

"We need to be going," said Fitzber, sobering. "If there's one thing I noticed, it's that this city is ill-prepared for its defense. I do not believe the walls will hold for more than 30 seconds, maybe not even that."

"You're right," said Dantes. "They've probably already fallen, and we need to get going. I've been here before. The port is just over this hill; hopefully, we can find transportation there."

As the noise of the city diminished behind them, the group could hear shouting and screaming coming from the other side of the hill, in male voices as well as female, and in young as well as old. The group hurried to the top of the hill. Reaching the crest, John saw a winged creature headed away from them. It was enormous and colored a dark red that tended to brown in spots. As they watched, something fell from its claws and cartwheeled down almost 500 feet to impact the surface of the bay. John realized with horror that it was a man. He hit with an enormous splash and didn't resurface.

"Dragon!" Fitzber yelled, the first to recognize it, and the group ran down the hill to the port. If the dragon heard him over the screaming, it gave no indication as it made a lazy turn over the harbor to survey the results of its attack. Apparently it was pleased, as it continued its turn and headed out to sea, winging off quickly to the south. The devastation in the harbor was nearly complete, the group saw. Most of the ships had been sunk at anchor and now rested at the bottom of the bay, with only the tops of their masts above water. Only one ship was still afloat.

On a good day, that ship would have been beautiful. A three-masted xebec, its foremast leaned slightly forward, while its main and mizzen masts leaned slightly back. Each of the masts was built to carry a large triangular sail on a yard that was at a 45 degree angle to the mast. A long prow projected from its bow, giving it a look that implied speed.

Today wasn't a good day, however, and the look was greatly diminished by the fact that more than half of its main mast was broken and leaning overboard, causing the ship to list to starboard at a large angle. A number of crew members were working on the mast.

"I think our choice of ship has been made for us," said Dantes.

"Were it whole," said Father Telenor, "that looks like it would be a fast trading ship."

"Or a fast smuggler," said Dantes, catching sight of the vessel's name. "Ghorza, does that ship say what I think it says?"

Ghorza shook her head in disgust. "Yeah, it does," she said. "It's the *Pole Dancer*."

"Ghorza and I have had dealings with its captain in the past," said Dantes. "He styles himself to be a merchant while in port, but at sea he is also known as a pirate and a smuggler. That ship suits his life style; its speed and design help him to outrun what he can't outfight."

"A pirate?" asked Lady Ellyn. "Surely there is someone else more respectable that we can get to take us to Salidar."

"Look around," said Dantes. "Do you see any other ships available? We would have to go through the elven lands to the Commonwealth of Forgol to find another ship that could take us. That would take weeks, even if we could get safe passage from the elves. Then, we would start out further north, and the journey would take even longer. Who knows what the enemy forces would do with the extra month? They would certainly make it to the Mountain of Frost before us. Not only that, but finding someone that will take us to Salidar, especially now, is going to be extremely difficult. With the forces of Salidar already moving, no respectable captain in his right mind will want to go anywhere near there. I suspect that we will need someone that is a little more...notorious...if we hope to reach our destination."

"I would like to accomplish this as quickly as possible," said Lady Ellyn, "so I can get back to the defense of Norlon. If doing so means using *that* ship and *that* captain, then that is what we shall do." Although she agreed, her face looked like she had swallowed something sour. "Who is the captain?"

"The man's name is Philip Meyer," said Dantes. "Captain Meyer is a professional scoundrel. He only participates in things that make him money. He is successful at what he does, and he always pays his crew well, so his crew is one of the best around. Ghorza and I had to interview him as part of a case we investigated. Captain Meyer wasn't guilty of the crime, but he did transport goods that he probably knew were stolen and shouldn't have accepted."

The group jogged down the hill and through the port toward the pier that the *Pole Dancer* was tied up to. Mayhem reigned throughout the port, with fires burning in several places. People shouted throughout the port as they coordinated rescue efforts to pull people from burning buildings or the bay. In many cases they were already too late; rescue often became recovery as people that couldn't swim drowned.

"Shouldn't we be doing something to help?" puffed an out-of-breath John.

"Ordinarily, yes," replied Dantes, "we would stop and help." He could see in the eyes of Father Telenor and Lady Ellyn how much it pained them to keep going when every fiber of their being wanted to stop and help, to ease the misery of the people they were passing. "In this case, no," he added lowering his voice. "Not only are we on an urgent mission, but the forces of Salidar are right behind us. It won't be long before refugees come streaming over the hill, looking for a way to get out of here. With only one ship left, there will be a panic, and the ship will likely be overrun and swamped. As much as it hurts, we must not stop and help, or we will be trapped here, and our quest will be unfulfilled."

Dantes led the way onto the pier, stopping at the *Pole Dancer's* gangplank. The activity onboard the ship was as chaotic as the port in general. "Ahoy, the *Dancer*," Dantes called. "Permission to come aboard?"

A harried sailor looked down at them from the ship's railing. "Permission denied," he said, seeing the official looking party. "We're too busy at the moment for inspection."

"We're not inspectors," said Dantes. "We have an offer of employment for your captain that we'd like to discuss."

"He's not taking visitors at the moment," replied the sailor. "Come back later."

Dantes snapped his claw, and a flame sprang up on his palm. He looked at the flame to focus the sailor's attention on it for a couple of seconds and then said, "Your captain will be even busier if I set the ship on fire. It is urgent that we speak to him, and that we speak to him *now*."

The sailor looked back over his shoulder as if looking for someone of a higher rank to take responsibility for the visitors, so that the decision wouldn't be his. "Stay there," he ordered, seeing no one. "I'll go get him."

The sailor left the rail.

"*Pole Dancer?*" asked Father Telenor.

"Yeah, he named it after his last wife," said Dantes. "Don't mention it; he's very sensitive."

No more than a minute later, another head appeared over the railing. The new person had long curly hair, which poured out from under a swashbuckler hat. Where the first sailor had been missing teeth and generally looked somewhat rundown, this person appeared to be a man of some wealth. At almost six and a half feet tall and nearly 250 pounds, he was a big man who had an equally large air of authority. "Who is it that's threatening my ship?" he roared. He rested a crossbow on the railing. Although it wasn't pointed at the group on the pier, it wouldn't have taken much effort to aim it down at them.

"Good to see you again, Captain Meyer," said Dantes. He nodded to Ghorza. "I'm sure you remember Ghorza and me. It looks like you're having some problems at the moment that you need to attend to, so I will come straight to the point. We are not here in an official capacity, but we would like to make you an offer of employment."

"You're not here in an official capacity? Wonderful, then you can piss off because I've got nothing to say to you. You couldn't pay me enough to do business with you." He turned to leave.

"Before you go," Dantes called, "I think it important to tell you that even though I don't intend to destroy your ship, it will be destroyed within the next half hour if you don't hear me out."

Captain Meyer turned around. "Oh? In what manner will it be destroyed?"

"Trust me when I tell you that you don't want me to yell it out," Dantes replied. "Come down here, and I will tell you all about it."

Captain Meyer raised an eyebrow. "Really?" he asked. "Come down *there* where there are six of you and only one of me? I don't think so. Why don't you just go ahead and tell me."

Dantes turned to Lady Ellyn. "Can you promise on your word that he won't be hurt? We're wasting time we don't have."

Lady Ellyn nodded and stepped forward. "Captain Meyer," she said, allowing all of her goodness to shine through. John was once again reminded of the sun shining. "Surely you recognize me as a paladin, whose word is bond. I give you my solemn vow that if you come down, I will do everything within my power to protect you and restore you to your ship unharmed. I will not allow anyone to hurt you or take you captive while you are under my protection."

"Paladin, eh?" Captain Meyer asked, trying to fight the effects of her aura. "If you're giving me your word, I guess I can spare a minute or two." He came to the gangplank and walked down. "Now, what is all of this talk about my ship being destroyed? I take it you mean something else beyond what has already befallen the shipping in this port?"

"Aye, indeed I do," said Dantes. "The city of Harbortown is about to fall; the army of Salidar is at its gates."

"The gates are strong," replied Meyer. "How do you know they will fall? Are you a military expert now, too, as well as a policeman?"

"I am an expert," interrupted Lady Ellyn, "and I tell you that the city *will* fall. The mayor has already switched sides and has a dark knight as his counselor. The gate was open as the army of Salidar approached. We got it closed, but the army here is criminally unprepared to fight. They have neither the equipment nor the training required to turn back an army of this size. If the combined might of the Silver Swords couldn't stop them, there's no way that the Harbortown rabble is going to. I don't know what the enemy's plan is, but I know that the assault will not be a straightforward one. When they captured Norlon they purchased the contracts of several mercenary units, which switched sides in the middle of the attack and opened the gates for the enemy to enter. Once the hill giants and trolls were inside the gates, it was a slaughter."

"And you think they will do something similar here," said Meyer, chewing on his lower lip.

"Think? No," said Lady Ellyn, "I *know* they will do something sneaky. It is how they think and how they fight. They might have more people on the inside, they might have tunnels already dug under the walls; I don't know. All I know is that they've been planning this for a long time, and they have a plan that will work to capture the town." She paused, looking him in the eye. "When the town falls and the rout starts, where do you think the citizens are going to go?"

Captain Meyer looked nervously in the direction of the town. Several pillars of smoke could already be seen. The attack had commenced. "They're going to come here," he said. "And when they do, they will swamp the only ship they still see afloat." He nodded, as if accepting the logic, even if he didn't like it. "Okay, that answers the question of my ship being destroyed. You mentioned employment. You can't seriously want to employ the *Dancer*. You see the condition she's in, right?"

"Yes, we can see it," replied Dantes, taking back the conversational lead. "You're going to have to cut loose the main mast and put to sea. We are on a quest from the queen and need transportation. Let's focus on getting underway before the mobs get here. We can discuss our destination and your terms once we're at sea."

"No businessman I know ever made a profit by discussing terms once he allowed armed soldiers aboard his ship," replied Captain Meyer. "In my experience, that is a good way to find yourself held hostage on your own ship."

"We. Don't. Have. Time. To. Argue," said Dantes. In counterpoint, a woman screamed from the shore where she was gathering goods that were floating in from the ships that had been sunk. The group looked and saw her pointing at the crest of the hill where a dark knight holding a large saber sat astride a large, black horse. It was the same knight from the mayor's audience hall. The first group of Harbortown's civilians crested the hill at the same time, giving the knight a wide berth. As they looked down into the harbor, all of them turned to head straight for the *Pole Dancer*.

"Time just ran out," said Dantes. "We can help defend the ship until we get to sea, *but you've got to go now!*"

"Aye," said Captain Meyer. "Indeed I do." He turned and started up the gangplank, stopping suddenly as he made a decision. "Come along," he added. "I'll take you where you need to go."

"You heard the captain," said Dantes, "let's go." He started up the gangplank.

"No," said Lady Ellyn, "not this time. I have overlooked much in this quest so far, but this I cannot abide. That knight must die." She strode down the pier.

"Be right back," said Father Telenor as he broke into a run to catch up. "This won't take long," he yelled back over his shoulder. "I hope."

Dantes looked up and saw that the black knight had begun killing the fleeing civilians. As he watched, the knight caught up with a man that was running down the hill away from him carrying two long loaves of bread. The knight's saber flashed as he passed, and the man's head was separated from his shoulders in a spray of red.

"I challenge you by the one true god," called Lady Ellyn, reaching the shoreline. "Come and fight me!" Somehow her voice or her presence carried to the dark knight; he wheeled his horse in her direction and charged. Lady Ellyn held her ground as the knight galloped down the hill, building speed.

"She's dead," said Ghorza, who had witnessed such charges before. Ghorza turned away. She didn't want to watch.

"No!" said Dantes. "Look."

Lady Ellyn had chosen her position for a reason; a broken piece of spar from one of the ships had come ashore where she waited. With only seconds until impact, she bent down and grabbed the six-foot long piece of wood. As big around as her forearm, the spar was jagged on one end where it had been broken off the ship. The other end was smooth, and she slammed that end into the ground and braced it with her boot. She tilted the jagged end toward the charging knight at a 45 degree angle.

The knight's horse saw the improvised pike at the last second and tried to shy away to the right, but it was too late. Instead of impaling itself in the chest, the spar lanced into the horse's left shoulder, stopping the majority of its momentum and catapulting the dark knight over its head. The knight somersaulted through the air to land on his back in about six inches of water, momentarily stunned.

Although it broke the knight's charge, the spar wasn't up to the task of stopping the horse completely, and it snapped. The upper piece was driven into Lady Ellyn's chest armor, and she flew backward through the air to land in the water also. Neither knight got back up.

"M'lady," said Father Telenor as he ran up, "are you all right?" He lifted up the visor of her helmet and saw that her mouth was open and she was gasping for breath like a fish out of water. "*Ostium Mortis*," he said, casting his Death's Door spell to determine her condition. He was relieved to see that she was not near death.

"Just...got...wind...knocked out...of me," Lady Ellyn said. Father Telenor could see a three inch dent in the center of her chest armor; she was lucky to have only had the wind knocked out of her. It could have been much worse.

"Look out," yelled Dantes.

Father Telenor looked up to see the black knight rising from the bay, water streaming from his armor. Father Telenor started to cast a Hold Person spell on the knight.

"No," said Lady Ellyn. "My challenge. I will finish this. No helping."

Both knights made it to their feet at nearly the same time, but Lady Ellyn fell into the throes of a violent coughing fit and leaned forward, her hands on her knees. The black knight couldn't take advantage, as he had lost his sword when he flew over his horse. He searched through the water near his landing spot and, after a couple of moments of looking, found the saber. Picking it up, he turned and charged the paladin, drawing his dagger as he ran.

Lady Ellyn overcame her coughing fit and took a defensive pose, drawing her sword and dagger to meet the dark knight, who was similarly armed. Although difficult to determine in full plate armor, the dark knight appeared to be at least six inches taller and a good deal more massive.

Disdaining finesse, the dark knight came in fast, hoping to overwhelm the paladin before the cleric could help her. He tried an overhead slash, using his momentum to try to break through Lady Ellyn's defense. Used to fighting men that were larger and physically stronger, Lady Ellyn knew that her best defense was speed and maneuverability, not meeting the dark knight in a battle of strength versus strength. She feinted right and then dodged left, guiding the knight's saber to the side with her sword.

The knight hadn't expected her maneuver and overextended himself, and she stepped forward and thrust her dagger up into his right armpit where there wasn't any armor. Sensing what she intended, he used his momentum to roll away, but was only partly successful. She wasn't able to stab him deeply enough to kill him, but the blow still landed. Blood began flowing down the side of his armor.

The dark knight disengaged, so that he could switch his sword to his left hand. Having made the swap, he came back in on the attack. Wounded, he moved more cautiously this time. He knew time was on his side; the rest of his unit would crest the hill shortly. When that happened, they would slaughter all of the people trapped in the port area.

Lady Ellyn saw the knight's eyes twitch toward the hill and knew he was expecting additional forces. Regretting her choice to come and fight the knight, she advanced on him to end the battle. Recognizing her intention, the dark knight began backpedaling to stay out of reach and stall for time. This worked for a bit, but there was too much debris in the shallow water and he stepped on something, lost his balance and went down.

The knight twisted as he fell, landing on his left side, rather than his back. He rolled to his stomach and pushed himself up, trying to rise before she could get to him. Lady Ellyn knew she was out of time so, disdaining protocol, she stepped forward and swung her sword with all of her might at the defenseless knight. Killing the knight from behind was against her code, but that was not her intention. Instead, she turned the sword as she swung. With a loud 'clang,' the flat of her sword hit the knight's helmet, putting a large dent in both the helmet and his head. Unconscious and concussed, the knight fell face forward into the water.

"M'lady, we've got to go," said Father Telenor running up. Lady Ellyn looked up to see civilians streaming down the hill...and three more dark knights coming over the crest.

"Yes, I believe we should, at that," she said, reaching down to take the knight by the collar. "By the one true god this knight is heavy," she added as she pulled him forward three steps to get him out of the water. Dropping him to the sand, she broke into a jog.

More screaming ensued as the knights on the hill began slaughtering the town's citizens. Lady Ellyn tried to shut out their shrieks, but they went through her ears and into her soul. She knew she would hear them for the rest of her life.

"Run faster!" yelled Dantes as she reached the pier. Lady Ellyn could see that he was looking behind her, and she put on a last burst of speed. With a splash, the top half of the *Pole Dancer's* mainmast was hacked loose and fell overboard, righting the ship. She reached the gangplank and slowed to go up it. When she reached halfway, the mooring lines arced over the side of the ship to the pier, and the ship started to move.

The gangplank started to slide off the ship and Dantes didn't think that Lady Ellyn would make it aboard, but with a small jump, she cleared the side of the ship as the plank fell away to splash in the growing gap between the pier and the ship.

"Couldn't wait for me?" she asked.

Dantes was once again staring behind them. "No," he said. "Look!"

Lady Ellyn turned. The three knights were no longer slaughtering the town's inhabitants; instead, they were galloping toward the ship. "They're not going to make it," Dantes asked. "Are they?"

"No, I don't think so," she replied.

As the knights reached the pier, the two trailing ones pulled up short, but the one in the lead only spurred his mount faster, urging it to greater speed. A massive warhorse, it was black as night and was moving swifter than anything of its bulk had a right to go. Halfway down the pier, Lady Ellyn realized it wasn't a horse. She could see flames wreathing its hooves, and smoke streamed from its nostrils with every giant breath. Two strides later, she saw its bright red eyes…which matched the gauntlets of the knight riding it.

"Oh gods," she swore softly. "*Kazan!*"

She knew he would never give up. It wasn't in his nature. "He will make the jump," she forecast, drawing her sword.

"He can't make that jump," said Ghorza, judging the distance and the ship's rate of movement. "We're 10 feet up, and the gap is going to be easily 20 feet across when he gets to it."

"He will make the jump," repeated Lady Ellyn, drawing her dagger.

"Not if I can help it," replied Dantes. "*Globus Incendi!*" A bead of fire streaked toward the knight, detonating into a fireball just in front of him. If the knight noticed or cared, he didn't give any indication, nor did his nightmare steed; the two took three more strides and, reaching the end of the pier, launched themselves into the air.

"Boarders incoming!" yelled Dantes. All eyes turned in time to see the dark knight and nightmare soar over the port rail of the ship, smoke trailing from the nightmare.

The horse and rider crashed to the deck. Although they made the jump, the ship was narrow, and the nightmare immediately began skidding as it tried to stop itself from going over the opposite railing. Trailing flames from its hooves, the horse turned left to change its momentum, but there wasn't enough room. It hit the side rail, its momentum carrying it overboard.

The knight, however, was more agile. Seeing that his steed was going over, he pulled his feet from the stirrups and pushed off the saddle, vaulting from the beast. As the nightmare went over the railing, the Dark Lord Kazan landed next to the starboard rail. He still had some of the momentum of his steed, and he flailed his arms to regain his balance. It looked like he was going to make it.

"*Molaris!*" Dantes shouted, and two force missiles shot out from him. The large missiles didn't have enough room to grow to their full size, only achieving eight inches before striking the knight in the chest, but they were big enough. The missiles exploded simultaneously, denting the knight's armor and overbalancing him. He followed the nightmare overboard, making a large splash as he hit the water.

The companions looked back to see the knight treading water. Although they couldn't see his eyes, they could feel the heat and force of his gaze as he stared at the ship. After a moment, he turned and began swimming toward shore in the wake of his steed. "Shouldn't he sink in all that armor?" asked John.

"No," said Lady Ellyn, a far off look in her eyes, "it's magic armor and barely weighs anything." She turned to Dantes. "You should hope that you never meet him again. You have just made an enemy of the most powerful man in the world."

Chapter Forty-Two

"You took time off during the attack to go swimming?" asked Solim, walking into the former mayor's audience hall to find Kazan removing his armor. Water dripped from all of it. A piece of seaweed dangled from one of his boots. "Did I have the attack planned out so perfectly that you had time to sun yourself on the beach, too?"

"No," replied Kazan, dumping out a boot. "I tried to kill the outlander for you, but only ended up in the bay for my troubles."

"You let them get away?" asked Solim. "I thought you were so tough, you and all of your dark knights. You can kill *anything*." Sarcasm dripped from every word. "I heard the paladin bested one of your dark knights, too."

"I no more let them go than you did, every time you had the chance to kill them but failed," said Kazan. He pulled off his other boot and turned it over, dumping out several ounces of water that hadn't drained out on their own. He glared at the seaweed, and he removed it, before looking back at Solim. "Be warned, pipsqueak, that my patience has limits. Even though our masters have bid me not kill you out of hand, if you sneer at me again, I *will* kill you, regardless of my instructions."

"Really?" asked Solim. He met Kazan's eyes and focused his power through the crown. "You will not do anything to harm me."

Kazan dropped the boot, stood up and walked over to stand in front of Solim. "I will not do anything to harm you," he intoned.

213

"That's more like it," said Solim.

Kazan laughed, long and hard, before reaching over to take the crown off Solim's head. He inspected it for a minute and then threw it aside. It made a soft tinkling sound as it came to rest against the wall. "Don't ever try to control me again, either," he said, looking down at Solim. "It won't work because you are *not* my intellectual equal. All it's going to do is piss me off." He started to turn away, but then faced back toward Solim. "One last thing," he said. "If you ever say anything disrespectful about my troops again, I will personally pull off each of your limbs and beat you to death with them while you watch. Do I make myself perfectly clear?"

"I hear what you're saying, Kazan, and you may scare everyone else, but you *don't* scare me. I have power, too, and am not afraid to use it on you."

"This power that you speak of... is it the same power that you've used to kill the outlander? If so, I'm confused, as it hasn't worked very well. How many times have you tried to kill him now and failed? I'm afraid I've quite lost count as there have been so many." He poked Solim in the chest with his index finger. "We are supposed to co-rule...for now. At some point, though, something unfortunate may happen to you, and there's nothing your 'power' is going to be able to do to save you. Don't. Piss. Me. Off. Again."

"My mistake was counting on others to kill him for me...like you, who failed so miserably that you were tossed into the bay. This time, I am not going to rely on anyone else. I have a ship coming that I will use to chase him down before he reaches the Mountain of Frost. After I kill him, I will claim the prize he is after as my own, and I will bring it back here. When I return, all will bow down before me."

"If you return," said Kazan.

"*When* I return," said Solim, "even *you* will bow before me."

Chapter Forty-Three

"Now that we have made it to open water," said Captain Meyer, "what direction do you need to go?" he asked.

"Southeast," replied Dantes.

"Southeast?" asked a female half-orc sailor that Dantes had seen directing some of the sailors earlier. "There be no land in that direction. In fact, there be no land short of Salidar, and we not be going there." The half-orc had a full sailor's accent, which seemed odd coming from someone with her heritage.

"She's got that right," said a tall broad-shouldered man standing behind her.

"That is not entirely true," said Dantes, "The Mountain of Frost lies in that direction. That is our destination."

"No," said the half-orc. "It cannot be done, and we won't be doing it."

"She's got that right," the tall man behind her added.

"And who are you to say what will and won't be done?" asked Dantes.

"The woman's Tanja Cilia," replied Captain Meyer. "She's my second mate. She used to have her own ship, and she sometimes forgets that she isn't the one making the decisions onboard the *Dancer.*"

"I'm the first mate now, though, aye?" asked Cilia.

Captain Meyer pursed his lips in thought as he stared at the half-orc. "Aye, 'tis true," he said, "but don't be getting a bigger head than you already have. If you do, I'll throw you overboard myself." Captain Meyer turned back to Dantes. "Tanja just got promoted to first mate. The dragon you saw in the harbor carried off our first mate and dropped him in the middle of the bay. Even if he survived the fall, he couldn't swim, and I saw him go under. The tall man behind her with more muscles than brains is the new acting second mate, John Rowntree."

"Okay, first mate," said Dantes, "why can't this ship go to the Mountain of Frost?"

"There be two reasons. Firstly, the *Pole Dancer* is too light to take out across the ocean. "She's made for speed and maneuverability inshore to get her goods to port. She's not made for the storms that lie out on the open seas, and it'd be extra dangerous now to try it without her main mast."

Dantes couldn't help himself. "And what goods are we transporting?" he asked.

"Legitimate goods," replied the captain. "If you must know, we've got a full cargo of none of your damn business, comprised of equal parts of piss off, sod off and bugger off. You're not a policeman on this ship, you've got nothing on us, and we've got a lot of work to do to make this ship seaworthy again. Keeping your nose out of our business would be a good habit to get into if you want us to even consider what you're saying."

Dantes nodded to the captain, acknowledging the point. "Sorry," he said, "old habits die hard." He looked back at the first mate. "And the second reason?" he asked.

"The second reason is that, even if the *Dancer* was whole, you wouldn't be getting us to go there," replied the first mate. "Those waters be haunted. No one that goes there ever returns." Several of the sailors that were working in the area spoke up in agreement, while making signs to ward off evil.

"Still," said Dantes, "that is where we must go."

The captain cleared his throat. "The first rule of leadership, especially with *this* crew, is never to give an order which you know won't be obeyed. I have a hard time believing that I will be obeyed if I tell the helmsman to steer toward the Mountain of Frost. Unless you're hiding a big bag of coins that's going to make it worth our while?"

"Unfortunately, no, I don't have a bag of gold for you at this moment," said Dantes, "but if we accomplish our quest, I'm sure there will be rewards aplenty when we return."

"Aye, it's always good to risk your neck for people that are likely to die, on the hope that; one, they somehow won't actually get themselves killed; two, they will be successful in their quest; and three, they will remember to ask the king for your reward when they're done. When I said that I would take you where you needed to go, I meant somewhere in the civilized world. I never intended to go on a trip with no return."

"We are the only hope Tasidar has," said Dantes. "If you don't take us to the Mountain of Frost, there won't be anything to stop the forces of evil from killing everything that is good in this world. What you just saw in Harbortown isn't going to stop. The forces of Salidar are on the move, and they won't stop at anything short of Tasidar's complete destruction. They have been ordered to take over the world...and they intend to do it." He lowered his voice. "We have information that there may be a way to stop them, and we are on a quest to figure out how that may be done." He nodded to John. "This boy is the key to it although we're not sure how yet."

Captain Meyer could tell that many of the members of his crew were listening even though they were pretending not to be; one of the sailors had been swabbing the same patch of deck for five minutes now. Those crewmembers that weren't actively listening would probably be told about it within a couple of minutes of the conversation ending. He knew he'd have to be careful with how he handled it. "Even if I believed you, which I'm not saying I do," he said, "we certainly wouldn't want to help save the world, only to find ourselves penniless in it. I, for one, could use a new mast for my ship. While masts may come from trees, they don't grow on trees, if you take my meaning."

"I'll pay you 1,000 gold crowns if you take them to wherever it was that they wanted to go, prior to dropping us off," said a new voice. Dantes turned to find a man standing in the doorway of the captain's cabin. Two little girls could be seen standing behind him, hiding behind his legs.

Captain Meyer sighed. "I'd like you to meet our cargo, the merchant Gary Mathison and his daughters Samantha and Shelby. We had just taken them aboard when the dragon attacked the port."

"I heard about what happened in Norlon and knew Harbortown would be next. I decided it was time for my daughters and me to leave." said Mathison. "I had contracted with Captain Meyer to take us to Evenfar to avoid the Salidarian hordes. If what you say is true, though, they won't stop with just Norlon. They'll keep coming until they have killed us all. There's no place that we can run that will be safe."

"Unfortunately, that is true, Merchant Mathison," said Dantes. "If we are unsuccessful in our quest, there is nothing that will keep them from taking over the entire world."

"Then it is worth what money I have left to aid you in your quest," said Mathison. "I can always make more money. What is the value of money, though, if you aren't around to spend it?"

Chapter Forty-Four

"Hey, Fitzber," said John, "can you show me how to use all of this?" He had opened the parcel that Fitzber had given him to find a chain mail top to go along with the sword and dagger. Asking Fitzber for assistance made sense; not only had the unassuming gnome given the gifts to him, but he was even shorter than John and less intimidating than some of the others in the group. All of the others in the group, actually, if the truth were known.

"Aye, sure'n I can," replied Fitzber. "It wouldn't be much o' a gift if'n I didn't show you how to use it now, would it?" He took the armload of things from John and laid them out on the deck. "This goes on first," he said, handing John a thick padded shirt with long sleeves.

"I need a shirt under the mail?" asked John. "Can't I just wear the chain mail over what I have on?"

"I guess you could," replied the gnome, "But that wouldn't be the brightest thing to do. What do you know about mail?"

"Not a whole lot, actually," said John, struggling into the shirt. "In my world, we don't have anything like it. No one wears armor anymore."

"How do they stop a sword thrust then?"

"No one carries swords. We now have these things called guns. They are kind of like bows in that they launch a projectile, but it goes a lot faster than an arrow and can be shot a lot further. They are also

223

a lot more powerful and go through armor like it is nothing." John decided that he didn't want to try to explain the kevlar armor that soldiers wore. "There isn't a need for armor anymore."

"Well, it's needed here, and that's the truth," said Fitzber, handing him the mail shirt. "Okay, this goes on top o' the padded shirt, and you'll see the necessity for the shirt in a moment."

John slid the mail shirt on. The mail came down to about his elbows and to mid-thigh.

"If you look at the mail," said Fitzber, handing him a sword belt to go around his waist, "you can see that it's made with lots o' wee interlocking circles o' steel, so it's going to be good at stoppin' sword or knife cuts. This mail is well made, so it will be difficult to penetrate, and it will stop most thrusting or piercing weapons. If a blow doesn't hit perpendicular to the mail, it will usually just glance off. Even with a well-placed strike, the mail ringlets will absorb the blow by bending rather than breaking. You get a lot o' defense, even though the mail doesn't weigh a whole lot. That's the good part."

"What's the bad?"

"The bad part is that mail isn't very effective at stoppin' impacts," said Fitzber, adjusting the sword so that it sat correctly. "In order to help save you from the force o' the sword attack, or to help ward off blows from weapons like maces, you wear the padded shirt underneath it. That will protect you, at least somewhat, from hits that would kill an unarmored man." He gave a couple of tugs. "There you go; that is how it should all be put on."

"Thanks a lot," said John. "I'm not sure how I'll be able to pay you back for all of this. In fact, I don't even know what you use for money. How much did all of this cost?"

"Don't say anything to Lady Ellyn, but it was extremely cheap today; we'll just call it a 'going out of business' sale that I took advantage o', even if the owner didn't know he was having it. Right now, I doubt he'll be missing it." He looked John over with a critical eye and then adjusted where the dagger sheath sat on John's right side. "Okay, so you've got a sword and a dagger o' your own now. Do you know how to use them?"

"I've never even held a sword before, much less tried to do anything with one. I'm afraid I don't know anything about them."

"Well, sure'n I better teach you a few things, or you're going to be more o' a danger to yourself and the rest o' us than you will be to the enemy. Let's see you draw the sword."

John tried to pull the sword out of its scabbard, but it wouldn't come out. "It's stuck," he finally said, giving up. He heard a choking noise from Fitzber and looked over to see the gnome doing his best not to laugh. "What?"

"Well, laddie, if'n you want to pull the sword out of its wee scabbard, you need to pull it straight out, rather than trying to bend it 90 degrees. You can use your left had to hold the scabbard if you need to."

John tried it again while holding the scabbard with his left hand and was able to pull the sword out.

"You've never done this before?" asked Fitzber. "Ever?"

"No, I've never done this before. Why?"

"Oh, nothing laddie, nothing to worry your wee little head about. I expect you'll be sore tomorrow, though..."

Chapter Forty-Five

Fitzber had been wrong, thought John. He wasn't going to be sore tomorrow; he was already sore *right now*. His sword-fighting injuries woke him up in the middle of the night, and they were preventing him from going back to sleep. He wished he had a handful of aspirins he could take, but they were on another world...somewhere else.

He struggled out of the hammock he had been given in the hold of the ship. Because of his height, or mostly because of his lack thereof, he had been given the bottom hammock. Father Telenor was snoring loudly above him in the upper hammock. John thought that he could still probably have gotten back to sleep...if every part of his body didn't hurt so much.

John now understood the need for the padded shirt; if anything, he wished it was heavier. Even though Fitzber had pulled his strikes to keep from hitting John as hard as he could have, getting slapped with a sword, even at half speed, was still enough to hurt. A lot. Dantes said that a few bruises in training were better than cuts in combat, but John was no longer so sure; if you were dead, they wouldn't hurt as much. As he started moving, he realized that all of his muscles hurt even more than the places he had been hit and bruised. As much as it hurt to lie in his hammock, moving around hurt even more.

John went topside to get a breath of fresh air and to see if anyone had something that would dull his pain. Seeing a couple of shapes at the back rail of the ship, he went to join them. As he walked aft, he recognized Dantes' distinctive shape (the horns were a giveaway) and then that of the ship's captain.

"How much longer do you think it will take us to get there?" Dantes was asking as John came within hearing distance. "Even without the main mast, it doesn't seem like we are making very good time toward the island. Am I wrong?"

"No, you are not mistaken," said Captain Meyer, looking into the darkness behind the ship, a troubled look on his face. "There is something wrong with the weather. When we left Harbortown, the winds were lighter than they should have been for this time of year. About the time that night fell, the winds fell off to almost nothing."

"Any idea why?" asked Dantes. "Is there a storm approaching?"

"I don't know," replied Meyer, "and that's what bothers me. The winds always blow from the north at this time of the year. Always. They should be pushing us toward Salidar. But not since we left Tasidar. It's almost like something is holding them back. They're there, but they have nowhere near the force that they normally do. It's not natural."

Dantes sensed a presence next to him and turned. "How's our newest swordsman?" he asked.

"I hurt all over," said John. "I don't know which hurts worse, the bruises from getting hit or the muscles from overexertion."

"The muscles will get better as you move around," said Dantes. "The bruises will get better, too...in time. Better a few bruises in training..."

"...than cuts in combat. Yeah, I know. Blah, blah, blah. That doesn't make it hurt any less. Do you guys have anything for pain relief? An aspirin or two?"

"I don't know what aspirins are, but you could see the second...I mean, the first mate," said the captain. "Usually she has a tub of some sort of cream for things like that."

John woke up in the morning, feeling a little better. After talking with the captain, he had found Tanja Cilia and her tub of cream. He didn't know if the ointment was magical or not, but it did the trick; he was much less sore as he went up onto the deck. Seeing most of the members of his party clustered around the aft rail with the ship's captain and first mate, he went to join them.

"What's going on?" John asked.

"That," said Dantes, pointing to a dark spot on the horizon off the starboard quarter.

"What's that? A storm?"

"Aye," said the captain. "It's a storm, but there's also a ship that it's pushing."

"I can't see it," said John.

"It's there," said Ghorza. "I used a far-seeing spell to look. We're being chased by a warship."

"A warship? Do you suppose someone sent us an escort?"

"That's unlikely," said Dantes, "since no one knows where we are or where we're going."

"So that's the enemy?"

"Aye," said the captain. "Based on the description, it's probably an orc marauder. It's got the black sails of the Reaver clan."

"Can't we avoid them somehow?" asked John.

"No," said Captain Meyer. "Without our mast, their ship is faster than ours, and they have more of the wind helping them to intercept us. We can make it take longer for them to catch us, but catch us they surely will." He turned to nod in their direction of travel. "'Tis too bad. We almost made it." John turned to look and could see the top of a large mountain on the horizon. The mountain's snowcapped peak glowed brightly in the early morning sunshine although most of its base was shrouded in clouds.

"The Mountain of Frost," said Dantes. "You don't think we can beat them to it?"

"If our mast was whole, we could sail rings around that pig of a ship," replied Captain Meyer. "As it is, no. We will be close, but they will overtake us 'ere we get there."

John looked at the mass of black clouds behind the enemy vessel. "What about that storm? Do you think that we can stay away from them long enough for the storm to catch up with us? Maybe we could lose them in it."

"If only it were that easy," replied Meyer. "I'm pretty sure there's someone on that ship controlling the storm. It has stayed in the same position behind them ever since we first saw it."

"Growing up, I heard tales of shamans who were capable of manipulating the weather a little to help the crops," said Ghorza, "but I never saw any that were ever actually able to do it. I always thought they were just that...tales. The power required to manipulate the weather is beyond anything I have ever seen before. The only shaman I ever saw that could do anything close was Ragula, who could sometimes coax a rain from a cloudy sky, but nothing like this. And besides, he was thought to have died a long time ago."

"Did you see his body?" asked Lady Ellyn.

"No, I did not," Ghorza replied. "He went missing just before my father fled with me. I never heard what happened to him."

"What do you have to defend the ship?" asked Lady Ellyn, changing the subject to one she was more familiar with. "Beside us, that is."

"Sadly, not much," said Meyer. "We have some cutlasses and clubs, and a few crossbows, but nothing big enough to keep them off of us. If you can't do anything to stop them from getting next to us, you'll have to kill them as they come aboard. Based on the size of their ship, there are going to be more of them than there are of us when they come over the rails."

"Even though there aren't many of us, we will make them pay dearly for every foot that touches the deck of this ship," promised Lady Ellyn. "Very dearly."

Chapter Forty-Six

Like an avalanche the ship grew in size slowly and inexorably throughout the rest of the morning and afternoon. The closer it came, the more wind spilled over to the companions' ship, and the rate of closure dropped as the orc ship neared.

"Is that a picture of a campfire on their flag?" asked John.

"No," replied Captain Meyer. "As I feared, the ship is one of the Reaver clan's. The picture on the flag is a bunch of broken leg bones stacked together. The red you see is the blood coming out of the broken ends."

"Gross."

"Aye," said the captain. "They don't leave anyone alive when they capture a ship, nor do they leave a single body unbroken. They are as horrible an enemy as you would ever want to come across. Sometimes they take prisoners, but I can't imagine life under them would be very pleasant, or very long." His voice trailed off, leaving John to imagine all sorts of horrible things that would be done to him if captured. He vowed he wouldn't be captured...and hoped he would be able to fulfill that vow.

"There's a halfling in the front of the boat," said Fitzber who had the best natural sight of anyone in the group. "'Tis the spitting image of the halfling I caught in the woods with the orcs when they attacked us. The rest of the boat's crew looks to be orcs, generally bigger than normal ones, if I had to guess." He looked a little longer.

"They appear to be armed with swords and battle axes, all except for the skinny one in the back of the boat that's jumpin' up and down with his staff."

"What does his staff look like?" asked Ghorza.

"It's an odd one," replied Fitzber. "It isn't straight up and down; it's got a wee bit o' a curve to it and all sorts o' wee markings and writing on it, if that means anything."

"It *can't* be," said Ghorza. "*Focus!*" she added, casting her far-seeing spell. "By the gods! That *is* Ragula. He uses a troll's leg bone as a staff. He killed it when he was young. He's carved all of his spells into it, along with words of power to increase the potency of his spells. Do not underestimate him; he may look like some backcountry shaman, but he is very powerful."

As the group watched, there was a flurry of activity from the other ship.

"What are they doing?" asked John.

"Getting ready for battle," said Father Telenor. "I know. I used to serve on ships when I was young. They are setting up its weapons." He pointed to the front. "For example, it looks like they have a couple of onagers in the bow."

"What's an onager?" asked John.

"It's a light catapult. Onagers aren't big, but they're effective. They can throw a 20 pound load over 1,200 feet."

"20 pounds?" asked John. "That doesn't seem like much. Shouldn't the sides of this ship be able to withstand getting hit by rocks that small?"

"Oh, I doubt they'd throw rocks with it," said Father Telenor; "I wouldn't, anyway."

"What would you throw then? They aren't going to launch their men with them are they? Like to get them up into our sails and rigging?"

"No," said Father Telenor with a laugh, "I doubt they'd do that, either. I imagine they're more likely to launch clay pots full of demon fire."

"Demon fire?" asked Ghorza.

"Yes, it's a mix of resins and oils that, once ignited, is extremely difficult to extinguish. They'll lob them over here and get our ship burning. Then, while we're busy trying to put it out, *that's* when they'll board. If boarding is their intention, anyway. They could also just stand off and watch us burn. It's not a good way to go."

"We're surrounded by water, though," said John. "Can't we rig a hose or something to put out the fires? Like with a pump or something?"

"I don't know what this 'pump' thing is of which you speak, but trust me, once you get demon fire on board, it is very hard to put out. You can expect to lose all of your rigging. You may keep enough of the hull together to float, but there won't be much." He indicated several sailors that were rolling barrels around the deck of the *Dancer*. "Those are barrels of sand that they will use to smother any flames. Throwing water on demon fire just tends to scatter it all over the place."

Father Telenor looked back at the other ship. "They've also got six ballistae," he said, pointing to where the orcs were mounting three of the weapons on each side of the ship. "Those will be fairly accurate today, since the water is smooth, with a range of about 1,500 feet."

"How accurate is accurate?" asked Dantes.

"Inside of about 1,000 feet, a good ballista operator can pick off individual targets," said Father Telenor.

"That's pretty accurate," Dantes replied.

"Are these orcs any good?" asked John.

"The Reaver clan? They're the best," replied Captain Meyer, walking up to look at the enemy. "If they want us dead, the odds are that we're going to be dead in short order." He nodded to where several of the *Dancer's* sailors were leaning crossbows against the rail. "We've got a few surprises of our own," he added. "We'll get a few shots off; we'll just have to make them count, since we won't be out-running them today."

"If you can kill the shaman in the back of the boat," said Ghorza, "that will release the weather to let it go back to normal."

"Aye, he will be the first one we kill," agreed the captain. "If we get the opportunity."

"Why don't you go down below," Dantes said to John. "No sense letting them know that you're here." John didn't look happy to be sent below, but left the rail without too much grumbling.

The vessel approached until it was just outside of bowshot, at which time the shaman in the back of the ship put down his arms. All of the wind ceased, and both boats coasted to a halt. There weren't even any waves; both boats were completely becalmed. The orc shaman and several of the largest orcs moved to stand with the halfling, aft of the onagers.

"The crown!" said Ghorza as she got a closer look at the group. "The halfling is wearing a crown. It's got to be Milos!"

One of the orcs handed the halfling a hailer, a cone of metal that helped to focus a speaker's voice, allowing it to travel further. "Ahoy, the *Pole Dancer*," he called. "I would like to talk to the outlander."

"Ahoy yourself, Milos or Solim, or whatever you're calling yourself these days," said Dantes. "I'd like to say that it's good to see you again. I'd like to, but that would be lying. Something you're good at, I guess."

"So you recognize me, do you? No matter, it's too late for you to do anything about it."

"It's never too late," Dantes replied. "Why don't you come on over here, and we can discuss it?"

"No thanks," Solim replied. "I have a feeling you might bear me some ill will. I think that I will stay over here with my friends." He looked at the *Dancer*. "Tell you what. If you send over the outlander, I won't bother sinking your vessel. It's obvious that the ship is in no danger of catching us; I'm surprised that it hasn't already sunk on its own."

"Outlander?" asked Dantes. "What do you mean by outlander? We're all from Tasidar. The only people from Salidar are on your boat."

"You know who I mean," said Solim. "The person that I framed as the Spectre. I don't know how he was able to use the mirror, but I know that he followed me through it. I've been watching you through a seagull, and I know he is with you. If you send him over now, I won't destroy your ship. You have five minutes. If he isn't on this ship by then, we will sink you."

"Have you found your brother yet, laddie?" asked Fitzber. "If not, I'm happy to be tellin' you that he died on my blade." He smiled. "I'm right here if you'd like to come avenge him."

"He was my half-brother," said Solim, "and I never really liked him much. You have four minutes left."

"You wouldn't sink a ship with women and children on it, would you?" asked Lady Ellyn.

"If that's what it takes to get the outlander, then yes, I would," said Solim. Several of the orcs said something to him. "My friends would be happy to take whatever women and children you'd like to send across. In fact, please feel free to send them all over." The orcs began laughing. "Two minutes. If he isn't in the water within the next minute, we will sink your ship."

"I'm coming!"

The companions turned to see John coming out the door from below.

"If you promise to let them go, I will come with you."

Dantes intercepted him on his way to the railing and lifted him off the deck. "No," he said. "I won't let you go."

"I don't want all of your deaths on me," said John. "I'll go over there, and you can figure out a way to rescue me...somehow. Maybe I can escape. You've all been so good; I can't let you sacrifice yourselves for me." He lowered his voice. "Besides, the Mathison girls are still down below. They'd be killed, too."

All of a sudden, Dantes understood why John had come up on deck. He would have happily sacrificed himself for John, even if that meant fighting the orcs, but he didn't want the little girls to be killed either. He nodded. "Go then. We will follow you and get you back." He set John back down on the deck.

"I know you will," said John, kicking off his sandals. Flipping one leg over the rail and then the other, he pushed off the railing and fell to the sea below. He hit the water and came up sputtering. The water was *cold!* He forced himself to keep moving although every fiber of his being wanted to huddle into a ball to retain what little heat it could. Although John had learned to swim when he was younger, he hadn't done it in a very long time and was forced to dog-paddle his way across to the orc ship while everyone watched. Better a little embarrassment than having the little girls get killed, he thought as he continued to stroke his way over. If only it wasn't so cold!

A line came down from above as John reached the side of the orc ship. The rope had knots in it for climbing, as long as the climber had the upper body strength to pull himself up. Cold and out of energy from the swim, John didn't, so the orcs pulled him up instead.

"So," said Solim as John was brought over the railing, "there's more to you than I thought. I don't know how you were able to figure out the mirror, but you have been a thorn in my side ever since you got here. No more, though." He looked at two of the orcs standing nearby. "Grab him. Search him."

The orcs' eyes glazed over. "Yes, highlord," they intoned, and each grabbed one of John's arms. Six and a half feet tall and 250 pounds, the orcs were giants compared to John; there was no way he could break free of them. The orcs searched him, but didn't find anything. They shook their heads.

"What are you planning on doing with him?" asked Dantes from the other ship. "You know that even killing him won't stop the Prophecy."

"Why would I want to stop the Prophecy?" asked Solim. "I'm *counting* on the Prophecy." He started laughing. "Silly people," he said, when he could talk again, "why is it that you hero-types always think everything is about you?" He said 'hero' as if it were some lower form of life. "The Prophecy isn't about this boy. How could it be? The Prophecy is about *me*. I came back from another world. I am gathering all of the Items of Power. And I will be the one to end the world as we know it and re-make it in my image. An image where the tall bow down to those who aren't. Everyone will bow down to me. Even you would have bowed to me...except that you will all be dead and will miss seeing it."

"What do you mean?" asked Lady Ellyn. "We gave you the boy like you asked; you said that you would let us go. Have you no honor?"

"No," replied Solim. "I gave up my honor long ago. I'll make you a deal, though. I know that you still have the spell book that the Magistra gave the outlander. If you give me that, we will be on our way, and you will be free to go."

Onboard the *Pole Dancer*, Ghorza stiffened. "You can't give that to him," she whispered. "It's worth more than even the girls' lives. You *cannot* give it to him."

"I know," Dantes whispered back. To Solim he yelled, "We don't have it. The boy lost it somewhere in the escape from Norlon. It's probably in the tunnels there if you want to go look for it."

"If you don't have it," Solim replied, "then there is no longer a reason to keep you alive."

"I challenge your captain to a duel," called Captain Meyer. "Man to orc, with the winner to take both ships."

Solim started laughing, followed by all of the orcs that were topside. "Why would he want to do that?" asked Solim. "Have you *seen* what your ship looks like? Pathetic." He laughed again. "No, I think there is only one fitting end for that collection of broken timbers you call a ship...and that is to turn it into driftwood."

Even across the gap between the ships, the companions could see Solim's eyes go unfocused.

"Stand by the crossbows," said Captain Meyer. Crewmembers edged closer to the weapons leaning against the railing. They didn't have the range to shoot across to the other ship, but if they were attacked, the crossbows would prove deadly to at least a few of the orcs.

"You have heard of Scylla and Charybdis, I hope," said Solim, his voice strangely flat. "Meet Scylla!"

Chapter Forty-Seven

A scream sounded from behind the group, and they spun around to find a creature out of their nightmares rising from the water. Scylla was enormous, with six dragon-like heads on long, serpentine necks. Each of its heads was 10 feet long and could open up wide enough to swallow a gnome sideways. Their mouths had three rows of shark-like teeth, top and bottom, for seizing their prey and cutting it to ribbons. The heads were almost hypnotic as they rose swaying from the water on their 60-feet-long necks. The body remained mostly under the surface, but its underwater shadow was far larger than even the orc ship. A shadow passed in front of the sun as the monster's tail came up from the water on the other side of the ship. It rose 50 feet into the air and then fell across the ship, crushing two of the crewmen who had the misfortune of being underneath it.

As everyone turned to see the tail sliding across the deck of the ship, the closest of the heads struck forward to seize one of the crewmen, and it pitched the unlucky sailor headfirst down its gullet in a single bite. The other five heads screamed as they approached the ship, making coordination among the crew impossible. "*Empathia Feri!*" called Fitzber, casting Wild Empathy on the head that was looking at him, preparing to strike.

"I don't think so," said the head in Solim's voice. Fitzber dove out of the way as the head snapped forward, biting down on the empty air where Fitzber had been a split-second before. Fitzber came out of his roll already nocking an arrow to his bow string. In one smooth motion he drew and fired. His jaw fell open as the arrow ricocheted harmlessly from the scales on the monster's head.

Within seconds, heads were everywhere, striking at people along the length of the deck, as Scylla's tail continued to wrap itself around the *Dancer*. The starboard railing couldn't take the weight of the monster's tail and snapped with a loud crack.

"'Ware the tail!" yelled Captain Meyer. "If we don't get it off, it will crush the ship!" The sailors dropped the weapons they had been using to fend off the heads and grabbed knives and axes and went to work on the tail. The scales on the beast's tail were nearly as strong as steel, though, and the sailors' weapons had very little effect on them. The monster's heads flashed down, and two more sailors were carried screaming from the deck. One of the heads tossed its sailor down its throat in a single bite; the other one paused, holding the screaming human, and another of the beast's heads reached in and bit the sailor in half at the waist. Freed of the extra weight, the first head tossed the other half of the sailor up in the air and swallowed it with no problem.

The companions were not having any better luck fighting the monster than the sailors. "*Globus Incendi!*" shouted Dantes, as he hurled a fireball into the open mouth of the head that was attacking him. The mouth snapped shut as the fireball burst, but then opened up again to scream in pain. Dantes could see that the fireball had charred portions of the monster's tongue, but it was otherwise unharmed.

The head attacking Dantes decided that it didn't like having hot things thrown into its mouth and went in search of easier prey. It turned and saw Second Mate Rowntree, who was fending off another head with a boathook. Similar to a pike, the boathook was an eight-foot long pole that was used for docking and undocking. Although similar to a pike, it was far less effective as a weapon as its tip was blunt (for pushing away from the dock), and he wasn't able to penetrate the monster's scales. He was jabbing ineffectively at another of the monster's heads when the second head took him from behind, biting him in half as it lifted him off the deck. His legs and torso created a red stain as they fell into the water below.

"*Flagra!*" cried Father Telenor, unleashing a flame strike on another of the creature's heads. The divine flames were more effective against the monster's slime coating than Dantes' fireball had been, and the flames burned out the eyes of that head, blinding it. The monster slammed its head down on the deck, breaking several of the planks.

"Not on my ship!" said Captain Meyer, charging up to it with his cutlass drawn. He stabbed the creature in the eye, causing it new waves of pain. It reared back and then slammed its head back to the deck, hoping to squash the human that had stabbed it. It missed and slammed its head down on the remains of the main mast. Several large splinters of wood protruded from the end of the mast; these knifed through the monster's throat, up through its mouth and into its brain. The head died, and the ship rocked precariously as its weight pulled the ship down to port.

The sea monster began squeezing the ship, and the hull groaned as it endured forces it wasn't meant to withstand. Hearing a little scream, Ghorza turned to see Gary Mathison and his girls come out onto the deck from below. Boards were already being sprung by Scylla's squeezing, and the family had come up to avoid the water rushing into the hold. The smaller of the two girls, Ghorza couldn't remember if that was Samantha or Shelby, screamed again at the sight of the giant six-headed monster that was fighting the crew across the length of the ship. One of the heads looked over and, in a flash it struck, picking up the girls' father. It bit him in half and swallowed both pieces.

As the head turned back to look at the girls, it found itself cut off from them by Ghorza and Lady Ellyn, who positioned themselves in front of them. "*Celeritas!*" said Ghorza, casting Haste on the paladin before scooping up the two little girls to pull them out of the way.

The Scylla head hadn't fought any of the little shiny ones before, and it circled Lady Ellyn warily, just outside of her sword range. The head moved back and forth, up and down, looking for an easy way to get to its prey without having to go through the pointy thing that the prey was holding in front of it. It paused, turning sideways to Lady Ellyn to inspect her more closely. This gave the paladin the opportunity she had been waiting for. Switching weapons, she used all of her Hasted reflexes to throw her dagger, and it buried itself in the monster's eye. The head reared back in pain and screamed.

While it was distracted, Lady Ellyn turned part way around toward Ghorza. "Give me your sword," she said. Without hesitation, Ghorza pulled out her scimitar and tossed it to Lady Ellyn. The paladin turned to meet the monster, armed with a sword in each hand. Enraged, the monster struck down at Lady Ellyn, intending to eat her whole. As the mouth came down toward her, she jumped back out of its grasp with her Hasted reflexes, and the head snapped shut within inches of her chest. Lady Ellyn stabbed Ghorza's sword into one of the beast's nostrils and used it to climb up onto the monster's head. Before it could react, she drove her sword into one of its ear holes and into its brain, killing it. The monster spasmed, its head rearing back and up, and Lady Ellyn was thrown 100 feet into the air. She splashed down into the water several hundred feet behind the monster.

Another head took its place in front of Ghorza. She tried to draw her sword, but realized that she had given it to Lady Ellyn. As the head drew back to strike, she realized that she didn't have any spells that would work on the monster, either. She pulled out her dagger, but it seemed woefully inadequate to the task. Reaching behind her, she found one of the girls. "Move," she said over her shoulder, while keeping her eyes on the monster. The monster's head circled, looking for the best angle to get at Ghorza. It decided on one.

It attacked.

Chapter Forty-Eight

Onboard the orc ship, all of the orcs had moved to the railing to watch the fight, with the exception of the two holding onto John, who had not relaxed their grip or moved at all. The way they held onto John, his arms dangled alongside their weapons, his right hand next to the sword of one of the orcs and his left hand next to the other's dagger. He smiled. His time below decks hiding from the orc ship hadn't been wasted.

He twisted his arms slightly so that he could get a finger on both of the weapons. *"Calefacite!"* he said under his breath. For a few seconds nothing happened, and he wondered if he had pronounced the spell correctly. Then he saw the handle of the sword start to change color and John knew that he was okay. Within a couple of seconds, both weapons started to hiss as the heat of the metal began to eat into their scabbards. Although the orcs at the ship's railing couldn't hear the hissing, the two holding him could, and they looked down to see their weapons glowing. The one on John's right tried to grab his sword, but immediately dropped it after touching the white-hot metal. Realizing they couldn't touch the weapons, both of the orcs let go of John so that they could take off their sword belts.

That was all John needed, and he sprinted toward the rail of the ship. The orc with the hot sword was too busy trying to get rid of it before it could fall on the deck and set the ship on fire, but the other enemy saw where John was heading. "Look out!" it yelled, loud enough to be heard over Scylla's screams. The orcs along the railing began to turn away from the rail to see what was happening.

"*Spira!*" John shouted as he crashed headfirst into the chest of the shaman. Smaller than the rest of the orcs, the shaman wasn't much bigger than John and was much older and wizened. As they went over the railing, John had a hard time holding onto the orc. The creature wasn't much more than skin hanging loosely over bones, and he was hard to grab. They hit the water with a splash, and John drew a breath as the cold water rushed over him. The shaman was less prepared, and he got water up his nose and began coughing.

The two wrestled, and the shaman showed that, while old, he still had a wiry strength about him. He was, in fact, stronger than John, and kept fending him off as he tried to clear his lungs. As the shaman's coughing passed, John knew he had to do something, or he was going to die in some nasty way. Although the shaman pushed him away, John succeeded in wrapping his legs around the shaman's waist and drew him in.

The shaman opened his mouth to cast a spell, but John put both of his arms over the shaman's head, and pushed him under the water. The shaman began struggling as John held him under. John was fine, as he had cast a Water Breathing spell as he went over the rail, and he had no problems breathing. What he hadn't counted on was how strong the shaman was, nor how hard he punched, even under water. Although John was able to breathe under water, he quickly lost the ability to do so as the shaman threw punch after punch into his chest and stomach, without seeming to wear out. Finally, aiming lower, he punched John in the groin.

John's legs opened of their own accord as he doubled up, fighting several waves of nausea which threatened to incapacitate him. Almost out of air, the shaman pushed his way free and began struggling toward the surface. Seeing that the shaman was going to get away, John cast the only spell that came to mind. *"Fluxum Geli!"* he said, casting the Ice Ray spell.

Emanating from his hand in a stream, the water froze in a cone toward the shaman and encased his head. The shaman stopped trying to make it to the surface and began clawing at the block of ice that covered his head. Already out of air, the shaman's struggles soon slowed, and finally ceased. The shaman was dead.

It suddenly dawned on John that he had just killed someone, and the realization threatened to overwhelm him. He hadn't meant to kill the orc, he thought...well, that wasn't entirely true; he had intended to drown him, which would have killed the shaman just as dead...but John hadn't really thought about the fact that he was going to kill the shaman. John knew that they couldn't get away while the shaman lived, and he was the only person close enough to do something about it, so he had acted. Mostly without thinking, he had done what needed doing. And he had killed the shaman...who was evil and would have happily killed John and everyone else aboard the *Dancer* without a qualm. John didn't have a choice; it was either kill him or have everyone he knew in this world be killed.

A spear flashed by him, bringing him to his senses. Launched by one of the ballistae, the crew had obviously seen that the shaman was dead and were now able to shoot at John. He turned and dove deeper, so that the orcs wouldn't be able to see him. He saw a couple more spears flash by, but they both missed.

He had accomplished his first goal of avoiding pursuit, but like his first night on the planet, he had evaded the pursuit only to get lost in the process; he wasn't sure how to get to the *Dancer*. He could tell which way was up, because he tended to float in that direction, but that was it. After a moment's consideration, he decided it was better to go a little way in the wrong direction than to surface and get speared, so he swam off in the direction he thought was right. He knew he needed to hurry; his teeth were beginning to chatter in the cold water.

Chapter Forty-Nine

The monster's head dove at Ghorza, only to draw up short as Tanja Cilia stepped in front of Ghorza with a boat hook. "I've got this," she called. "You take care of the girls."

Having grown up on an island, Cilia had been on the water since she was a little girl and was very familiar with the use of a boathook as a weapon. She began spinning it hand over hand like an airplane propeller, and it spun faster and faster until it was nothing more than a blur. The monster decided that the staff had evaporated and struck out at the first mate.

The staff hadn't disintegrated, though, and Cilia used the staff's spinning momentum to swing it up and slam it down on the monster's nose as it dove in for her. Although she didn't break through the monster's scales, she did deliver a stinging blow to the end of the monster's nose, and it jerked back in pain and surprise. It came back a second time, its mouth open to swallow the half-orc. Unable to dent it from the outside, she waited until it was about to engulf her and then jammed the boathook into the roof of the monster's mouth. Although not pointy enough to break through Scylla's scales, it was sharp enough to penetrate the roof of the creature's mouth, and about a foot of it wedged in its nasal cavity.

The boathook was designed with a downward pointing hook for holding onto things, and the monster was unable to shake the boathook out. Deciding it needed to bite it in half, the creature bit down on the boathook as hard as it could, but only succeeded in driving the boathook further into the roof of its mouth and then into its brain. It fell lifeless to the deck.

"Ha," the first mate said, walking up to spit into the monster's flat black eye. She didn't see another head rear up behind her. The head swooped in and snapped her up in a single bite. Before Ghorza could do anything, Cilia was gone.

"Why don't you try that on me?" yelled Captain Meyer. He was the only one of the *Dancer's* officers left; he knew it was up to him to kill the beast and save the passengers. He had tried cutting Scylla's tail, but his axe had only drawn sparks when he chopped down on it. The only way to stop the beast was to kill the heads. Snatching up a boathook, he brandished it at the monster, which turned and dove at him.

Meyer had seen the success his first mate had with stabbing the monster in its mouth, and figured that was his best chance to kill it. He dodged to his right as the head came down at him, just like he had planned; what he hadn't planned was to step in the puddle of blood and entrails left on the deck by one of the monster's earlier kills. He slipped and went down. The head shifted its strike and grabbed the captain by his legs. Lifting him up, the monster bit off his legs and his torso fell to the ocean, 50 feet below. The last thing he saw was the boathook as it fell from his numb fingers.

The sea monster now had two coils wrapped around the ship, and Dantes could feel the effect its squeezing was having on the ship. The hull of the ship vibrated with the pressure. With a loud crack, the port railing broke, and the deck groaned ominously. Dantes knew that he needed to do something before the entire ship came apart. While there were only three Scylla heads left in the fight, there were fewer and fewer people fighting them as the monster ate the crewmen or tossed them into the cold water. The closest head was fighting Fitzber, who was dodging in and out of the rigging to avoid the creature's bite. When the creature would withdraw, he would pop out to fire arrows at it. His tactics had proven somewhat successful; he hadn't been eaten yet, and the monster had lost one of its eyes to an arrow. After Fitzber had shot out the creature's eye, the fight had become a stalemate. Fitzber wouldn't give it much of an opportunity to catch him, but neither would the monster look at Fitzber with its good eye long enough for him to put an arrow into it.

"*Molaris!*" said Dantes, casting his Force Missile spell at the head. Both missiles impacted on the creature's nose, tearing bloody chunks out of it when they exploded. The head screamed and turned toward Dantes.

"You!" the head screamed in Solim's voice. Without waiting for an answer, it dove on Dantes and caught him in its bite. Smaller than most humans, the monster had no problem with him. Tossing its head back, it swallowed him whole.

Chapter Fifty

John could feel currents in the water and knew he must be close to the monster. He paused. His plan had ended with drowning the shaman and escaping; he hadn't thought about what he'd do if he actually made it back to the ship. When he had last looked, the monster seemed to be having its way with the *Dancer* and its crew. If he came up alongside the ship, there probably wouldn't be anyone available to pull him on board. They'd either be dead or still fighting Scylla, so getting aboard the ship was going to be difficult. That left either helping with the fight against Scylla from the water or going back to the orc ship. As going back to the orc ship was certain death, he ruled that out.

That left helping with the fight against Scylla, but he had no idea how to go about it. He didn't have his sword, dagger or armor. They wouldn't have been much help if he had them; it would have been hard to swim with their weight dragging him down.

He had a few spells left, but didn't know how well they'd work under water. Lost, he didn't even know where to go to find the monster. For that matter, he didn't know if the fight was still going on. Maybe his friends had already killed the monster. He didn't want to contemplate the other outcome. John knew he needed to come to the surface to find out what was going on and which direction to go.

John surfaced about 20 feet from the side of the *Dancer*. In his short time underwater, the sky had darkened considerably. The death of the shaman had freed the storm that had been following the orc ship, and it was surging forward to claim them. Lightning flashed and thunder rolled, but it wouldn't get there soon enough for the crew of the *Dancer*, John saw, as the fighting was all but over. The creature was unstoppable. He turned toward the ship in time to see the half-orc first mate get eaten by a head that she never saw coming. The head then dipped back down and came up with the ship's captain. The monster cut him in half, and most of the captain's torso fell into the water, along with whatever weapon he'd been carrying. He couldn't find Lady Ellyn. Always where the fighting was the heaviest, if he couldn't see her, she was already dead or eaten. Or, most likely, both.

He found Ghorza. She was huddled with the two Mathison children behind the captain's cabin. It looked like she was trying to console them so that she could get back into the fight. She was certainly needed; John could hear the ship's timbers cracking from the monster's constriction. John couldn't see Fitzber, but he could tell where he was. One of Scylla's heads had an arrow in its eye and was screaming in frustration. John had seen the way Fitzber frustrated Dantes; Fitzber had to be harassing that one.

As he thought of Dantes, John saw him run up to assist Fitzber. Two force missiles streaked upward to blast pieces from the monster's nose. It screamed again, but this time it was in pain, not frustration. Before Dantes could launch another spell, though, the head snapped down with the speed of a cobra. It rose back up and Dantes was gone. Dantes must have dodged to the side, John thought; he was too good a fighter to let the monster get him that easily, wasn't he? John was horrified moments later as the head flipped back and opened slightly to swallow what was in its mouth. There was a flash of red, and Dantes was gone.

NO! John couldn't let the enemy win. He *wouldn't* let the enemy win. If nothing else, he wasn't going to let the orcs get the little girls. He'd kill the monster, somehow, would escape with whoever was still left, somehow, and would use his spell book to complete the quest. Somehow. He'd figure it out as he went, but first he had a monster to kill and a friend's life to avenge.

John needed a breath, so he dropped down below the surface. The motion saved his life as a spear shot through the place where his head had been. The orcs on the ship had seen him, and the spear rocketed past him, skipped once on a wave and wedged in the side of the *Dancer*, only a foot above the waterline. Perfect, John thought, not worrying about how close he had come to dying; just *what I need.*

He went under and swam to the side of the ship. He knew that he would have to be quick; the orcs were surely searching for him now. Looking up, he could see the spear above the ship's water line. Most of its energy had been spent prior to hitting the ship; John didn't think the spear was stuck too far into it. Even better, the blade of the spearhead was vertical, so it should come out fairly easy for him. He reached up out of the water, grabbed the end of the spear and pulled down. Success! It came out of the ship in his hands, and he quickly submerged with it.

Thwack! Thwack! Thwack! Three spears took the place of the one he had just removed. The orcs had guessed that he would try to get the spear and had aimed all of the ballistae on that side of their ship at it. If the spear had been stuck, or if John had been exposed for any length of time, he would have looked like an oversized pin cushion.

Taking his new prize, he swam under the boat to the side of the monster. As he approached, he got the scare of his life; one of the heads was waiting for him. He froze in shock and fright. There was no way he was going to beat the monster in its own element. He closed his eyes; he didn't want to see it coming. When nothing happened after several seconds, he opened an eye. The monster continued to look at him with its unblinking eyes, but didn't attack. When John saw the hilt of Lady Ellyn's sword sticking out of its ear hole, he understood. This head was dead. He swam up to the head, experiencing a brief moment of terror when Scylla moved, causing the head to shift as if it was alive. John decided the sword would work better than the spear, so he let the spear go, and it vanished into the depths before he had time for a second thought.

Grasping the sword, John pulled on it, but it wouldn't come out. He tried using one hand to brace himself on the head and the other to pull, but it was wedged in tightly. John needed more leverage, so he grabbed the sword with both hands and put both feet on the creature's head. Pulling with all of his might, he was finally able to withdraw the sword.

Now that he had a sword, he was once again stumped as to what to do. He had to kick hard to counter the weight of the sword, so he grabbed onto the head to hold himself steady while he considered. He laughed as he saw his handhold. It looked like someone had stuck Ghorza's scimitar into the monster's nostril. He palmed his face as the realization dawned on him. All of his friends were attacking the monster in the places that it was best able to defend, where it was bony and covered in hard scales. Someone, probably Lady Ellyn, had figured out how to attack the heads—stab them in soft places where it would do the most damage.

John needed to do the same thing. He needed to stab Scylla somewhere that it didn't have a lot of defense, but it also needed to be somewhere that it would do the most good. His friends were stuck attacking it head by head; by virtue of being able to breathe water, though, he was able to attack the body. The problem, John realized, was figuring out where to attack that would do the most damage. The monster's body was over 100 feet long; there had to be some places that would be better to attack than others.

It had to be the belly. That part would probably be the least well defended; if there was a place that the scales were easier to penetrate, it would probably be there under one of its flippers, John decided. That would be its most vulnerable spot. He might not be able to kill it outright by stabbing it in the belly, but maybe he could perforate some organs and kill it...although it was debatable whether or not he would last long enough to enjoy the victory. In the movies, people that were gut-shot always died, but sometimes it took a while. If he could stick the sword all the way into Scylla, he was pretty sure he could kill it.

He hoped this would work, as he knew most of his spells wouldn't be effective against the monster. Although the freeze ray worked well against the shaman, he doubted that it would have much effect against something as big as Scylla. The only thing he had that he thought might work was his second Heat Metal spell. If he could heat up the end of the sword so that it was really hot, maybe that would help him penetrate the monster's belly and cause a little extra damage once it was inside.

It wasn't a great plan, but it was all he had, and he knew time was running out. The sound of wood snapping carried to him clearly through the water. Scylla was about to destroy their ship, and then it would eat the rest of its passengers and crew. He had to act, and he had to act now.

John swam forward along the creature's side. He wished that he hadn't dropped the spear so quickly. Made of wood, it wouldn't have been as heavy as the sword, and he would have been able to stab deeper into the creature, potentially doing more damage.

He finally reached the forward left flipper, which was slowly stroking to hold Scylla in place. Growing tired from all of the swimming he'd done, he didn't stop to contemplate. He touched the point of the sword and cast the Heat Metal spell. *"Calefacite!"*

It didn't take long for him to see the problem with his plan. As the metal began to heat, the water worked to draw off the heat. The monster's moving fin caused currents that made the heat loss worse. The beast's sides expanded and contracted several times while the metal heated, causing additional currents. He could tell that it was taking too long; the spell would end before the sword got white hot. The spell just didn't work as well in water as in the air. He realized that there *was* one positive effect; by drawing off some of the heat, he was able to hold onto the sword longer than he would have been above water. As the water heated up, he also found that he was warm again for the first time since he jumped into the water.

As the tip of the sword passed 101 degrees Celsius, he found that he had another problem; the sword started boiling the seawater, turning it to water vapor and causing bubbles. John didn't know if Scylla would feel the bubbles, but they were super-hot, so he tried to keep them away from the creature. The boiling water surrounding the sword did allow the sword tip to heat faster, though, and also kept more of the heat in the sword. While the hand heating the sword was magically protected from the effects of the spell, in no time the sword became almost too hot for his other hand to hold. He had to use the sword before he was forced to drop it.

He ended the spell and took hold of the sword with both hands. Before he could stab the monster, the flipper that John had been swimming behind shifted, lifting up so that one of Scylla's heads could see what was causing the water to heat up alongside it. John was suddenly face-to-face with a live head.

The creature saw John and the sword, and it knew what he intended. Without having to think about it, the head snapped forward at John. He was just as terrified as the first time he had seen one of the monster's heads, but this time he was armed. He held out the sword in front of him, hoping that the Scylla head would impale itself on it.

It didn't.

The head couldn't reach him; it came up two feet short. John knew this was his one chance. Now that the monster knew he was there, it would have all of the advantages and would eat him in short order. He turned to the beast's body as it took the biggest breath that John had seen, its side coming all the way out to him. John saw the tip of the sword was still a dull red as he stabbed the creature as if his life depended on it.

Chapter Fifty-One

Fitzber was down to his last two arrows, for all of the good they would do him. He looked down the length of the wreckage that used to be a ship. Three heads left to kill and three heroes left to do it. While he would never give up, the realist inside of him knew their odds weren't very good. After his last two arrows, he was down to his short sword and dagger. He didn't think that Scylla would notice either of them as it swallowed him. Father Telenor was fending off a second head with a boathook. Fitzber doubted that battle would last long. Ghorza was fighting the third head, and she unleashed her black enfeeblement ray. If Scylla noticed, it wasn't obvious to Fitzber.

"Come out, little gnome, and I will make it quick," said the Scylla head to Fitzber as he ducked back around the forward mast. Out of the corner of his eye, he saw the head Father Telenor was fighting bite down on the boathook and pull it from his hands. Father Telenor dove to the side as the head tried to snap him up.

"Not while I have arrows," said Fitzber, firing his penultimate arrow at the head. He made his shot, even with the gale force winds that had sprung up, and the arrow vanished into a nostril to prick the sensitive membrane inside. Unfortunately, the arrow caused the head to sneeze and the whole body spasmed. The port side of the ship gave way, boards snapping and wooden rivets popping in a spray of broken lumber. The ship had already been settling into the water; now it rolled to port as water flooded in the broken side. The aft mast, already weakened in the earlier dragon attack, snapped off. The ropes holding the sail parted, and the sail blew away, the canvas flapping in the breeze. The remaining companions and the two little girls were thrown overboard as the ship keeled over.

The head closed to within several feet of Fitzber so that it could look at the gnome with its remaining eye. "And now, I have you," it said. Lightning flashed as the head turned back to him and the mouth opened. Fitzber could hear the little girls screaming as the mouth came toward him. As the rain began pelting down, he saw that there was nowhere else to go.

Chapter Fifty-Two

Being swallowed alive was a totally shitty plan, Dantes thought; unfortunately, it was the only one he could come up with at the time. They had used up most of the crew and had only killed half of the heads; Dantes didn't see how the few remaining people would be able to kill the other three.

As expected, Dantes survived the process of being eaten. Solim had been so mad that he hadn't stopped to chew Dantes before swallowing him. The whole reason for the force missiles was to infuriate Solim enough to get swallowed whole. Dantes' skin was incredibly dense, due to his heritage, and he might have been able to withstand a little chewing without completely coming apart, but he didn't think that he would have enjoyed the process very much.

The acid in the creature's digestive system was slowly wearing away his skin as he slid down Scylla's esophagus. Full-blooded devils were able to withstand the acid pools in the first level of hell, so Scylla's stomach acid was less effective on him than if he'd been made of flesh. His father would have laughed at the weak acid while clawing his way out of the belly of the beast. Of course, his father wouldn't have been eaten in the first place, though, since he would have been on the orc ship with the rest of the evil creatures.

Dantes dropped into the creature's stomach. He tried not to think about the things he could feel bumping into him. Acid found a way into a cut he had received fighting the heads, and it burned. A lot. He figured that he had about three minutes until either the acid killed him or he ran out of air. Unfortunately, 'hard to kill' wasn't the same as 'impossible to kill.' He sighed. This really was a shitty plan. He hoped it worked.

"*Murus Incendi!*" he said, casting a Wall of Fire spell. A 10-foot tall curtain of deep-red flame sprang up in a five-foot radius around him. The light it cast danced and shifted, giving him a view of the inside of Scylla's stomach. Even for a half-devil, whose father had forced him to see many a disturbing sight, it was too much, and he closed his eyes.

The stomach acid and other assorted fluids came to a boil, and a toxic mist soon filled the beast's stomach and began pushing it out. As Dantes had hoped, the valves in the monster's digestive tract were all one-way. Things were pushed through, and then they closed and wouldn't let anything back up. While normally a helpful mechanism for a creature that swallowed live prey, it was not good if the beast needed to relieve gas pressure in its stomach.

He had learned this from his father. As it turned out, his father *had* been good for something. When Dantes was young, his father had taken him to the seashore and had given him some chalky tablets to feed the seagulls. The birds would fly up, expecting a treat, and his father would have him toss the tablets into the air for the birds to eat. After several had been fed, Dantes asked what he was feeding the birds. Even at a young age, Dantes had thought it seemed too nice an act for his father.

"Powdered seashell," his father replied. "It reacts with the birds' stomach acid and makes gas in their stomachs. Eventually they will burst because the birds don't have any way to get rid of the gas." Laughing all the while, his father had made him watch as the birds fell from the sky in agony.

"Don't ever trust anyone who seems to be giving you something for nothing," his father said in explanation when they were done. "They're hiding something from you that you just haven't figured out yet."

Scylla's stomach seemed to be made of stronger material, though. It didn't seem to be expanding any more, even though the flames continued to roar. Maybe a little more flame, he thought. *"Globus Incendi!"* he said, casting his last Fireball spell. It burst, cooking the lining of the monster's stomach and making it comfortably warm inside, but the lining still held together.

Acid had now found its way into a number of cuts and was wearing through in a number of other places. Dantes' remaining spells were useless. He could try to claw his way out, but the acid was starting to have a greater and greater effect on him. He didn't think he could get out before the damage done to him reached a critical level. He hoped that Scylla's stomach ruptured before the Wall of Fire went out; if it didn't, he was going to be in trouble.

The interior of the beast's stomach was plunged into darkness as the fire went out. Dantes started clawing at the stomach's lining, trying to break free, but he knew he was going to be too late.

Chapter Fifty-Three

John thrust the sword into the side of the monster, and the creature *exploded*, its skin tearing both up and down in an eruption of boiling gas. The force of the blast ripped the sword from his hands and drove it into his stomach, knocking the wind out of him. He doubled over as a wave of hot acid washed over him. His skin aflame, he felt himself being pelted with something. He straightened, opening his eyes to see that he was being hit by pieces of what used to be the *Dancer's* crew. He lost his lunch, adding to the already disgusting mix of...things...he was swimming in. At least he had killed Scylla, he thought, although he didn't know why the creature had exploded. The monster had stopped moving and was beginning to settle in the water as it started its trip to the bottom. "Good riddance," thought John.

He started for the surface, but caught a flash of red out of the corner of his eye. He looked back and saw a red hand holding onto the edge of Scylla's torn stomach. John knew it had to be a trick of his imagination; nothing could have survived the environment or the explosion.

Scylla's corpse started to pick up speed, and John watched it slide out of view. A second hand and the top of Dantes' head appeared just before the corpse went out of sight. John equalized the pressure in his ears, turned and swam downward, chasing the corpse. He saw that he wasn't going to be able to catch up to it; it was already going almost as fast as he could swim, and its rate of descent was still increasing. Scylla disappeared into the darkness. John knew that he was needed on the surface, but he decided to follow it a little further.

He was glad he did; seconds later he saw a small form flailing at the edge of his vision. He continued a little further and saw that it was Dantes. Although he struggled upward, Dantes wasn't making any progress. John swam down to meet him and moved behind the struggling teufling.

"Gotcha," said John, putting an arm around Dantes. He kicked toward the surface and understood why Dantes was struggling. Dantes body was incredibly dense, and he weighed a lot more than what he looked. He wasn't able to swim well enough on his own to make it to the surface. With John's assistance, they began making progress.

"Don't know if...I can make it," said John after about 30 seconds. He had already been swimming for a while and was quickly running out of energy. His entire front also seemed to be burning.

"Let me go," replied Dantes, struggling to talk underwater.

"No!" said John. "We're...going...to make it." As he said it, light flashed above them several times, indicating they were getting closer to the surface. John put all of his energy into one last burst.

Dantes looked up and could see a timber floating above them. He gave a few last desperate strokes and reached up to grasp the wood.

Exhausted, John let go, pausing about ten feet below the surface to recover.

They had done it.

Chapter Fifty-Four

"We must leave," said the captain of the orc vessel. "If we continue to stay here, the storm is going to swamp us." As if in response, several more strokes of lightning flashed nearby, and a roll of thunder hit the ship hard enough to shake it.

"I need the book," replied Solim, "but we don't need to stay here. The storm should take care of killing any of the ones that survived Scylla." He didn't know what had happened to kill the monster, but it had felt like its stomach burst. It was probably something that damned teufling had done. Solim realized he shouldn't have used Scylla to swallow the devil whole, but it really didn't matter now; the teufling was dead.

"You may proceed to the island," said Solim; "I will find the book."

Reaching out, Solim found a seagull nearby. He had to push hard to take over the bird; the seagull didn't want to fly in the storm. Once airborne, it didn't take long to find the wreck of the ship although the storm was spreading it out over an increasingly large area. The wind shear made flight difficult, but the seagull was used to looking for and identifying things on the water, and it made an outstanding search platform. A flash of lightning lit the wreckage and he saw it, sitting on a rectangle of wood that might have been a door. An artifact of magic, the spell book wanted to be found.

The lightning also illuminated the half-orc Ghorza, who was swimming toward the door. In another 30 seconds, she would have it. That would never do.

Solim landed the seagull on the door and walked over to the spell book. He was surprised at how plain it looked; he had expected the Spell Book of Aran-Than to be much more ornate.

"Shoo, bird!" said the half-orc, arriving at the floating door.

"If you insist," said Solim through the seagull. "I'm going to go ahead and take this, though." He had the seagull put a webbed foot on the book and thought about the book being in its smallest and lightest form. The book obediently shrank to a small cube the size of one of the dice that Solim had seen the sailors using.

The half-orc reached for it, but Solim already had it in the seagull's webbed foot, and he took to the air. He made one circle over the wreckage so that he could laugh at the few remaining survivors, and then flew toward the orc ship, which was already heading toward the Mountain of Frost.

Chapter Fifty-Five

John inhaled a lung-full of water and choked. He couldn't breathe. He had been resting about 10 feet below Dantes when his water breathing spell ceased suddenly. It didn't slowly end or give him any warning; it just cut off in mid-breath when he had a bunch of water in his lungs.

He struggled up toward the surface, but it was too far off. Doubled over, gagging, he couldn't swim. He couldn't breathe. Somehow he made it to the surface, but it didn't help. He couldn't get the water out of his lungs. He was too tired.

Too weak.

Dantes saw him and tried to grab him. He missed, and the blackness closed in on John. He was out of air and couldn't clear his lungs to get a breath.

He was done. His head went under.

The last thing John heard was Solim's maniacal laughter, somehow blown to his ears by a trick of the gale.

Epilogue

John came back to consciousness bit by bit. He was lying on his back, he noted without opening his eyes. He took stock of his situation. If this is what being dead feels like, he thought, it sucks.

He hurt all over. The light breeze irritated his skin for some reason, causing a burning sensation across most of his body. His stomach hurt worst of all, but he couldn't think of why that would be.

In contrast to all of his aches and pains, his feet felt good and seemed to be floating in some water. They bobbed up and down as small waves came in.

He realized that he could feel the ground all along his back. It felt like sand, but what was strange was that he could feel it all the way down his back.

He was naked.

With that realization, he flipped over and opened his eyes. Movement irritated his skin and caused new areas of his skin to come in contact with the sand, which hurt. He looked at his arms and saw they were red and blistered all along their length. He had no idea how that happened.

He shook his head once, but stopped. Shaking it made it hurt too much. Looking to the right, he saw that he was lying on a beach. There seemed to be an abnormal amount of driftwood and debris along the waterline. Looking to the left he saw a similar collection of debris, along with a figure in silver armor. The visor was up, and he could see that the silver armor held a beautiful woman. Lady Ellyn.

It all came back to him. The battle with Scylla. His stomach hurt because the monster had exploded when he stuck the sword into it, and the sword had been driven back into him. Hard. At least he understood that pain; he had no idea why his skin burned all over. He had then gone down to rescue Dantes, and then he had drowned. He remembered the water breathing spell ending suddenly and getting a mouthful of water. And then the laughter…he would always remember the laughter.

"I see you're back among the living," said Dantes. John looked up to see the teufling standing in front of him holding a tunic.

"Barely," replied John taking the tunic. He turned away and sat up so that he could throw it over his head. It hurt, but he managed it. Partially clothed, he stood up. As many injuries as he had, the process of standing took a while. "What happened? I feel like crap."

"What's the last thing that you remember?"

"I remember the water breathing spell ending as I got you to the surface, and then I think I remember drowning."

"The spell didn't end," said Dantes. "Solim took your spell book. Ghorza saw him get it. When he did that, you dropped two levels and you were no longer able to cast the water breathing spell, so it ended. You did drown, but Ghorza dove in and brought you back up. Fitzber fashioned a raft of sorts, and we were able to collect everyone from our group, as well as the two little girls. Over the course of the next four days, we were able to sail the raft to the island."

"Four days?"

"Yes, you've been out for four days. Lady Ellyn has, too. She took a blow to the head during the fight and hasn't awakened since." Seeing the questioning look on John's face, he added, "Apparently her armor is magical. It kept her afloat while she was unconscious. Anyway, the current was against us, and we weren't able to make a sail, so it took a while for Father Telenor, Fitzber, Ghorza and me to paddle our way to the island. I wasn't much use for the first couple of days until my skin regenerated. I lost most of it to the creature's stomach acid while I was inside it."

"Stomach acid? Is that why my arms and face are burned? After I stabbed Scylla, it blew up in my face."

"I imagine so. I had cast a couple of fire spells to make its stomach burst, but it was too strong. It didn't blow until you stabbed it. When you did, all of the burning acid must have sprayed out in your face."

"Well, that makes sense. Is Father Telenor around? I would love a healing spell or ten."

"He will be back soon. He went into town with the rest of the group to get a wagon to transport you two, while I stayed here to watch over you. Sorry about having to leave you unhealed; it took all of the healing spells that Father Telenor had memorized to save Lady Ellyn and me. We lost all of our gear and spell books in the wreck of the *Dancer*, so he wasn't able to re-memorize any of them until we got here and he could use one of the local priest's spell books."

Looking around, John saw a snow-capped mountain in the distance. "Well, it wasn't pretty, but at least we made it to the Mountain of Frost," he said nodding toward the mountain.

Dantes nodded, frowning, but didn't say anything.

"What?" John asked. "Why are you making that face?"

"We made it here," Dantes replied; "however, we were the second group to arrive. We met one of the townspeople when we came ashore, and he told us that Solim and his orcs landed here three days ago. They drove off a small force of local troops and went to the mountain. Solim and a much smaller number of orcs came down from the mountain yesterday. They've already left."

"So, we're too late?"

"We're too late for getting here first," replied Dantes, "although no one knows whether they got the scepter or not. It doesn't matter, though. Our quest was to go to the Mountain of Frost, and I still intend to. I don't know what we'll find, but the Magistra told me to go, and I intend to do so."

John looked up at the mountain. He wasn't sure he could walk a hundred feet, much less scale a mountain, but that wasn't going to stop him now that he'd come this far. "If you're still going," he said, "then I am, too." He gave a wan smile. "But I'd still like to get those healing spells, first."

# # # # #

The following is an
Excerpt from Book 2 of the War for Dominance:

Chasing the Past

Chris Kennedy

Available from Chris Kennedy Publishing

Summer, 2015

eBook, Paperback and Audio Book

Excerpt from "Chasing the Past:"

Although there was no source of illumination that could be seen, the end of the tunnel stood out as the companions approached. The tunnel ended in a flat stone wall, into which the outline of a doorway was carved. The floor directly in front of the doorway was stone in a three-foot square, with a six-inch band of metal that surrounded the block in a large "U." A metal plate stood out from the front of the doorway at what would be eye level for a gnome or halfling or at a human's waist. In the plate were five depressions in the shape of a right hand's fingerprints.

Dantes moved to the side of the tunnel and made a sweeping motion with his hand toward the door. "It's all yours, 'Unchosen,'" he said with a smirk.

John glared at him, but walked past him to the doorway. As he stepped onto the square stone area in front of the doorway, it depressed slightly with an audible 'click.' John froze where he was. "Did everyone else hear that?" he asked.

"Aye, laddie," said Fitzber, who got down on his hands and knees to look at the floor more closely. "It sounded like a trap arming."

"What should I do?" asked John. "Step back off it?"

"That is the last thing I'd be doing," said Fitzber. "Right now, your weight is holding the trigger down; if you get off, it will activate."

"So what do I do?"

"Isn't it fairly obvious?" asked Father Telenor. "What do you suppose that plate is for?"

283

"Oh, I see," John said, turning back to the wall. He reached out to the metal plate with his right hand. He noticed that his fingers were shaking. Timidly, John placed a finger in each of the depressions.

He vanished.

"Where did he go?" asked Lady Ellyn.

"I think he's still there," replied Ghorza, holding out her hands. "Some sort of force field just sprang up that is blocking our sight of him. I could feel it come into being. It's like when an air mage casts a Wall of Force spell." She leaned forward on it, and the invisible wall supported her weight. "The metal band on the floor is projecting it, but I don't know what purpose it serves."

"If we can't see him, it also probably blocks his ability to see us," Dantes observed. "If he can't see us, we can't help him. His success or failure is riding on his abilities, alone."

"I don't think he's ready," Ghorza said. "He's only done a couple of the cantrips once. What if he can't remember one of them or gets it wrong?"

"I would imagine that he dies," said Dantes. "Probably the rest of us, too."

The companions heard another 'click,' and then Ghorza fell forward as the force field dissipated. Off balance, she stumbled all the way to the wall across the empty stone block.

John was gone.

* * * * *

ABOUT THE AUTHOR

A bestselling Science Fiction/Fantasy author and speaker, Chris Kennedy is a former naval aviator with over 3,000 hours flying attack and reconnaissance aircraft. Chris is currently working as an Instructional Systems Designer for the Navy.

Chris' full length novels on Amazon include the "Occupied Seattle" military fiction duology ("Red Tide: The Chinese Invasion of Seattle" and "Occupied Seattle") and "The Theogony" science fiction trilogy ("Janissaries," "When the Gods Aren't Gods" and "Terra Stands Alone"). Chris has also released "Chasing a Spectre," a short story that is a prequel to the "War for Dominance" fantasy trilogy.

Additional Titles by Chris Kennedy:

"Red Tide: The Chinese Invasion of Seattle"

"Occupied Seattle"

"Janissaries: Book One of the Theogony"

"When the Gods Aren't Gods: Book Two of the Theogony"

"Terra Stands Alone: Book Three of the Theogony"

"Chasing a Spectre: Book Zero of the War for Dominance"

"The Search for Gram: Book One of the Codex Regius" –
Coming Soon

* * * * *

Connect with Chris Kennedy Online:

Facebook: https://www.facebook.com/chriskennedypublishing.biz

Blog: http://chriskennedypublishing.com/

Want to be immortalized in a future book?
Join the Red Shirt List on the blog!

www.ingramcontent.com/pod-product-compliance
Lightning Source LLC
Chambersburg PA
CBHW062133170626
46813CB00002B/680